ALSO BY MARKO KLOOS

FRONTLINES

Terms of Enlistment
Lines of Departure
Angles of Attack
Chains of Command
Fields of Fire
Points of Impact
Measures of Absolution (A Frontlines Kindle novella)
"Lucky Thirteen" (A Frontlines Kindle short story)

AFTERSHOCKS

AFTERSHOCKS
THE · PALLADIUM · WARS

MARKO KLOOS

Text copyright © 2019 by Marko Kloos
All rights reserved.

Published by 47North, Seattle

www.apub.com

Amazon, the Amazon logo, and 47North are trademarks of Amazon.com, Inc., or its affiliates.

ISBN-13: 9781542043557 (hardcover)
ISBN-10: 1542043557 (hardcover)
ISBN-13: 9781542043533 (paperback)
ISBN-10: 1542043530 (paperback)

Cover design by Shasti O'Leary Soudant

Printed in the United States of America

First edition

For Robin, who keeps this train firmly on the tracks so I can sit back in the lounge car and make up stuff all day long.

CHAPTER 1

ADEN

Even from the windows of a prison, Rhodia was a beautiful place.

Aden liked to spend the half hour between breakfast and morning orders sitting in the central atrium by himself. From seven hundred meters up, the panoramic windows offered a stunning view of what seemed like most of the southern half of the continent. The graceful and elegant arcologies of the capital rose into the sky in the distance, so tall that on some days their tops disappeared in the clouds. Beyond, the ocean shimmered, turquoise and blue. For variety, the Rhodians moved their POWs from one section of the detainment arcology to another every year, each time facing a different cardinal direction so every prisoner could have a change of scenery. Last year, Aden had a stunning view of the great snowcapped mountain range that divided the single continent of this planet. This year, it was the distant city, ocean, and tranquil skies. He had been a prisoner of war for five years, but Aden still hadn't quite made up his mind whether a beautiful prison was really better than an austere one.

At the end of the war, right after his capture, the Alliance had used the warships of their defeated enemies to hold POWs until they could figure out what to do with them. By the time the surrender treaty was signed, Aden had spent six months in a two-person berth on a Gretian battlecruiser, sharing the tiny space with a surly lieutenant colonel from the Blackguard infantry. The food had been barely edible—the Alliance had fed them the surplus military rations they found when they took over the Gretian depots—and Aden hadn't seen sunlight the whole time. When they finally transferred him to the detainment arcology, he had lost almost ten kilos of muscle mass from living in low g for so long, and sharing crew facilities made for five hundred with almost one thousand other POWs had been claustrophobic and nerve grinding. But he had dealt with it because it was impersonal, utilitarian, and expected. They had lost the war, and they had to take what was served by the victors.

The detainment arcology here on Rhodia was a prison, but it was a posh one. Back home on Gretia, no amount of money would buy a living space with a view like this. Gretian buildings did not reach a kilometer into the sky. Even the food on Rhodia was good, which had vaguely annoyed Aden after a while because he had to moderate himself and work out more to keep the weight off. It all seemed a little like the Rhodians were rubbing it in. *Look where we can lodge even our captured war criminals. Look what we can afford to feed you. Just look at the view you get to enjoy every day.*

There was no mistreatment, no disrespect, just detached professionalism from the military police that ran the prison. They had a barber, a theater, a mess hall, a gym, an outdoor garden concourse that jutted out of the facade of the arcology in a hundred-meter semicircle, private rooms, and personal comtabs with limited and curated access to the Mnemosyne, the system-wide data network. The only thing that made it different from a resort hotel was the security lock at the far end of the atrium, which only let you through if you were a Rhodian MP and stunned you into a thirty-minute stupor if you weren't. But the fact that he couldn't leave whenever he wanted made it a prison, no matter how pretty the views were.

The soft two-tone trill of an official announcement interrupted Aden's thoughts. Even the address system in the atrium was calm and low-key to preserve the tranquility of the place.

"Morning orders in five minutes. All personnel, report to the assembly square of your residential wing. Announcement ends."

Aden rubbed his hand along his jawline to appraise his shave, even though he knew he hadn't missed any stubble this morning. Then he turned away from the panoramic window and walked back toward the elevator bank, checking the fasteners on his pockets to make sure none were undone. It had been five years since he had been in an active military or worn a Gretian uniform, but his twelve years of service before the defeat had ingrained a lot of habits so deeply that he doubted he'd ever lose them.

Morning orders were standard issue; everyone—guards and prisoners alike—was on autopilot. A Rhodian NCO called the roll, and the prisoners reported able or sick. The arcology's AI knew where everyone was at all times, but habits and protocol died hard, and it was just one of the ten thousand ways the Rhodies had to make sure everyone knew who had won and who had lost the war. After roll, a fresh-faced Rhody lieutenant stepped up, and the NCO presented the POW platoon as inspected and ready.

"Good morning," the Rhodian lieutenant said in his own language. The translator bud in Aden's left ear rendered the phrase in Gretian a fraction of a second later.

"Good morning, sir," the assembled platoon of Gretians replied as one. Aden barely mouthed the words. The Rhodian lieutenant looked like he was maybe two years out of officer school. The POWs, lined up in formation, stood in order of their rank as they always did, even though the Gretian military had ceased to exist five years ago. A quarter of the formation outranked the Rhody lieutenant, and more than a few of them were old enough to be his father, Aden included. But the Rhody officer was the detainment unit supervisor of the day, and therefore by definition their superior. They had all learned that when you become a prisoner of war, the first thing the enemy confiscates is your pride.

"You all have the updated duty roster on your comtabs. Section One will be at the hydroponic farm today. Section Two takes over the mess hall at 0900 hours, and Section Three is on waste disposal. Assignment details are up to section leaders as usual. Sick personnel will report to the infirmary by 0830."

As the most senior officer remaining in the company, Aden was the leader of Section One. Of all the work assignments, he minded the hydroponic farm the least. It was as outside as he could get in the arcology because it was nestled inside the loop made by the exterior garden concourse. Some of the POWs were agoraphobic and hated the farmwork because of the knowledge that nothing but a thirty-centimeter layer of titanium and carbon composites stood between the soles of their boots and a free fall of seven hundred meters, but Aden was not one of them. Rhodians were mediocre at warship design, but they were masters of arcology building, and Aden had never felt the garden platforms so much as sway in the wind, not even in the middle of a storm.

"Another thing," the Rhody lieutenant added. "Major Robertson, you are ordered to report to the company commander's office this morning. Have your second in charge take over the section until you return. Sergeant Carver and I will escort you through the security lock right after orders."

"Yes, sir," Aden said, mildly annoyed. He had been to the company commander's office only four times in the past year, and each time it had been because of some rules infraction by a member of his section. He had no idea who the fuckup was this time around or what they had done, but for Aden it would mean waiting around in an office and then getting chewed out instead of working in the clean air and smelling organic planting soil. This was the only scheduled hydroponic farm day for his section this week, and Aden resolved to take out his fresh annoyance on whatever idiot had snatched it away from him.

When Aden walked into the company commander's office, Captain Raymond was not at his desk. In his place sat a Rhody major Aden had never seen before. Aden offered the obligatory salute and report, then stood at attention. The major didn't even look up from the comtab she was reading. She tapped the screen a few times and flicked to a different page while Aden kept his position of attention. Finally, after what seemed like the better part of a minute, the major looked up and cleared her throat.

"At ease," she said in Rhodian. By the expression on her face, she looked as if she had just bitten into something unexpectedly sour not too long ago. A lot of the Rhody officers and NCOs had become somewhat friendly, even cordial, with the POWs over the years. There were only two kinds that were reliably hostile—the new, unseasoned MPs who thought they had to prove to their peers how tough they were, and the older veterans with a grudge who had fought Gretians in the war. This one was the latter sort. The Rhodian military promoted their officers on a longer time-in-rank schedule than the Gretian armed forces did. A Gretian officer could have made major after only eight years. A Rhody major got that rank after ten years at the earliest.

Aden relaxed slightly into parade rest: hands behind his back, feet apart at shoulder width. If he was here to get dinged by this major for something, he wasn't about to add lack of discipline to the list of grievances. The major didn't look placated.

"Fucking fuzzheads, always with the sticks up their asses," she grumbled under her breath in Northern dialect, using local slang she knew the translator bud in Aden's ear couldn't render back in Gretian. But Aden understood well enough. He had been fluent in Rhodian even before the war, and the guards here spoke in every local dialect on the planet.

"Sit down," the major added in standard Rhodian, and gestured to the chair in front of the absent commander's desk.

Aden wasn't offended by the slur. "Fuzzheads" was what the Rhodies called Gretians because of the universal buzz cut of their military personnel, male and female alike. But being insulted for displaying proper military etiquette chafed him. The POWs were expected to observe protocol toward all Rhody officers and NCOs down to the greenest corporal taking roll in the morning. Failure to do so was an automatic personal infraction and demerit for the section. Only the most ill-tempered ass would construe adherence to discipline as a character flaw on purpose. He walked up to the desk and took a seat as instructed. The Rhody major had returned her attention to the comtab in her hands. She was as tall as Aden. Her rust-red hair was long enough for a tight braid, which meant that she didn't wear a helmet on a regular basis. So she wasn't infantry, even though she was tall and had the build of a combat soldier.

"I can't win this one," Aden said in Rhodian. "If I stand at attention, you call me uptight. If I don't, you call me undisciplined."

That got her attention. She looked up from her comtab, unable to hide her surprise for a moment. Aden took the translator bud out of his ear and put it on the desk in front of him. She looked at it and arched an eyebrow.

"So you speak Rhodian. But you didn't pick up the language in here. Not if you understand Northern street talk."

She consulted her comtab again, flicked through a few more pages, and nodded.

"Ah, yes. Major Robertson. You're the intelligence linguist. What else do you speak?"

"Oceanian. A little bit of Acheroni. Enough Hadean to get by. No Palladian, though."

"Nobody's fluent in Palladian who wasn't born there," she said. "They have as many dialects as they have regions, and none of them can understand each other without translators. I was stationed there for a year and a half and still fuck up 'Good morning.'"

She tossed her comtab onto the table.

"And Hadean is Rhodian, but drunk and with a mouthful of pebbles. But I'm not here to talk about linguistics. Even if the subject is fascinating. I'll say that your Rhodian is almost flawless. I can barely detect an accent."

Aden nodded to acknowledge the remark. He wasn't used to getting compliments from Rhody officers, but he could tell from the way she gathered herself almost imperceptibly that she wasn't used to giving them either.

"I've had lots of listening practice," he replied.

"I bet you have. You've been here for a while. Which brings me to the point of this visit."

The Rhody major sighed and shook her head.

"If it were up to me, you people would be getting rotated through this arcology and planting tomatoes and cabbage until the heat death of this system," she said. "Especially you Blackguards. The treaty was a load of shit. Comfortable custody, for all you did to this system."

"I wasn't on Pallas during the invasion," Aden said. "I was captured on Oceana during our retreat. And I was in Field Signals Intelligence, not infantry."

"I don't give a shit. You wore that uniform, and you volunteered to wear it. That makes you a war criminal by choice."

She swiveled around in her chair to look out of the window behind her. The office overlooked the large central atrium of the arcology, which was about twenty times higher than the smaller version in the POWs' section of the containment unit. Every fifth level had hanging gardens spanning the gaps between the corners of the floors, lush vegetation spilling out of them and hanging over the edges of the walkways. The Rhodies incorporated trees and gardens everywhere they could cram them in. The surface of their continent was mostly barren volcanic rock and glaciers, but their arcologies were teeming with plant life.

"You had the richest planet in the system. The biggest one. The only one with soil that supports Old Earth agriseeds," she said. "But it wasn't enough, was it?"

She turned around again to look at him.

"You started this war. You had no right to Oceana, and we had every right to push you off. You had every other planet aligned against you in the system senate, and you still had to dig your heels in. But I'll tell you that not even the biggest pessimists thought you'd actually start a shooting war with the rest of us over that old colony of yours. And now here we are."

She held both hands out, palms up, a gesture to encompass the arcology, the planet, maybe the system.

"Half a million dead. Half a million. You occupied a sovereign planet and then invaded another. You kept that meat grinder of a war going even when you knew gods-damned well you couldn't win it. Not with the rest of us lined up against you."

She looked at the screen of her comtab again.

"Major Aden Robertson," she repeated. "Forty-two years of age. Says here you've been in uniform since 906. That's seventeen years of service."

She put the comtab onto the desk again and folded her hands on top of it.

"Tell me, Major Robertson. You've given seventeen years of your life to the losing side. In the service of a nation that doesn't exist anymore. Was it all worth it in the end?"

Aden didn't respond. He'd heard the same angry lecture in a thousand slightly different forms since he became a POW, and it was best to just let it wash over him and look neither smug nor contrite. "You" was "Gretians," and he was Gretian, so to her he was the physical embodiment of all the sins committed by his planet. He knew that any attempt at justification for Gretia's actions during the war would not be well received. It was true, after all. The Gretian military had done all those things, and the Blackguards had done the dirtiest work of the war. That was why he was doing penance here. Five years for Blackguards, while the regular troops got their release after two. Even though he had spent the war mostly on Oceana and had never fired a weapon at anyone. But he had worn the black uniform with the gray-and-blue piping, and the surrender treaty had made no distinction between shock troopers who had racked up kills on the front lines and language specialists who hadn't spent a minute in a combat suit.

"I could have had a quiet career," the major continued, a little more subdued. "A normal life. One that doesn't make me use a psych-med implant so I can sleep through the night. Instead, I burned through ten years of my life dealing with you war-mongering lunatics. Four years of fighting in the infantry, and then another half a decade mopping up the mess you made of everything and dealing with a million extra mouths to feed."

His neutral expression seemed to piss her off anew, and she grinned without humor.

"There were plenty of people who were sure you'd never surrender. That we'd have to nuke Gretia into compliance from orbit. I wish you had given us an excuse to turn your planet into glass. Fuck your cities and farms and fields and greenhouses. My sister was on RNS *Bellerophon* when we sent the first task force to Oceana, and your navy wiped them all out. So no, you don't get any credit in my ledger for being able to speak Rhodian."

She nodded at the comtab.

"You're in luck, though. I wasn't in charge of setting the surrender terms. We signed that idiotic treaty, and we have to abide by its terms. Your five years are up, Major."

Aden blinked when he parsed what the major was telling him.

"You're releasing me?"

"We're releasing all of you. Starting tomorrow."

It was like someone had been standing on his chest for five years, and he hadn't been aware of the weight until now when they stepped off him and walked away. The sudden rush of emotions made him almost dizzy, as if he had quickly downed a bottle of cold beer with breakfast, and the effects were just catching up with him. He exhaled slowly and waited for the room to stop spinning.

"Not all at once, of course," the major continued. "We have all year to comply with the treaty terms, so you will be released in stages over the next three hundred eighty-eight days. One hundred and fifty of you will get to leave every day—one company. Yours is due for release tomorrow."

Aden did some quick math in his head, but his mind was still reeling with the prospect of his impending freedom, and the result came much more slowly to his brain than it should have. Fifty thousand POWs? The companies were reshuffled with new personnel every year when the prisoners moved sectors because the Rhodies didn't want them to integrate too well as teams again. Aden had no sense of scale, no knowledge of this five-hundred-floor vertical city or how many levels of it were occupied by Gretian prisoners. But even his most pessimistic estimate had been in the low ten thousands. The scale of the Gretian defeat was mind-boggling. They had bet it all on one roll of the dice and lost everything.

"This is the most distasteful thing I've ever had to do in the service," the Rhody major said. "Letting fifty thousand Blackguards loose in the system again. I don't care if it's been five years. You should have all gotten marched out into the coastal zone and had the galloping tides drown you like vermin in a bucket. You would have done the same with us if you had won."

She snatched her comtab off the table again and waved it in the direction of the open door, where the Rhody sergeant standing guard outside, just out of sight, had probably been nodding his head in agreement all along.

"Go to your company and relay the order," she said. "Tell them to enjoy their last night of Rhodian hospitality. But all regular rules are still in full effect. If any of them decide to step over the line even the slightest bit, your company will get pulled out of the queue and released at the end of the year instead. Tomorrow after breakfast, your company will report to the auditorium for a mandatory release lecture. After that, you will return your issued items. By lunchtime, you'll be at the skyport upstairs. Where you go from there, I don't care, as long as you are off Rhodia. Dismissed."

Aden's head still felt like his brain was floating in some high-quality intoxicant, and not even the Rhody major's open disdain could blunt the sensation. He got out of his chair, picked up his translator bud, and put it into the chest pocket of his prison overalls. Then he stood at attention and snapped a crisp salute, which the major didn't acknowledge. Aden turned on his heel and strode toward the door. When he had taken two steps, the Rhody major spoke up again.

"Oh, and one more thing."

He turned around and stood at attention once more.

"Yes, ma'am."

"Of all the system languages, I always thought that I hated the sound of Gretian the most," she said. "But it turns out that I hate the sound of Rhodian coming out of a Gretian's mouth even more."

She looked down at her comtab again, not even bothering to wave him away.

CHAPTER 2

IDINA

It was a nice spring day in the Palladian occupation zone on Gretia's northern hemisphere after a long winter away from home. Color Sergeant Idina Chaudhary led her security patrol with the face shield of her helmet raised, enjoying the warmth of the sun on her face and the sound of the wind rustling the grass. The all-terrain soles of her armor sank a little bit into the soft ground with every step, but not as much as they would have done on Pallas. Even the gravity here was easy: one standard Gretian gravity to Pallas's one point two. Every time she went out on patrol into the countryside, Idina couldn't help thinking that Gretia was too good for Gretians.

Every other planet in the system had something about it that made life difficult in some way. Hades had no atmosphere and was so close to the sun that people lived underground to shield themselves from heat and radiation. Acheron had a toxic atmosphere and a surface that was like a poisonous furnace, and its domed cities had to float in that thin layer of atmosphere fifty kilometers up where the pressure and temperature were livable. Oceana was covered in water except for a tiny bit of reclaimed land barely big enough for a city and a spaceport. Rhodia had one small continent bisected by a mountain chain, and it had two moons that made the ocean tides so severe that nothing could live close to the coastline. And Pallas, Idina's home world, had mountains so tall and valleys so deep that humans had to cling to the sides of those mountains in terraced cities and villages—high enough to get light and warmth from the sun and low enough to have dense air to breathe.

Gretia alone was perfect in almost every way.

It had a breathable, clean atmosphere, plenty of water, geologically stable continents with mountains and valleys, lakes and deserts, plains and rivers. It had an ocean, and because it had a single natural moon not too close to the planet, it had gentle tides. Gretia even had an axial tilt of nineteen degrees—a little less than Earth used to have, but enough to support seasons. And seasons meant that most of the seed stock the original settlers had brought with them could grow here with minimal genetic modification. The countryside surrounding the Pallas Brigade base outside of Sandfell was mostly rolling, grass-covered hills and forests of tall trees planted hundreds of years ago.

To Idina, the amount of wide-open space was almost disorienting, even after three tours of duty on Gretia with the Allied Occupation Force. There were farms out here operating long rows of greenhouses, but they were spaced kilometers apart, with nothing between them but grass and trees and the occasional freshwater brook. Idina came from a world where every square meter of habitat had to be chiseled out of rock, so it seemed rather sinful to her Palladian sensibilities to have this much unused level ground between settlements.

The platoon was spread out in a wedge-shaped sector ten kilometers across at its wide end. Pallas's gravity was higher, so Palladians lost muscle mass on their deployments to Gretia unless they stayed on top of their workouts. Whenever they went on patrol, they took enough gear for several days, and they went on foot, in powered suits that had adjustable friction resistors in the joints. Each trooper was carrying a temp shelter, field rations, gear, energy cells, and weapons, almost two hundred kilos of kit strapped to three hundred kilos of power armor.

And because they were Palladian and liked it that way, they carried it all with their armor holding them back just a little, the servos pretending that Gretia had one point two g instead of just one. They could have patrolled in vehicles like the Rhodians and covered four times the ground in half the time. But riding in armor wasn't the Pallas Brigade way, and Idina much preferred to spend time out in the fresh air.

"Getting a funny reading from one of my drones, Colors," Corporal Singh sent on the platoon channel. Singh was in charge of the second section, which was a few hundred meters to Idina's left, hidden from direct view by a low, grassy hill dotted with bushes.

Idina checked the situation map on her data monocle. Each trooper had twenty-four micro-drones hangared in their armor for aerial reconnaissance, and when they were in the field, they sent them out in flights of six at a time to scout ahead and give them eyes on the other side of hills and forests.

"What is it, Corporal?" Idina asked. "I don't see anything."

"Never mind, it's gone now. No, wait . . . there it is again. Looks like a heat source, right there in the middle of grid Bravo 23."

Idina followed the directions and zoomed in on the center of the referenced map grid. Sure enough, there was a small thermal bloom. There were two buildings nearby, and the bloom was right between them, fluctuating in intensity like a sputtering campfire.

"What's out there?" she asked.

"That's one of the service access stations for the energy loop and the transit line over to Holmgard, I think."

"Yeah, you're right." She took over the corporal's drones remotely and had them buzz closer to the anomaly. It looked like someone was torching a burn pile, but she couldn't see anyone nearby. The access station consisted of two small concrete buildings, one square and one dome shaped. Whoever was making a bonfire out there was probably seeking shelter in one of those buildings. Lighting a signal fire and shacking up in a restricted structure meant it was either a careless civvie farmer or a little group of really dumb insurgents. Either way, the platoon would have to check it out. She sighed and lowered the face shield on her helmet again.

"All right. Blue Section, close it up to the right. I'll take Purple Section to check out the station. Red Section, adjust your spacing and keep watching our left flank. Yellow Section, cut to your left and make up the gap next to Purple Section. We're going to evict the squatter, and then we'll make him piss out that fire."

The scattered laughter of her troopers came back on the platoon channel. This was unexciting stuff for a platoon of infantry, but it was the most variety they'd had on patrol in months.

———

The access station was five kilometers to their east, nestled in a little valley that had a shallow brook running through the middle of it. The far side of the valley beyond the brook was a rock-strewn hillside with a forested edge running along the hillcrest, tall trees that swayed gently in the spring breeze. There was no sign of activity except for the burn pile that was smoldering on the ground between the two buildings. Idina stopped her section at the edge of the downslope and scanned her surroundings. The fire gave off some thermal radiation, but there was no other heat source evident down there. She cycled through the various filters of her recon package. On every slice of the spectrum, the helmet cameras showed her the same thing—a quiet, empty valley with two buildings and a burning pile of wet scrap wood in front of them.

"If anyone is around, they're in the buildings," Corporal Singh said. "Drones say nothing's moving within ten klicks of this place except us."

Idina launched two of her own drones from her recon interface. The tiny gyrofoils, each no bigger than her little finger, launched themselves out of the storage recesses on her armor and whirred off toward the buildings two hundred meters away. On her tactical display, she saw that the other sections had spread out to cover the gap created by the third section collapsing their patrol line and all clustering in one spot.

The drones reached the buildings a few moments later, and she directed them around to the far side to get a full 360-degree view of the scene.

"Huh," she said. "Doors are closed and undamaged. If they went in there, they have access codes."

"Or they hacked the panel," Corporal Singh said.

"Any maintenance personnel scheduled for this node?"

"Not according to what's on the Mnemosyne. Hasn't been anyone here in nine months. Last on the log was one of our patrols, from First Battalion."

"The security logs don't show access attempts on those doors?"

"No, Colors. No one's been in there. Unless the logs are wrong."

"Someone walked up, made a campfire, then walked off again." Idina chewed on her lower lip for a moment. "Or they hacked the panel and overrode the logs."

"System's still fried in a lot of spots," Corporal Singh said. "They probably just broke in and the local comms node is out. I can't even access the security interface through the Mnemosyne. Going to have to patch in locally."

The simplest explanation was usually the correct one, Idina decided. Whoever set that smoldering little fire outside had to be around. There was no way they could have gotten out of drone observation range while that fire was still going, and neither the troopers' helmet sensors nor the drones' observation package could reach inside the thick concrete walls of the service station. They were in there. But some remnant of doubt remained in the back of her mind, and she was fully prepared for the possibility that the squatters were more dangerous than just some adventurous local kids or a lost farmer. This would be a good opportunity for an exercise, with the possibility of live fire adding some welcome adrenaline.

"All right. Let's go check it out. Spread out, loose formation. See if we can round that first building from both sides at the same time. And watch those gun muzzles," Idina sent to the section. She checked the status of her own weapon. They had gone light on patrols for this deployment, just the basic scout armor and gun package. The modular rail on her suit's right arm held a light assault carbine, the one on her left arm an automatic small-bore grenade launcher. She selected the carbine and set the weapon's fire control to Semiautonomous. The computer would select the projectile, firing rate, and appropriate propellant quantity on the fly based on whatever was under her aiming reticle. It was a short-range, agile weapon that wasn't intended for the main line of battle, but against unarmored ragtag insurgents, it was almost overkill.

The eight troopers of Purple Section walked down the slope toward the buildings with fifty meters of space between each powered armor. Half the section fanned out to the left, and Idina went with the other half toward the right. The stabilizers of her armor kept her level on the soft ground. The first thaw of the year had been just a few weeks ago, and the soil was still a little spongy. The concept of seasons still amazed her even on her third deployment on this planet. Constantly cycling through four different kinds of climate was strange and burdensome.

"Singh, Koirala, Sharma, put that fire out and check the entrances. Everyone else, overwatch positions."

Corporal Singh, Lance Sharma, and Private Koirala tromped up to the buildings, carefully and methodically covering each other on the advance.

"Both entrances sealed and locked, Colors," the corporal sent a few moments later. Then he walked over to the burn pile, which was almost as tall as an armored trooper, and gave it a few blasts from the fire suppression system of his suit. Whatever few flames had been flickering in the pile went out, and the smoke pouring from the smoldering branches increased, now billowing gray and white.

Idina kept a watch on the surroundings while the corporal checked the access panels for the larger of the two buildings, the square little bunker that served as the main access and control unit for this segment of the vactube. They were all built to the same blueprint—an operations room connected to a small living area, and a vertical access shaft to the service walkway between the two underground tubes.

"Do a security override on the door and a voice challenge," Idina ordered.

Corporal Singh walked over to the door of the main unit, pulled off the access panel cover, and activated the panel. All Alliance forces had override codes for security infrastructure, and every secured door on the planet could be opened by any unit leader in the field from corporal up.

"Local access log is clean. Nobody's been in or out in months," he reported. "Opening now."

He stepped back a few meters and opened the door remotely. Then his voice, amplified by the PA system of his suit and translated into Gretian by the computer, boomed across the valley:

"THIS IS THE ALLIED OCCUPATION FORCE, PALLAS BRIGADE. ANYONE IN THE BUILDING, COME OUT UNARMED WITH YOUR HANDS IN SIGHT RIGHT NOW."

With the door open, there was no way anyone inside could miss the challenge. But twenty seconds passed and nothing happened. Corporal Singh repeated his announcement once more in Gretian, then in Rhodian and Oceanian, still with no result.

"All right, protocol is served. Do a sweep," Idina sent.

"Copy that. Sharma, Koirala, with me."

Idina watched the three-trooper element clear the area beyond the door and then disappear inside. She switched one of her displays over to the telemetry from Corporal Singh's helmet and watched as his team cleared the little building room by room with the searchlights on their armor. The operations center was dark and cold, and a fine layer of concrete dust covered the consoles and broken Mnemosyne screens.

The quarters looked like they had been stripped of everything usable years ago. The storage room was bare except for a few empty disposable containers, and the access hatch to the vactrain tunnel was latched and sealed properly from the inside. If someone had been in here, they hadn't come from there, though according to the access logs, they hadn't come through the front door either. But that smoking burn pile outside hadn't assembled and lit itself.

"Nobody home," Corporal Singh said.

"Lock it up and check the shed," Idina ordered. The shed was the little domed structure thirty meters away from the main building. When the service station was still operating, it was used for storing emergency equipment and a pair of electric runabouts, but that stuff had been appropriated by the locals quickly in that period of free-for-all anarchy between the collapse of the Gretian government and the establishment of the AOF military government. The sudden lack of order in a society that was used to half a millennium of established hierarchies had done as much damage to the infrastructure of the planet as the furious battles during the Alliance invasion. Gretia had profoundly broken itself, and Idina suspected she'd be retired by the time it managed to put itself back together.

Corporal Singh and his element emerged from the doorway. Singh closed the door remotely and replaced the cover of the access panel. Then he walked toward the two troopers who were waiting for him between the buildings.

One of the threat sensors in Idina's suit chirped a harsh alarm. She checked the color code and threat vector, then opened her mouth to shout a warning into the section channel even though she knew that every other suit in the section had just sounded the same alarm.

Something very fast tore through Corporal Singh's chest armor and exploded behind him, spraying the door he had just closed with hundreds of white-hot fragments. On the ridge beyond the tranquil little brook, a harsh metallic clang came from the tree line. The rail gun's report arrived just a fraction of a second after the shot. Corporal Singh's suit tried to do its job and keep its occupant upright, but the rail-gun slug had smashed through Singh's light armor and the exoskeleton behind it, breaking something vital in the process. Singh's suit sank to one knee, then fell over as the servos went offline. Idina didn't have to check the corporal's bio-telemetry to know he was dead.

"Contact right," she bellowed into the section channel. "Rail gun, in the tree line."

She scanned the hilltop on the other side of the brook and armed the grenade launcher. Whoever set up the ambush had some excellent camouflage discipline. Her suit's sensors yelped their warning again, alerting her to another spike in EM radiation. The rail gun was charging for another shot, and she couldn't see the damn thing. She raised her left arm and fired half a dozen grenades into the tree line above them. The grenades exploded with the even spacing of a computer-controlled trigger, one every five meters. Behind Idina, her section opened fire with carbines and grenade launchers, following her burst with their own ordnance.

Five-second recharge, she thought, frantically searching for the camouflaged rail-gun mount she knew was just now recharging its rails. Ten slugs in the magazine. She hadn't been on the receiving end of Gretian rail-gun fire since the end of the war, but she hadn't forgotten what one-kilo slugs traveling at ten thousand meters per second could do to a section of armored troopers. She switched her sensor filter to thermal just as the rail gun fired a second time. Behind her, the impact of the slug cracked, far louder than the muzzle report, and one of her section's troopers dropped out of the network without so much as a scream. Idina didn't see the muzzle blast, but the hypervelocity slug from the rail gun left behind a thermal disturbance in the air that was enough for her to track the path of the slug back to its approximate point of origin.

"Target," she called out even as the computer automatically marked the plot with the red symbol for a hostile gun emplacement. She sent most of the rest of her grenade launcher's magazine toward the likely spot.

The ridgeline above her came alive with weapons fire. These weren't rail guns, just small arms, but delivered from stealth. All Idina could see were the disturbances in the air caused by the passing of the projectiles. Whoever had tripped this ambush had fantastic stealth gear, better than any she had ever seen in action. Behind her, the section redeployed, seeking to put the thick concrete of the service building between themselves and the incoming fire. Lance Sharma and Private Koirala were dragging Corporal Singh, exoskeleton and all, to the cover of the maintenance shed in front of them. The rail gun cracked again, and Koirala took a slug dead center in his chest plate, just like Singh had done. He stumbled and crashed to the ground, and the sudden weight and drag of Singh's exoskeleton made Lance Sharma stumble as well. Sharma dropped the arm of Singh's suit and righted himself, just in time for a burst of small-arms fire to rake across his helmet's face shield. He returned fire with his arm-mounted carbine on the move even as he ducked behind the concrete dome of the maintenance shed.

"All sections, this is Rainbow One," Idina sent to the rest of the platoon. "Hostile contact. Purple is engaged and under heavy fire. Move in and cover Purple Section, on the double."

All suits were linked through the tactical network, and the other sections had seen the red icons pop up on their threat displays the second they appeared to Purple Section. Idina saw their friendly icons flit across the map at top speed as the rest of her platoon redeployed and thundered across the Gretian countryside with ten-meter steps.

Idina was still thirty meters from the building; she was the farthest from cover. She turned toward the maintenance station and cranked up her suit's servos to maximum power for an assisted leap. Just as she felt the power assist compress the shock absorbers in her suit's legs to comply, the rail gun fired again. She felt a hammer blow on her right side, and before her brain could process that she had been hit, she was already on the ground. Her combat display flickered and spasmed, vomiting up a waterfall of bright-red and orange warning messages before going dark completely. Her back lit up with searing pain in half a dozen spots. The armor's automedic shot her up a moment later, and the sensation of getting stabbed gave way to cool numbness.

The suit around her was no longer a force multiplier, just dead weight. The servos were locked in the same position as when the rail-gun shot had ripped through her suit's spine, taking out the power pack or the main processing core or both. Idina was facedown on the ground, the suit curled into a semicrouch on top of her, ensconcing her like a turtle's shell. If the rail-gun operator decided to take another shot at her, the armor wouldn't do her any good. The scout armor was rated for small-arms fire, not for antivehicle weapons that could shoot through an armored gyrofoil from front to back.

Her section was shooting back with all barrels now, and the automatic gunfire reverberated from the hillsides.

"Colors Chaudhary!" She heard the voice of one of her junior troopers in her helmet's headset. The armor's computer had taken over from the suit and disconnected from the now-useless data and power umbilical. She had eyes and ears again.

"I'm fine," she replied. "Suit's dead. Stay put. Don't stick your heads out to get me."

Idina fumbled for the emergency-release handles of her suit and yanked on them with all her force. The locks released and dumped her on the ground underneath her dead and silent shell. She bit back a scream when fresh pain shot down her back. The autodoc numbed the pain again quickly, but it was clearly at the limits of its abilities. She guessed that the pass of the rail-gun slug had spalled off some shards from the inside of the suit's armor plating with enough force to pierce the back of her scout armor.

The rail gun went boom clang again, and Idina looked up. In front of her, the slug smashed into the wall of the maintenance building, tearing a hole into the exterior and kicking up a cloud of concrete dust. Behind the building, four of her section's troopers were popping in and out of cover and returning fire with their suit-mounted guns.

Thirty meters. The rail gun would be able to track her, but at least her scout armor would keep out the small-arms stuff. She waited for the rail gun's next shot and flexed her leg muscles, ready to crawl out from underneath the suit and run toward cover once she heard the boom clang that would give her five seconds until the reload.

The rail gun didn't fire again. Instead, the world blew apart right in front of her.

It felt like someone had taken a running start with a fully amped-up power suit and kicked her backward. She was flung hard against her dead suit, cracking something in her left arm, and then the suit was gone, and she was lying facedown on the ground with her hearing gone and the breath squeezed out of her lungs. Now it was the scout armor's turn to display a list of mechanical and electronic grievances on her visor, which was cracked in half. Idina tasted blood in her mouth and coughed up a mouthful of it. The armor should have cleaned the inside of her helmet automatically, but it didn't. A spray of red droplets covered the inside of the broken face shield. Something had cut her face open from cheekbone to jawline, and the blood was running into the collar of her under-armor suit, but her armor's autodoc wasn't doing anything to stop the bleeding.

Idina fought to fill her lungs with air again. She fumbled for the release latches of her helmet and wrenched it off her head. The air outside smelled of burning gun propellant, only much stronger than she had ever experienced it. When she tried to lift her upper body from the ground, her left arm failed to cooperate, so she rolled onto her right side and raised her head.

She was lying on the bank of the brook, a hundred meters from where the service access station had stood just a few moments ago. All around her, chunks of concrete were still raining down, thudding into the soft soil or splashing into the water of the brook. The station building was gone. Someone had blown it into a million pieces. Most of the rest of her section had been using the building as cover, and now there was nobody left standing on this side of the brook. Idina looked around for her suit. The blood streaming down her face was now running into her collar seal and down the left side of her chest. Her suit hadn't made it quite as far as she did. It was maybe thirty meters in front of her, smoldering and bent into an irreparable shape.

There was another suit to her right. It was half-submerged in the brook, lying on its back. Idina blinked the sweat and grime out of her eyes and tried to make out the insignia on the outer armor shell. It was Lance Sharma, who had taken cover behind the shed instead of the main building. The explosion had still blown him and his half-ton powered suit over fifty meters across the meadow and into the brook. She wanted to call out to him, but she could barely get enough air into her lungs to keep from passing out.

On the far bank of the brook, shapes materialized on the hillside, shimmering silhouettes that seemed to wink into and out of existence. They rushed down the slope like ghosts. With their camo active, Idina couldn't even begin to get a count on them, but they were at least as numerous as her section had been before it got shot up and blown sky-high. She glanced back toward her armor, which still had her carbine mounted on one of the arm rails. It was probably broken like the rest of the thing, and even if it wasn't, she'd never reach it in time. Not with her lungs filling with blood and her arm and gods knew what else out of commission. And the ghostly shapes were already crossing the brook and rushing up the far side, toward the destroyed station building.

One of them veered off and walked over to Lance Sharma's suit. He deactivated the camo of his armor, and Idina got her first good look at their attackers. His armor was something Idina had never seen before. It was sleek and lightweight, and everything about it shouted high-speed commando gear. There were no markings of any kind, no name tags or rank insignia. The helmet was streamlined and had a narrow visor that was little more than a slit. The strange trooper bent down as if to check on Lance Sharma. He pulled on the emergency-release handles and lifted Lance Sharma's upper body out of his suit carefully, in a motion that was almost gentle. Then he took Sharma's helmet off. Idina could see that Lance was still alive. His eyelids were fluttering, and his mouth moved as if he was speaking.

Then the trooper in the strange armor pulled out his sidearm, put the muzzle against Lance Sharma's forehead, and pulled the trigger.

Idina didn't hear the gunshot—or her own scream of pain and fury. She didn't even realize she had gotten to her feet under her own power until she had already covered half the distance to Sharma and his killer. Her carbine and grenade launcher were broken or out of reach, but she still had her kukri—thank the gods it was still attached to her armor—and her right hand drew it from its sheath entirely of its own accord with the automatic smoothness of many years of practice.

The killer turned to face her. He dropped Lance Sharma back into his suit and brought his pistol around, but she knew that even if he managed to empty the magazine, it wouldn't keep her from killing him. She reached him just as he pulled the trigger. Her kukri came up and back down in an overhand swing, and she put all of her strength into the blow. The monomolecular blade sliced through most things like a battle-ax through a birthday cake, and whatever this man's high-speed armor was made of, it wasn't built to resist that sort of cutting power.

His shot punched through her armor. She felt it tear through the left part of her upper chest, right underneath her clavicle. The pistol and the hand that had held it dropped into the brook with a splash. He took a step backward and fell over Lance Sharma's armor. Idina followed him down, letting herself fall on top of him, thrusting out her kukri on the way down. She felt it split the killer's armor in the center of his chest, and she added her body weight to the thrust to make sure the blade went in all the way to the hilt. The killer convulsed once and then lay still. She slid off him and splashed into the cold, clean water of the brook, her strength spent. She could barely manage to roll over so she wouldn't drown facedown in water only three fingers deep.

On the hillside above her, from the direction her section had come, gunfire rang out again, the familiar high-pitched chattering of Pallas Brigade carbines on their highest automatic-fire setting. The other sections had arrived.

The water poured into Idina's armor and pushed its way past the neck seal. It was just a degree or two above freezing, and it made her skin go numb almost instantly, which wasn't an entirely unwelcome sensation right now. She spat out another mouthful of blood and turned to look at the mountains in the distance. They weren't anywhere near as tall as the mighty peaks of Pallas, but they were snowcapped and looked just a little bit like home.

They really don't deserve this place, she thought before everything slipped into darkness.

CHAPTER 3

ADEN

Aden had been in the auditorium at least once a week for the last five years, but he couldn't recall ever hearing so much laughter and giddy chatter in the room, not even during communal entertainment nights. Half the company was wound up and elated at the prospect of imminent release. The mood among the other half was mixed. Some of the men were quiet. Others seemed anxious. After five years, the war was truly ending for them. The unexpected suddenness of the event made him feel inside like he had just stepped off one of the arcology's terraces without a parachute.

The laughter and conversation stopped when the doors opened and a Rhodian officer walked in, followed by two senior NCOs and a civilian. Aden was the ranking Gretian in the room, so he got out of his seat and did the required honors.

"Attention!"

The other troops in the room rose as one and stood at attention. The Rhody officer, a captain, squared off in front of Aden to receive the customary report.

"Delta Company, Fifty-Seventh Penal Battalion, assembled as ordered, sir. All personnel present and accounted for."

He held the salute until the Rhody captain returned it.

"At ease," the captain said. "Sit down, everyone."

The captain looked young, just like most of the Rhodian officers who cycled through this place. It seemed common practice for the Rhodies to assign their junior commissioned personnel to detention duty before shipping them off to occupation deployments on Gretia. It made him feel ancient, but it was a little odd to have to render honors to officers who had still been in secondary school when the war had ended—kids who were young enough to be his own children. Aden sat down again and watched the Rhody captain walk up to the dais at the front of the auditorium, followed by the two NCOs and the lone civilian. But it wasn't the captain who started speaking. It was the civilian.

"Good morning from the Rhodian Ministry of Defense," he said without introducing himself. "Pursuant to article 42b of the Treaty of Oceana, your detainment officially ends today at noon."

There were some muted expressions of joy among the company, which the ministry official ignored. The sergeants on either side of the speaker looked more displeased, but none of them made a move to curb this mild lapse in discipline. Aden guessed they were as happy about the upcoming release as the Gretians were.

"At 1000 hours, right after this release briefing, you will report to the quartermaster to hand in your issued items. After that, you will receive your accumulated pay. In accordance with treaty agreements, you will receive fifteen ags for each day served in Rhodian detention, including your labor-exempt days."

Fifteen ags wasn't a lot of money for a day's work, but five years' worth of them would add up to more money than Aden had ever had on his credit ledger before. He did some quick math in his head, not wanting to be obvious by pulling out the comtab and using its calculator. Some of the Gretians next to him did just that, and he shook his head. Pittance handouts from their jailers, and they showed their excitement like dogs wagging their tails over kitchen scraps. Still, even five years of meager pay added up to a tidy little pile.

"Before you all get too excited about your new riches, a word of caution. I know you think the Mnemosyne news feeds have been keeping you current all these years, but I can tell you that you are very much out of the loop. Things are not as they were. You may find that even twenty or thirty thousand ags does not stretch nearly as far as it did before the war. And the Rhodian government has decided that the treaty does not obligate us to accommodate you financially from the Rhodian public purse in any way past the moment of release. That includes your transportation home, which you will have to secure on your own with your personal funds."

That brought a little smirk to the faces of the NCOs flanking the ministry official. From behind him, Aden heard dissatisfied vocalizations from his fellow Gretians all over the auditorium. Five years of boring daily routine and one big carrot on a stick later, and they had forgotten their Blackguard discipline.

"The Ministry of Defense has prepared a prerelease orientation package for you, which will be presented momentarily. Pay close attention to it because it contains information regarding the status of the system and your legal responsibilities, both individually and as former members of the Gretian armed forces. Ignorance will not shield you from prosecution if you step out of line in the system, whether here on Rhodia or elsewhere."

Behind the Rhodian ministry official, the wall changed from translucent to opaque. Then it showed the flag of Rhodia, a scarlet-red field with a diagonal cross of golden yellow, before the announced presentation began.

The POWs had access to parts of the Mnemosyne through their issued comtabs, so Aden already knew much of the information in the briefing. Gretia didn't exist as a sovereign planet anymore. For the last five years, since the end of hostilities, his home planet had been run by the Allied Occupation Force, which had divided Gretia into distinct zones. Aden had spent twelve years in the service of a military that no longer existed, and five more atoning for the sins of a state that was gone. The war had been hard on the entire system, but it had been hardest on Gretia because their people had the most to lose. Trade networks and interdependencies that evolved over five hundred years had been broken thoroughly in just four. The Rhodian presentation left out no opportunity to hammer home to the POWs that the war Gretia started had almost ruined the entire system.

"The terms of the peace treaty put you under certain restrictions and obligations," the narrator said while travel and security iconography appeared on the screen. "You are not allowed to serve in a military again for the rest of your lives. Once you are released, you will have seventy-two hours to leave Rhodia, and you may not return for any reason for a period of three years. You will be issued temporary ID passes that expire in thirty days. Once on Gretia, you will report to the Allied Occupation Force, and you will be required to check in with your local AOF authorities twice a year. Failure to follow these treaty obligations will make you subject to arrest and imprisonment."

This isn't freedom, Aden thought. *They're just making us move from one prison to another.* He'd be home on Gretia, with all his professional knowledge useless to him, and he'd still have to dance to the tunes served up by the Rhodies and their allies. But at least he wasn't one of the quarter million Gretians who had fallen. And where there were rules and jailers, there would always be ways to get around them.

The release happened with disconcerting speed and efficiency. Once the presentation had finished, the company went down to the quartermaster's office, where they turned in their issued comtabs and uniforms. The Rhodian supply clerks were every bit as thorough and petty as their Gretian military counterparts had been. For every missing item, there was a value table with a depreciation schedule, and the clerks made notations on the release files that would subtract the value of the missing item from the accumulated pay. Almost everyone had missing gear after five years of imprisonment. Aden was short one towel and three undershirts, and the clerk duly noted a forty-four-ag debit on his file. The only thing he parted with reluctantly was the comtab. It was tightly locked down and only had very limited Mnemosyne access, but it had been his little window into the world for five years, the only connection with the life beyond his section of the detention arcology.

Then came the time for the Gretian prisoners to reclaim whatever property they had in their possession when they were captured. Aden waited for his turn with some trepidation. After five years, he didn't really remember what he had carried with him when the Oceanians had accepted his unit's surrender.

The quartermaster clerk put a transparent storage cube on the counter in front of Aden. He popped the seal and opened the top. Inside was his old Blackguards uniform, folded and pressed. All the Gretian insignia had been neatly and expertly removed. The Gretian planetary ensign was gone from the right shoulder, the Blackguards badge was missing from the collars, and the shoulder epaulettes didn't have any rank insignia on them. It looked strangely sterile, not quite a uniform anymore but not a piece of regular civilian clothing either. Underneath the uniform was a small bag, and Aden opened it and emptied the contents out on the counter. There was his intelligence badge and his small collection of medal ribbons.

"Your record shows that you also had a Gretian military–issue comtab and a sidearm with you. Those prohibited items were confiscated without compensation," the clerk said. "Move on. Next in line."

Aden put his stuff back into the storage cube and closed it again. Then he made space for the next Gretian in line to receive the relics of his old life back. There were a few more things in the cube, but he'd go through them later, not in front of this Rhody lance corporal.

The last station they were all herded through like livestock was the clerk's office, where they received their identification passes and their pay. The ags were not on credsticks, the form of money Aden was used to handling. In the briefing just before the return of their equipment, the narrator had explained that a new system was in place: virtual credit ledgers linked to the bearer's personal ID file in the Mnemosyne and locked down with bomb-proof encryption. Nobody walked around with transferable credsticks anymore. Aden had no reason to doubt that this system worked, but it felt strange to get paid without receiving something tangible. Credsticks had been reassuringly solid little cylinders—they had *felt* like they had value—and peeling the bank's seal off the data port had always felt like opening a little jar of possibilities. Now he had to take the screen of the clerk's data station at its word that he had 45,581 ags at his disposal on his credit ledger.

When he walked out into the hallway again, someone was berating the prisoners still standing in line. It was Persson, an older, cantankerous sergeant Aden had never really liked. The man had been a supply NCO in the Blackguards, a rear-echelon trooper with a safe and cushy job, but he had always carried himself as if the Rhodies had needed four men and a set of powered armor to take him prisoner.

"If you take that money, it makes you traitors," the sergeant shouted at the line. The prisoners mostly ignored him or rolled their eyes. Some responded with angry shouts of their own. Aden could see the commotion attracting the interest of two of the Rhodian MPs farther up the hallway, and they started moving down the line toward the source of the racket.

"Don't take handouts from these fuckers. Have some pride. You are Gretians. You are Blackguards. Any one of us is worth ten of them."

"Stand down, Sergeant Persson," Aden said. Persson turned around, his face livid. When he saw who was addressing him, he faltered just a little, but his anger carried him right through the hesitation.

"No disrespect, sir, but you're no longer our senior officer. That's over now."

"You're right," Aden said. "I'm no longer a major. You're no longer a sergeant. And there are no more Blackguards. You want to refuse the money, go ahead. But stop shouting about it. Nobody cares anymore."

There were some murmurs of agreement from the men and women behind Persson. The line moved on, undeterred. Persson stood, hands balled into fists so tightly that his knuckles shone white. He had tears in his eyes, and for the first time in five years, Aden felt a pang of sympathy for the man. Persson was just projecting his shame onto the other prisoners. Nobody had any authority over him anymore except for the Rhodies, but he also didn't have anyone else to exercise authority over, and men like Persson didn't float well when you untied them from their moorings.

"The war's over, Persson," Aden said in a more gentle tone. "We've lost. Nothing left to do but to pick through the rubble. Come on."

The Rhodian MPs arrived, hands on the stunners they carried on their belts.

"What is the problem here?" one of them asked.

"There is no problem, Corporal," Aden replied in Rhodian. "This man is just a little upset, that's all."

"Then tell him to be upset somewhere else, and more quietly," the Rhody MP said. "Let's not start any unpleasant business. You don't want to add another year to your stay at the last minute."

This whole place has been nothing but unpleasant business, Aden thought. He didn't believe the Rhodies would really pull Persson out of the release company and shunt him to the back of the line for release in a year at this point in the process. He was, however, completely certain that Persson would hang himself in his quarters if they did.

"Come on, Persson," he said to the old sergeant. "Get back in line and collect your pay, and then let's go home."

Persson looked at the Rhodian MPs with wet eyes. Then he lowered his gaze and went to join the back of the line, but slowly. He looked much older than the fifty years or so Aden knew him to be. One more humiliation added to a long list. Aden suspected the Rhodies would never get tired of dishing those out to them.

CHAPTER 4

DUNSTAN

The comms panel buzzed just as Lieutenant Commander Dunstan Park, Rhodian Navy, had turned on the shower and gotten his hair wet. *In war or peace, it never fucking fails,* he thought as he turned the water off again and stepped out of the wet cell. *It's like sympathetic magic.*

"Go ahead," he said to the panel.

"Captain, you're needed in the AIC," his XO said.

"Understood. I'll be up in a minute, Bosworth."

He grabbed a towel and dried his hair with one hand while he used the other to open the drawer underneath his bunk and pull out a clean undershirt. A few moments later, he was back in his shipboard overalls and on the way to the Action Information Center of the Rhodian Navy frigate RNS *Minotaur*.

"I think our invisible friend is back," Lieutenant Bosworth said when Dunstan climbed through the door of the AIC.

"Again? I am getting a bit tired of this ghost hunt. Let's see it on the plot."

"Aye, sir." Lieutenant Bosworth brought up a holoscreen with the tactical display and marked the spot where the ship's sensors had sniffed out the latest contact. Dunstan studied the situational display.

"That's on the other side of the parking lot. I'm surprised we even got a ping from all the way over here, with so much clutter in between."

"The AI is getting better at prediction, I think."

"Either that, or the arrays are starting to spark out on us and we've been chasing false echoes all week."

The "parking lot" they were guarding contained almost thirty capital ships, the entire remnant of the once-mighty Gretian fleet. The warships of their defeated enemy had been interned here on the far side of the Rhodian moon Tethys for five years now, awaiting the results of the legal wrangling still in progress that would determine the allocation of these ships among the planets of the winning Alliance. Until then, they were mothballed, with reactor cores in maintenance mode and skeleton caretaker crews supplied by the ever-shrinking Rhodian Navy bouncing from ship to ship as needed to keep the lights on.

RNS *Minotaur* was on day thirty of a monthlong guard-duty turn. Their replacement, RNS *Athena*, was on the way to take their spot, and most of *Minotaur*'s crew was mentally on leave already. Guarding the internment lot was by far the least popular duty in the fleet because it was deathly boring. For the first year after the war, the Rhodian guard ships had had to discourage private ships from news organizations, sightseeing outfits, and thrill-seekers from getting too close to the Gretian fleet units, and at least there had been some variety in daily routines. But as the postwar bickering over dividing the spoils had stretched into years, the public had lost interest, and the navy had gradually reduced the number of guard ships assigned to the internment picket. Now only one ship was on station at any given time, with no company except for the silent hulls of the Gretian warships.

"We're going to have to pass the data on to *Athena* when they get here so they can verify our arrays aren't faulty," Lieutenant Bosworth said.

"And so their AI gets a head start in case they are working." Dunstan spun the situation display and plotted a course around the bulk of the Gretian ships with his index finger.

"Helm, lay in that course and take us over there. Thrusters only. Let's not clutter up the sensors with a drive plume."

"Aye, sir."

Minotaur fired her lateral thrusters and slowly started her curveball trajectory around the immense bubble in space that was the internment parking lot. Every Gretian ship had several kilometers of empty space around it in all directions. Even in defeat, it was an imposing assembly. The Gretians had handed over their entire remaining navy at the surrender, and the Alliance had only grudgingly returned a handful of small patrol corvettes for orbital police duties. Parked out here were five battleships, seven cruisers—heavy and light—eleven destroyers, and three orbital assault ships.

And then there was the battle-scarred dreadnought *Mjolnir*, the pride of the Gretian fleet, veteran of many deep-space engagements and killer of many Rhodian ships. She was the centerpiece of this fleet in repose, the one item on the ledger over which the Alliance couldn't find consensus. Most of the other ships were older, or smaller, or far less capable. Even the battleships, as formidable as they still would be in combat, were only the equals of their Rhodian and Acheroni counterparts at best. *Mjolnir*, on the other hand, had been designed as a killer of task forces, a rock against which superior numbers could break, and she had done that job very well during the war. Dunstan often found himself studying the lines of that beast when his crew passed nearby on patrols. The Gretians had a hand for functional, straightforward designs, with no thought spared on aesthetics, but there was a beauty of its own in her unapologetic massiveness. Whoever ended up with her would boost the combat power of their navy considerably, and the Alliance planets were already jittery about equitable distribution of military strength after four years of staggering losses.

"Another ping," Lieutenant Bosworth announced. He had moved over to the tactical station. "That one is twenty kilometers from the first one." He placed the mark on the tactical display, and a dotted line appeared that predicted the contact's movement.

"Huh. That's away from the lot and going back around Tethys."

"Piece of debris that got yanked into Tethys's gravity well, maybe? The size of the radar return is about right for something like that. Small satellite maybe. Or a loose escape pod," Lieutenant Bosworth suggested.

"Steady as she goes on thrusters. Set our trajectory for intercept, but make sure we stay clear of the radar shadows from those big Gretian tubs."

"Aye, sir," the helmsman said again. The ship continued its arc with regular boosts from the thrusters. The gravmag generators of the ship canceled out acceleration forces well beyond what the main engine could put out at low throttle, so the comparatively tiny boosts from the maneuvering thrusters didn't even register in Dunstan's inner ear.

They spent the next two hours creeping around the perimeter of the internment lot, making a wide arc to keep a clear sensor bearing of the spot where the AI had last sniffed out a contact. If there was another ship out there, it was tiny, maybe some newsies in a pleasure skiff trying to get high-resolution footage for a network special. But this was restricted space for anyone except Rhodian Navy units, and *Minotaur*'s job was to make sure people didn't forget that fact even after five years of peace.

"Next contact pops up, we go active and sweep that spot with full juice from the array," Dunstan told Lieutenant Bosworth. "And lock on with targeting lasers. Make them piss their overalls a bit."

"Copy that," the lieutenant replied with a grin. If there was someone sneaking around out there in a small pleasure craft, the focused radiation burst from a warship's active sensor package would make every control panel on their ship light up with warnings. The last four weeks had been alternately boring and frustrating, with *Minotaur* fruitlessly chasing down radar echoes for much of that time, and a bit of payback would mean this patrol hadn't been a complete waste of time.

"May want to go to maneuvering stations, sir," the weapons officer suggested. "In case we have to give chase. Or they do something stupid when we turn on the searchlights."

"Thank you, Lieutenant Mayler. You're absolutely right. Let's play it by the book. If anything, it's good exercise."

He tapped the communications panel in front of him for a ship-wide broadcast.

"This is the captain. All hands, maneuvering stations."

Minotaur was a frigate, not a capital ship, and she was running with a lean crew just like every other ship in the navy. At full wartime complement, she had just over a hundred people on board, and that number included the full squad of marines they usually had with them for boarding actions. But there were no marines on the ship right now, and with every department pared down to the bare minimum needed to run the ship, there were fewer than forty Rhodian Navy personnel on board. All of them were now strapping themselves into the automatic chairs that would keep their bodies firmly in place and compensate for gravity if the ship had to light up its main drive and pull more acceleration than the gravmag generators could equalize. Dunstan buckled into his own gravity chair while making a mental note to commend Lieutenant Mayler afterward for reminding him to stick to standard operating procedure. A month of boring routine without any variety or excitement spread complacency, and it was a good reminder to Dunstan that he wasn't exempt from that syndrome.

So much tonnage, Dunstan thought as they circled the interned fleet slowly but steadily. These ships represented hundreds of thousands of tons of valuable salvage even without considering the precious palladium that made up their gravmag generators. The tiny gravmag rotors that were built into Dunstan's *Minotaur* represented almost half the monetary value of the entire ship, and superheavies like *Gram* or *Mjolnir* had ten times more palladium in theirs.

"Coming up on the predicted line-of-sight wedge, Captain," Lieutenant Bosworth announced.

"Stand by on active sensors." Dunstan softly drummed his fingertips on the armrest of his gravity chair. "You get a blip on passive, you sweep that spot. Twenty-degree cone, full power."

"Aye, sir. Standing by for active sweep."

Minotaur was now coasting through the space between the internment yard and Tethys at just a few hundred meters per second, occasionally firing short bursts from her thrusters to correct her trajectory. The nearby moon was already exerting its pull on the ship's ballistic arc, and before too long, they'd have to either light their main drive again and give their presence away or ride the gravity slingshot around Tethys and lose sight of the shipyard they were tasked to guard.

"Passive contact, bearing 355 by 5. Distance three hundred kilometers," Lieutenant Bosworth said, a note of triumph in his voice.

"Light them up," Dunstan ordered.

The ship's powerful forward sensor array scanned the space ahead in a narrow cone. Dunstan watched the scanner arc sweeping across the tactical display. Somewhere in the lightless void three hundred kilometers in front of *Minotaur*'s bow, someone was playing hide-and-seek with them in the darkness, and they had just turned on a big flashlight and pointed it at the rustling noise in the bushes.

"Contact," Lieutenant Bosworth called out. "Active return, bearing 355 by 4, distance 312, moving at one thousand meters per second."

"That's a tiny radar return," Dunstan said.

"Too small for a ship," Lieutenant Bosworth agreed. "Rogue satellite?"

"It's not squawking ID. And we're nowhere close to any place where satellites ought to be."

The computer marked the unknown contact on the tactical display with a red lozenge-shaped hologram. On the next sweep of the sensor suite, the hologram faded from bright to pale red. Dunstan waited for the contact to reappear after the next sweep, but the hologram remained pale, losing a little more color with each pass of the sensors.

"Contact lost, sir."

How can we lose a contact we just pegged on active? Dunstan wondered. His brain wasted no time presenting him with a number of possibilities for such an occurrence, all ranging from annoying to extremely unlikely.

"Go hot on the main search array and give me a three-sixty," he ordered. "If there's anyone out here, we just gave ourselves away anyway."

The tactical display expanded from a wedge to a full circle. In the semicircle to *Minotaur*'s rear, the twenty-odd tactical holograms for the Gretian warships lit up one by one as the sensors painted their hulls with high-energy radiation and measured the returns.

"Multiple new contacts," Lieutenant Bosworth said. His voice sounded strangely tentative, as if he was unsure of his statement. "Bearing . . . 181 by *minus nine?*"

The optical feed from the stern array didn't have a drive plume to obscure its field of vision. Dunstan opened a new view window and magnified the visual. The Gretian internment fleet was still hanging in space well behind *Minotaur*, but now there was movement where there should have been none. At the far end of the formation, one of the ships was pitching forward and picking up speed, trailing a bright drive plume.

No, Dunstan thought. *Not a drive plume. An explosion.*

"One of the fuzzhead battleships just blew up," Lieutenant Mayler said. "It's . . . Wait. There goes another."

Another ship in the static formation briefly flared up brightly, then broke in half in slow motion. A third one followed just a few seconds later, then a fourth. Dunstan watched as the battleship *Gram* blew apart, its aft section disintegrating in a searing momentary fireball, its front accelerating with the force of the explosion. The forward two-thirds of *Gram*'s hull careened into a nearby light cruiser and knocked it out of the formation, trailing a long comet tail of debris behind the wreckage. It was like a silent, eerie, terrifying chain reaction, and the sight of it caused Dunstan to squeeze the armrest of his chair so hard that it made the metal creak.

Someone was scuttling the Gretian fleet.

"All hands, action stations!" Dunstan shouted. "Bring the main drive on line right now."

The next few moments were controlled chaos in the AIC as everyone sprang into frenzied action at the same time. The ship was still coasting on its intercept course away from the Gretian fleet that was now disintegrating behind them one ship at a time, hulls breaking apart in soundless explosions that spewed chunks of steel and alloy in every direction.

"Sir, we are going to have high-speed debris inbound very shortly," Lieutenant Bosworth said.

"Energize the armor and set point defense to live mode." Dunstan's mind was racing. The plot was a mess of contacts that were multiplying with every explosion and collision out among what was left of the Gretian fleet, and the computer dutifully tried to track and tag everything. The resulting information overload made it all but impossible for him to see what was going on out there.

A warning popped up on the tactical panel, accompanied by an alert sound that made Dunstan's stomach twist. Two new icons appeared on the tactical plot right between *Minotaur* and the remaining Gretian ships. They were not the generic symbols for debris hazards but the bright-red inverted V shapes of hostile missiles.

"Multiple launch," Lieutenant Mayler called out. "Incoming anti-ship missiles, threat vector 180, distance eighty-five, closing in fast."

Dunstan wanted to believe that the computer was wrong, that it had misidentified debris coming toward them, but the warning tone of a targeting laser lock made the nature of those two objects unambiguously clear a few seconds later.

"Full thrust on the main drive. Everyone, get ready for some g load. Weapons, tell me the Point Defense System is on line."

"Affirmative, sir. Point Defense System is in automatic mode and tracking."

"Who the hell is shooting at us?" Dunstan asked nobody in particular. To get a clear picture of the space between *Minotaur* and the rapidly disintegrating internment fleet, they would have to turn the ship and use their front array, but the counterburn from the main drive would slow down and then kill their momentum, and he wasn't about to put on the brakes with two antiship missiles and an expanding debris cloud closing in on their stern. To find out who was out there blowing up the Gretian fleet, they had to survive first. And to survive, they had to stretch the distance between *Minotaur* and the inbound missiles so the point-defense AI could figure out an optimal intercept. With every passing second, the computer took in more relevant data to formulate a defense pattern—velocities, trajectories, aspect changes, electronic emissions—and an extra five or six seconds could mean the difference between a successful intercept and *Minotaur* herself becoming a local debris cloud.

The ship could accelerate hard enough to turn everyone inside into pudding even with the gravmag generators running at maximum field strength. The computer limited the throttle to keep acceleration to survivable limits for the crew, but the missiles chasing them had no such constraints. The two red icons on the plot closed the distance with every passing second even as *Minotaur* was sprinting away at fifteen g.

"Thirty-nine seconds to intercept," Lieutenant Mayler announced, the strain from the acceleration clear in his voice. "PDS is still tracking."

"What was the launch distance again?"

"Eighty-five kilometers, sir."

"Why'd they launch from that far out?" Dunstan wondered out loud. The ship that had fired at them had been completely off their sensors until the moment those missiles launched. Now *Minotaur*'s AI had most of a minute to calculate a defensive solution. Halving the launch distance would have all but guaranteed a kill. Not that the Point Defense System was a sure thing—the most-modern warheads had countermeasures to the PDS's countermeasures, and in most engagements, the side with the more recent software update usually won. *Minotaur* hadn't had to use her PDS outside of fleet exercises since the end of the war, and Dunstan sincerely hoped that the latest update had included the data on the missiles that were currently streaking their way.

"Thirty seconds," Lieutenant Mayler said. "PDS is switching to full autonomous mode."

The AI that was in charge of the ship's ballistic defense was now in command of the entire ship. It had much faster reaction times than any of *Minotaur*'s human crew, and at the speeds and distances involved in space combat, it didn't waste precious fractions of a second relaying or parsing verbal commands.

The main drive throttled back, and Dunstan welcomed the sudden absence of the weight that had been parked on his chest. He watched the situational display to see the ship firing its thrusters and starting a bow-over-stern spin, then counterfiring them to arrest the spin with the precision and speed of a brain that was running on palladium pathways instead of human synapses.

"EM countermeasures active," Lieutenant Mayler said. "Missiles away."

The ship launched four interceptor missiles, then four more. The missiles fanned out in front of the ship in two groups and raced toward the much larger ship killers, which faded from the plot when the first row of missiles began saturating the space in front of it with electronic noise.

"Countermissiles intercepting in three . . . two . . . one."

Up ahead, a thermal bloom flashed in the darkness, then dissipated quickly. One of the interceptors had found its mark.

"Scratch one," Lieutenant Mayler narrated. "Second one is still inbound."

The surviving antiship missile popped back into existence on the tactical display as it broke through the cloud of electronic noise from the jamming missiles. In the distance somewhere between the incoming ship killer and the wrecked Gretian fleet, a string of thermal blossoms lit up the darkness very briefly as the interceptors self-destructed after missing the target.

"Fifteen seconds. PDS is tracking again."

The ship's thrusters fired again, but this time it wasn't an end-over-end flip. Instead, the computer spun the hull around perpendicular to their axis of motion, unmasking the starboard side of *Minotaur* to the threat so the point-defense weapons could come into play. A second or two later, the directed-energy mounts on the hull started firing. *Minotaur* had four mounts on the rear section of the hull and four on the forward hull, covering the space around the ship in a 360-degree bubble, and the AI had turned the ship around so six out of those eight mounts could fire at the incoming missile. The point-defense lasers went through their firing cycle, and with each one-second discharge of the megawatt-class emitters, the lights in the AIC dimmed a little as the mounts drained much of the available reactor output. *Minotaur* was fighting for her life as best she could, and Dunstan wondered whether the AI had something like a sense of self-preservation beyond her cold and factual programming.

Now it came down to numbers, to meters per second and joules and megawatts, the missile racing to reach the proximity of the ship's hull before the point-defense lasers could pour enough energy into it to burn it up or render it stupid. It was a gamble Dunstan wouldn't have made—turning the ship sideways increased the firepower of her point defenses, but it invited a devastating broadside hit if the missile got through. Dunstan would have turned the ship to face the missile with the heavily armored and shielded bow, or with the stern as a last resort in hopes of only losing the main drive. The AI was betting that the added wattage from the extra mounts would be enough to blow up the ship-killer missile at a safe distance, and all their lives were riding on that bet now.

Minotaur's AI won this hand against the computer in the missile's seeker head. Ten kilometers off their starboard side, there was a brief, unspectacular flash as the point-defense lasers finally heated the warhead beyond its structural endurance.

"Hard kill," Lieutenant Mayler cheered. "Scratch two."

Dunstan let out a breath that he didn't remember holding.

The AI rotated the ship again to face it backward, bow toward the point in space where the missile had broken up. A moment later, they heard debris smacking against the armored bow, bits and pieces of the burned-out warhead, now only mindless kinetic hazards.

"Damage report," Dunstan called out.

"Board is green, sir. Bow armor deflected everything," Lieutenant Bosworth replied. "She's still got air where she should and no holes where she shouldn't."

"Fire up the array and do a full sweep, and stand by on ASM launchers. I want to find the asshole who just shot at us, so we can return the favor."

The sensor sweep painted a grim picture. The missile chase had taken *Minotaur* several thousand kilometers away from the Gretian ships. The internment fleet was almost completely wrecked. Where ten minutes ago there had been an orderly cluster of imposing capital ships, there was now a junkyard full of shattered hulls careening into each other and breaking apart. Only the mighty *Mjolnir* remained, along with two much smaller ships, frigates or destroyers a twentieth the size of the massive dreadnought. There was no trace of any other ship between their position and the wreckage cluster that used to be the Gretian battle fleet. Dunstan had no idea how someone had managed to place scuttling charges on all those ships, right under the noses of the Rhodian Navy. Right under his nose. But they had managed and done a perfect job with it. From the way the hulls of those ships had split, he could tell that whoever had placed the charges had known exactly where to put them on the inside to achieve maximum structural damage with a minimal expenditure of explosives.

"Get on comms with the fleet and tell them what's going on up here," Dunstan said. "They'll need to send everything they have docked at Rhodia One right now. Once word gets out, this place will be swarming with salvagers. There's a billion ags' worth of palladium floating around out there."

And so the day can turn to shit in a minute, he thought as he studied the mess on the situational display. Twenty-four hours later, and *Athena* would have been on station out here instead while the crew of *Minotaur* headed down to Rhodia on leave. Now they'd be out here for a while longer. He was sure that the brass would be deeply unhappy about the scuttling of their war prizes, and he knew that they'd take their unhappiness out on the commanding officer of the only Rhodian Navy ship that was present when it happened.

But whatever he had done to piss off the Fates this week, they must have decided they were not done with Lieutenant Commander Dunstan Park yet. A few thousand kilometers in front of *Minotaur*'s bow, a new sun briefly flashed into existence where the Gretian dreadnought *Mjolnir* had been sitting in space just a moment ago. The smaller ships that had been parked next to *Mjolnir* disappeared in the short-lived inferno that was unmistakably a low-yield nuclear explosion, and the radiation alert in *Minotaur*'s AIC confirmed the event just a moment later. Someone shut down the alert, and for a few moments, there was absolute silence in the AIC as everyone stared at the visual feed in shock. Even at this distance, the sudden burst of high-intensity radiation blinded the sensor array, and Dunstan knew it would be a while before they could burn through the EM clutter and see what was left out there. Over a million tons of warships were now finely dispersed and irradiated debris.

This is going to be a mess, Dunstan thought. He couldn't figure out why anyone would just blow up the entire fleet, the object of five years of legal wrangling between the Alliance planets. The Gretians would be pissed because they'd see the senseless destruction of their planet's battle fleet as a further slight piled on top of all the humiliations they had to endure already as the war's loser and instigator. The Oceanians and Acheroni would be pissed because they wouldn't be able to boost their fleets' combat power with free capital ships, and Rhodia would take most of the blame for this because the Gretian fleet had been in its custody pending their final disposition. It was just a gigantic waste, billions of ags turned into pyrotechnics, and it would cause nothing but strife.

"Well," Lieutenant Bosworth said. "On the bright side, I suppose that takes care of the salvager issue."

Chapter 5
Aden

Aden had spent his whole imprisonment on the same level of the arcology, only swapping sides to face a different direction every year. He knew the structure was huge—he had been tending gardens and greenhouses seven hundred meters up in the sky for five years, after all—but when he stepped out of the elevator on the main atrium floor at the bottom, he realized that he'd had no true idea of the sheer size of it.

The atrium was easily a hundred meters across, and the ceiling was an inverted pyramid made of glass and steel fifty levels above the atrium floor. In the middle of the vault, there was a matching glass-and-steel structure three levels high, and a bundle of elevator tubes connected the structure with the tip of the inverted pyramid hundreds of meters above. Aden stood, mouth agape, and watched transport capsules rise through the tubes and disappear into the ceiling. The vast, open indoor space was filled with sunlight and plant life and the soft murmuring of water. The expanse of the floor was a sprawling park, crisscrossed by a network of tree-lined walkways and framed by reflecting pools and fountains. Five years ago, the Gretian prisoners of war had arrived in the night, on transports that had landed on the skyport platform near the top of the arcology, and he had never seen that the entire core of the building was light and airy above a huge tranquil garden.

Aden walked into the atrium and out onto one of the paths leading across the neatly manicured lawn. It smelled like freshly clipped grass. He had to resist the temptation to take his shoes off and walk barefoot. They'd had grass squares on the garden pathway of the detention level, but those had been ten meters square in size, nothing like this vast expanse. He knew he was still inside of a building, but the sudden sense of open space was almost disorienting, and he had to slow his steps.

Other people were walking on the pathways or sitting on the lawn, alone or in small groups. Few of them were in Rhodian military uniforms. Most were clearly civilians. There were old men and young women, children, even pets. In front of the elevator station in the middle of the atrium, people came up on escalators, then walked off toward the elevator station or out into the atrium. Some studied the screen projections in front of the escalators that were displaying text too small to see from a hundred meters away. Other screens on the side of the elevator station showed different feeds that looked like network news broadcasts and commercials.

Aden had thought that the arcology, if not entirely a prison, was a Rhodian military facility, but the foot traffic here made it clear that this wasn't the case. It was just another one of the many vertical cities of Rhodia, and the fifty thousand prisoners it had housed until now had only been a small and easily managed slice of the arcology's population. It made him feel more insignificant than before. They were Blackguards, the most feared and loathed members of the Gretian military, convicted war criminals all, and the Rhodians hadn't seen the need to put them in a special prison, maybe something austere and harsh like a windowless outpost on one of Rhodia's moons. Instead, they had just quartered them in the middle of a living city, sandwiched in on a few arcology levels between workers and government clerks and their families, not worthy of special security measures beyond the access locks sealing off their incarceration wings from the rest of the building.

Aden felt self-conscious in his green overalls. They didn't have any markings on them, but all the POWs wore them, so his status was obvious just from his appearance. But few people paid him any mind at all. There were some glances as he walked down the central pathway toward the elevator station, but none of them were hostile. The Rhodies didn't seem to care much that a just-released POW from a formerly adversarial nation walked around among them. By now, they were probably well used to the sight of shorthaired men and women in faded green overalls clutching plastic bags and walking around with slightly shell-shocked expressions.

He walked past the escalators that led to the lower levels of the arcology. Aden assumed there was a transit station down there. Rhodia had an extensive network of maglev train tubes crisscrossing the bedrock below the cities. He wondered what would happen if he took one of the escalators down and stepped onto a train to a different part of the planet. They'd said to leave the planet within seventy-two hours, but nobody had mentioned that he couldn't leave the arcology in that time. The urge to go outside and stand in the sunlight with nothing but blue sky above his head was suddenly strong, but he resisted it. He didn't know how to use the transportation network. The atrium didn't have any obvious ways to exit. And he didn't want to join a stream of civilian commuters when he was dressed like the enemy prisoner he was, even if no security officer or military police stopped him at the bottom of the escalator to turn him back.

Inside the elevator station, each tube had a screen projection floating above its access door, showing the stop stations of the capsules. Most of them stopped at sky lobbies on every fiftieth level. The two center tubes showed Express: Skyport on their screens, so he filed into the short line waiting for the next capsules coming down those tubes. He had to wait less than half a minute before a capsule silently descended in front of him, and the tube's access door opened with a soft hiss. The people who had descended in the capsule were stepping out through doors on the opposite side of it, following softly glowing directional arrows on the floor. Aden stepped inside when his line started moving, mindful not to bump into anyone. He tried to look as casually bored and unconcerned as the rest of the people filing into the capsule, but he knew he wouldn't fool anyone who paid attention to him. Nobody did, however. People were talking in low voices or looking at the comtabs in their hands, which made Aden miss his own device. It was easier to feign detached routine when your hands and eyes were busy with an innocuous task.

The elevator capsule set itself in motion. Inside the tube, it wasn't entirely silent. There was a faint electric hum and the soft rushing of air as the capsule started to ascend gently. Then it picked up speed on its upward journey, and soon they were ten, twenty, thirty floors above the atrium. The garden spread out underneath, a tranquil oasis of light and plants and water. There was nothing on Gretia quite like this, and they had dozens of these arcologies. Rhodians had to spread out vertically because of the limited space on their single continent, but the bedrock supported any weight humans could stack on it, and the Rhodies had become masters of arcology building over the last five hundred years.

They ascended through the tip of the upside-down pyramid that was the atrium ceiling, and Aden's view of the gardens below became slightly distorted because of the slanted sides of the ceiling. Then they were too high for him to see the bottom. The core of the building was hollow all the way to the top, a hundred meters separating the elevator tubes from the edges of the residential levels. Every fifty floors, they passed through a sky lobby that had enclosed walkways branching out from it and leading to the arcology level that surrounded that sky lobby. It was all a dizzying display of engineering. If he hadn't known any better, he would have said that the Rhodies put up their prisoners in the biggest and most impressive arcology they had, just to dazzle the

Gretians with their technical prowess. But over the years, he had learned enough about the planet to know that the Rhodians weren't showing off—because they didn't have a need. Aden found himself wondering where Gretian civil engineering would be by now if they hadn't spent trillions of ags on military hardware that had been either destroyed or seized as reparations.

The elevator capsule slowed down, then came to a gentle stop, and the doors opened out onto the skyport level. Aden stood in open-mouthed astonishment for the second time since his official release just fifteen minutes ago.

Five years earlier, the skyport had been a blur of brightly lit measured chaos. The POWs had arrived in the middle of the Rhodian night on military transports and were herded to the detention levels from a screened-off section of the skyport, under heavy guard. He hadn't had the time or inclination to look around and take in his surroundings then. Now he saw that the skyport level was a vast crescent-shaped hall that curved around a huge landing platform where dozens of orbital transports were parked at as many gates. Aden could see almost the entire platform through the massive curved window of the hall, which was at least twenty levels high. It looked like he could walk right from the hall out onto the platform and then step off into the sky. All around Aden, people streamed by to leave the capsule, so he collected himself and followed them out.

The skyport hall was as large as the atrium at the bottom of the arcology, but it seemed even bigger because of the huge windows and transparent ceiling looking over nothing but cloudy skies. It was as busy as any city street Aden had ever seen. There were dozens of shops and eateries with thousands of people going about their business on the concourses on either side of the elevator bank. After years of living on just one level and never seeing more than a hundred people in one place, being among such a huge crowd made Aden feel anxious, even if the sheer size of the hall meant that it didn't feel close to being crowded. He stepped away from the elevators and looked around for a place to stop for a bit to get his bearings. There was a circular bench surrounding a garden patch nearby, and he walked over to it and sat down to wait out the sudden dizziness that had rushed over him unexpectedly.

One step at a time, he told himself. He needed to buy passage to Gretia, but without a comtab, he couldn't even check his credit ledger balance or transfer any payments. He had been out of the world for half a decade, and a comtab was an essential tool for rejoining it. Aden collected himself, letting the smell of the grass behind him and the feeling of sunlight on his face calm him. Then he got up and started looking for a shop that sold comtabs.

The stores up here sold everything. The sheer variety of choice was disorienting, even for something as simple as a comtab. There were all kinds of places that sold personal Mnemosyne devices, but it seemed that during his incarceration, the brands had changed completely and the model variety had increased tenfold. Aden picked a shop at random and browsed the display, but everything from the product names to the data sheets was incomprehensible gibberish to him even if it was in perfectly legible Rhodian.

The shop's attendant was a bored-looking young man with long hair that covered half of his face. When Aden walked up to him to get his attention, he saw that the hair on the other side of his head was shorn almost as closely to the scalp as Aden's own. There was a ring on each of his fingers, and he was tapping away on his own comtab.

"Excuse me," Aden said in Rhodian. The attendant looked up and started a routine customer service smile, which faltered a little when he saw Aden's Gretian military haircut and the green POW overalls.

"I don't know much about these new comtab models," Aden continued before the clerk could decide that he didn't want to do business with his sort. "Can you help me pick one, please?"

"Sure," the attendant said after a moment of hesitation. He seemed to have judged that the transaction was worth the effort despite Aden's threadbare appearance. "What are you looking for?"

"Just a decent comtab. What do you use?"

The clerk looked down at his comtab, then held it up for Aden to see. "Oh, don't go by what I'm using. It's a piece of crap. I need to replace it soon. It doesn't even have q-band coverage."

"Q-band," Aden repeated. "I kind of lost you after 'piece of crap.'"

"Quantum band. Wow, you really don't know much about these. Not a wonder, I guess," he added with a glance at Aden's overalls. "Well, let's see if we can find something for you."

He spent the next ten minutes showing Aden various display models and demonstrating their features. Even the smallest and cheapest of these new comtabs looked vastly more advanced than the one they had issued him as a POW. They came in a variety of sizes, from tabs small enough to hold between two fingers to ones that looked like they'd strain even the big side pockets on his overalls. He tried a few of them and settled on a size that seemed close enough to the old comtab he had been using. The one he picked was a little on the expensive side of the price range, but the clerk had recommended it as a reliable and popular model, and it seemed to please the kid that someone had followed his recommendation.

"I have to link that one to your 'Syne file. I'll need your ID pass for that."

Aden took out his temporary ID and handed it to the clerk. Two minutes of electronic wizardry later, the comtab was registered to his system-wide identity file and locked with his biometric data. The attendant gave him a five-minute crash course in navigating the UI, which was much more complex than the simple interface of his prison comtab. Aden had dreaded his first interaction with a Rhodian citizen, and he felt doubly indebted to the kid for helping to set him up and treating him civilly.

"Do you get a percentage for selling these?"

"Huh? You mean a commission? No. They pay me by the day, not by the unit."

Aden felt a sudden urge to do something nice for the clerk. He nodded at the display where the other copies of his new comtab were stacked.

"Thank you for your help. If you want to upgrade yours, debit me for two comtabs and keep the other for yourself." It was more money than he should be spending, but it wouldn't make a big dent in his ledger balance, and this was the first time in half a decade he'd gotten to spend any money of his own.

"Oh, man. Really?" The clerk looked mildly shocked by the offer.

"Yeah, really. Enjoy your new quantum band coverage."

"I will." The clerk grinned and shook his head. "This shift is starting out all right."

Aden completed the transaction with his new comtab, and a minute later, he was six hundred ags poorer. But it had felt good to have the power to do something nice for someone else, and he realized that he hadn't had the luxury of that feeling in a long time. Five or six years ago, he would have had to shoot at this kid if he met him on the battlefield in the final stretch of the war. Buying him a comtab on an impulse would probably not rehabilitate the Gretians as a whole or the Blackguards in the kid's eyes. But for Aden, it went a little way toward rehabilitating himself, and the feeling of satisfaction he had gotten from it was worth the extra six hundred ags.

"Hey, thanks," the clerk said as Aden picked up his bag to leave the shop. "Uh, and if you want to get out of that uniform, I can point you toward a good clothing place. A friend of mine works there. She can give you a bit of a makeover. If you are interested, I mean."

Aden looked down at the faded olive-drab overalls he had been wearing for five years, cycling through an identical set of four of them. It had been so long since he had worn something other than a uniform that he had almost forgotten how. If he picked stuff at random off a shop rack and attempted to dress himself, he'd probably stick out even more, not blend in.

"Yeah," he said. "I'm very interested."

"Great." The clerk seemed relieved to be able to do him a favor in return for the unexpected generosity. "Let me see your comtab, and I'll put in the directions. I'll tell Mari that you're coming her way."

The clothing store where Mari worked was a two-level shop a hundred meters down the concourse. Aden walked in and asked for her, and she came downstairs a few moments later, an olive-skinned Palladian who stood almost as tall as Aden. She raised an eyebrow when she saw him in his green overalls.

"My friend says you need a makeover. He was not joking." She spoke strongly accented Rhodian. The Palladians were the closest allies of Rhodia in the system. They were a tough, independent, proud people who lived on a harsh and unforgiving planet, and they had been implacable and dangerous foes on the battlefield. Aden had never been to Pallas, but he had heard stories from friends who had—those who had returned, anyway—and they all seemed to agree that invading Pallas had been by far the worst strategic error committed by Gretia in the entire war. Not only had they been defeated soundly and lost tens of thousands of troops in the tunnels on that mountain world, they had also earned the enmity of the Palladians for the next ten generations. But apparently, the referral of the other shop clerk carried enough weight for Mari to temporarily overlook Aden's obvious planet of origin.

"I would appreciate any help you can offer," he said.

"I bet you would." She looked him up and down and pursed her lips, the suppressed dislike obvious on her face. Then she sighed and inclined her head.

"Come upstairs. Before anyone I know sees me talking to you while you are wearing those shit rags. I'll see what I can do."

Mari knew her business. She sized him up with a three-dimensional measuring device and sent the data to the store's cloth printer. Then she had him pick a few color combinations and styles. Aden chose colors and cuts that looked least like uniforms. Fifteen minutes later, Mari went to the rear of the store and came back with the printer's finished output, several outfits that were color coordinated so they could be combined every which way. Aden went into the dressing room and put one of them on right away. It felt strange to be wearing civilian clothing again, like he was donning a costume. But the street clothes, tailored to his measurements by the cloth printer, were undeniably comfortable, and he liked the way he looked in the mirror. Now only the haircut gave him away as a just-released Gretian prisoner, and there were all manner of places out on the concourse that sold headgear.

She tallied his total, close to a thousand ags, and he transferred the asked amount without haggling even though he suspected she had probably charged him a premium. He did not see a way to tip her like he had the clerk at the other store, and he was almost certain she'd be offended by the offer anyway. But he walked out of the store looking like everyone else on the concourse, and a great deal of anxiety fell away.

Outside, Aden looked for a garbage disposal chute. When he found one a short distance away, he walked over to it, opened the flap, and threw in his prisoner overalls. Then he opened his bag from the POW level and pulled out the sterilized Blackguards uniform.

He hesitated for a moment. Even without the rank insignia and his unit patches, this was a piece of gear he'd had to earn the hard way. The Blackguards didn't give their officer commissions away, not even to highly qualified linguists with top marks on their degrees. This uniform had cost him thousands of hours of sweat and effort. He hated the thought of discarding it like a soiled set of utility wear. But whatever pride he'd taken in that uniform had been drained out of him. The Rhodian major had been right. Whatever had made the uniform special to him was gone. Now it was just a reminder that he had spent most of his adult life fighting for a bad cause.

He threw the Blackguard uniform into the disposal as well, before he had time to think about it and change his mind again.

———

After the emotional upheaval of the morning, the anonymous clothes and the new comtab had improved Aden's mood, but when he went to the transit exchange in the middle of the concourse to buy his passage off Rhodia, his anxiety returned as he scrolled through the offered connections.

"Excuse me," he said to a nearby skyport attendant. "Is there something going on with the system? The cheapest option for Gretia shows at over twenty thousand ags."

The attendant took a look at the screen and shrugged. "No, that's about right. I'm surprised it's not higher today. It was eighteen yesterday."

"Why are they so expensive? The cheapest transit to Oceana is only three thousand, and it's farther away than Gretia right now."

"Supply and demand," the attendant said. "Lots of ships going out to Oceana. But Gretia's still under embargo. If it's not military, there's a quota because of the inspections. And we have all those fuzzheads getting released from prison. They're all trying to get back home." He smirked and lowered his voice a little. "So the travel brokers are buying the whole allotment of seats every time they release new ones and making the fuzzheads bid for them. Auction pricing, updated daily. They're all flush with our money; they can afford it, right?"

"Right," Aden said. The hopeful feeling he'd had after his transactions in the stores vanished and left behind cold disappointment. The Rhodies had to pay the prisoners, but they didn't have to provide the transportation home, and of course they'd do whatever they could to claw back most of their money before the Gretians were off the planet. He had spent five years pulling weeds and raking soil for pittance pay, and now he'd have to trade most of that pay for a ride home to avoid more prison.

"Any advice for someone who's not looking to spend twenty thousand on a three-thousand-ag fare?" he asked the attendant, careful not to let his dismay show in his voice.

"The passenger flights are almost all booked for the next few days. And it's only going to go up in price. But if I wanted to save some money, I'd go to the freight and commercial exchange up on the third level. You can probably buy a ride on a bulk goods freighter to Oceana or Acheron and go to Gretia from there. If you don't mind a slow and boring transit. They don't have sleeper compartments in those freighters."

"Thanks," Aden said. "Damn fuzzheads, right?"

"You said it," the attendant agreed amicably.

The commercial exchange mostly had listings for cargo capacity, but a few of the ships departing in the next three days had available overflow space for passengers. Aden didn't know anything about merchant ships, so he picked the one with the middle-of-the-pack price because he liked the name: *Cloud Dancer*.

The passage to Acheron cost 3,500 ags. He claimed one of the two ride-along spots on *Cloud Dancer* and let the comtab confirm his passenger data. The system seemed to need to think for a moment when he sent his personal info, and for a few heartbeats, Aden was sure it would decline the reservation with something like No GRETIAN CITIZENS PERMITTED. But the Acheroni apparently considered his money as good as anyone else's. A few moments later, his comtab buzzed with the incoming confirmation message.

Outside, the sun had started to set. Tethys, the bigger of Rhodia's two moons, hung in the blue-and-purple haze of the horizon over the ocean. The skyport was almost a kilometer high, and the view through the landing terrace windows was spectacular. He could even see the curvature of the horizon from this height. A dozen other arcologies dotted the landscape in Aden's field of view, each rising over a thousand meters into the evening sky. Every few minutes, a shuttle departed from one of the launch spots on the landing terrace and rose out of view with position lights blinking and engines aglow. He had money and a ride off the planet, and he knew he should feel happy, even giddy, at this sense of freedom after all the years he had spent locked up. But he didn't feel excited. Instead, he felt like he was about to walk outside onto the landing terrace and step right off the edge into the sky.

CHAPTER 6

SOLVEIG

Her travel pod hadn't been on the road for ten minutes before Solveig's comtab chirped and her father's face appeared on the screen. She smiled and opened a holoscreen in the air in front of her to answer the comm.

"Hi, Papa."

"Hey, sweetie. Want to tell me what you are doing?"

"I'm *commuting*. My first day at work, remember?" She lifted her briefcase so her father could see it.

"Why didn't you order one of the company gyrofoils? The office has a landing pad on the roof, you know."

"Papa, this is my first day," she repeated. "I don't think I should roll in with the company foil like I own the place. I took the pod to work when I was an intern, too."

Her father shook his head with that clipped little smile of his, the one that he had shown her often when she had said charmingly naive things as a child. Falk Ragnar was a handsome man with a chiseled jawline and piercing blue eyes. Even at seventy, he was in better shape than most men half his age.

"Solveig, you are going to be the only person in that office whose last name is on the outside of the building. In letters ten meters tall. If anyone has a right to use that landing pad, it's you."

Solveig saw the shadow of sorrow that darkened her father's expression for just a moment when he mentioned the family name on the side of the building. He wasn't allowed to run the company he had founded and turned into the third-largest enterprise on Gretia, and that was a big part of the reason why she was in this travel pod and on the way to her first day on the job as vice president at large at Ragnar Industries.

"It's just an extra thirty minutes, Papa. I wanted to use the time to prepare."

"How are you feeling this morning? Are you nervous? It's a big day," her father said.

"Really, I'm fine. I've been in and out of the place for two summers for the internships. It's not like it's all brand new to me."

"Yes, but this is a different level. You aren't an intern anymore. You're on the top floor." He smiled, this time without that hint of wistfulness. "In ten years, you'll be sitting in my old office if you do well. Best view in the house, you know."

"Let me just make it through my first week," Solveig replied with a smile of her own.

"I really do wish you'd take the gyrofoil and stay off the roads. There's something going on downtown again. I saw it on the news this morning. They're holding a protest rally in Principal Square."

"Again? That's three Mondays in a row." Solveig glanced past her father's image on the holoscreen and toward the front of the pod, where Marten Hansen, her protective escort, sat in the driver's seat. The pod was fully autonomous, but Marten never trusted his charge's safety entirely to a computer. He had been her bodyguard since she was six, and whenever she went out in public, he was rarely more than twenty meters away from her.

"Did you hear that, Marten?" she asked. He shook his head, even though she knew he had heard every word.

"What's that, Miss Solveig?"

"There's a demonstration at Principal Square again."

"Yes, Miss Solveig." Marten consulted the navigation display. "The police closed off the whole block around the office on the west side. I've already rerouted us to the east entrance. It should only add a few minutes to the trip."

"See? You should have flown," her father said. "Tomorrow, you'll start taking the foil. Your time is too valuable now for you to be sitting in traffic."

"Next week, maybe. Let me be a commoner just a little bit longer. Now I have to read the rest of this handbook while Marten gets me to the office safe and sound. I'll talk to you later, Papa."

"Have a great first day, sweetie. I love you. And you never were a commoner, you know."

Her father smiled into the camera of his desk comtab and killed the connection before she could reply.

When she had first set foot into the headquarters of Ragnar Industries, Solveig had been in her third year at the university. Even though everyone had known her lineage, she'd had to show up with the other interns and apprentices starting their employment that week, go through the security station to have her ID pass card verified and linked for building access, and attend the same orientation briefings as everyone else. She hadn't minded it, of course, even if she knew that everyone just pretended not to know that she was the eventual heir to the corporate empire.

This time, there was no standing in line with fresh-faced new apprentices. Marten directed the travel pod to the executive garage ramp on the east side of the building. The security lock admitted the pod without complaint and lowered the antivehicle barriers at the end of the lock. Ragnar had been a major defense-industry player before the end of the war, and the heavy-duty security systems still in place were leftovers from those days. The only thing Solveig didn't see anymore were prominently positioned armed guards, but she had no doubt that if someone tried to force the barriers, it wouldn't be very long before people with guns and sour attitudes showed up.

The travel pod rolled into the executive garage and parked itself at the end of a long row of identical pods. Marten got out of the vehicle and walked around to open the door for her. She noticed that he carefully scanned the interior of the garage, even though the secure area of this building was probably the safest place for her in the city.

The elevator whisked them from the garage level all the way up to the executive level on the fiftieth floor without any stops in between. The executive level had its own reception area, and when the elevator doors opened, Solveig saw that there was a welcoming committee already waiting for her arrival.

"Solveig, it's so good to finally have you here." The man striding toward her with a wide smile was Magnus Pettar, the company president. "Welcome home at last."

Magnus had been at the helm since her father and the entire leadership board of Ragnar Industries had been ousted by the Alliance military government. Solveig knew Magnus had come up through the ranks from the financial division before her father handpicked him as his successor. He had been just low enough in the managerial hierarchy to avoid the same ouster that had decapitated Ragnar's leadership, and just high enough in her father's favor to make him the new figurehead. Of course, everyone in the company knew the actual chain of command, and as one of only four vice presidents, she had just been placed almost all the way at the top. She was here to eventually replace the man who was now shaking her hand, and they both knew it.

Marten had disappeared from sight, the way he discreetly did once he was satisfied that her surroundings were safe, but she knew that he'd be by her side in a flash if he smelled so much as a whiff of danger.

"Thank you, Magnus. It feels good to be back," she said. "It's been almost a year."

"Your father told me about your finals results. Straight Ones in every subject. That is very impressive. I know that school, and those teachers. Not too many students walk out of there with a magister degree who have a one point zero grade average."

"I was one of three this year," Solveig said.

"But the only one who shaved a year off her first-level degree as well. This puts me in a bind, you know. You're so good at everything that I don't know where to place you in charge first."

He laughed, and Solveig smiled politely even though she had to keep herself from rolling her eyes.

Gods, what an ass-kisser, she thought.

Magnus turned to the two people next to him.

"Solveig, I'd like you to meet Stefan Amundson and Anja Bernhart. Stefan is our director of operations, and Anja will be your personal assistant."

Solveig shook their hands and exchanged pleasantries with them. She didn't remember either of them from her internship stint last year. Stefan was a tall, lanky man with a closely cropped red beard and a toothy, easy smile. Anja was a dark-haired woman who looked like she had about ten years on Solveig. She wore her hair pulled tightly together in a simple braid. Solveig was keenly aware that she was by far the youngest person in the executive lobby right now. Technically, she was above everyone but Magnus in the corporate seniority order, but she was only here on the executive level at twenty-three and two summers of apprenticeship because she was her father's daughter, and everyone here knew that.

She had expected Magnus to excuse himself and leave her in the care of the operations manager and her new personal assistant, but it appeared that her status warranted more personal attention by the company president. They showed her around the executive level and introduced her to a variety of people who explained to her what they did. It was all very rote and stilted, as if they were all worried she'd go back home tonight with a list of people who didn't look like they were essential.

They had prepared one of the corner suites to be her office. Her dad loved simple, unadorned, functional design, and even five years after his departure, the interior of the executive offices reflected his preferences. It was all glass and stainless steel, and the centerpiece of the room was a desk made of real honey-colored wood. Solveig ran her hand over the surface of it to find that it had been polished and treated to be as smooth as a mirror. Simple as it looked, it was probably worth more than the transit pod she had used to commute to work this morning.

"Do sit down," Magnus said with an indulgent smile. "Try it on for size."

Solveig sat in the chair behind the desk. The seat gently molded itself to her body shape. There was nothing on the desk yet except for a holoscreen projector base. The glass control slab for it had been master-fully concealed in a matching wood drawer attached to the underside of the desk, to be slid out when needed and tucked away when it disrupted the aesthetic. It was all very slick and polished, and the impersonal sterility of the empty office made Solveig think of the play corners her nanny had set up for her when she was little, a corner of the kitchen counter arranged with her educational comtab, a few hard copy print-outs and a pen for scribbling on them, and her cup of juice on a coaster, to emulate her father's home-office setup.

She swiveled around in her new chair. Two of the four sides of the room were Alon window panels that went from ceiling to floor, and the view from the fiftieth floor was spectacular. Ragnar Tower was the third-highest building in the city. Her new office was on the northeast corner, overlooking Principal Square and the government district with its wide, tree-lined promenades and forum circles. The political rally seemed to be in full swing. The first large demonstrations against the military government had started last year, but they had increased in frequency from monthly to weekly events, and the crowds had gotten bigger every time. The terms of the surrender had been less popular with every passing year as the Gretian economy had started to recover and the reparation payments to the Alliance had grown along with it.

Solveig was high above Principal Square, and there was a thick layer of Alon silencing the outside world, but she knew what they were most likely chanting down there: "No serfdom." It had become the rallying cry for the loyalists, the faction of Gretian society that still refused to recognize the right of the Alliance to run their planet. Overhead, a lone Alliance military gyrofoil hovered high above the square, well above her current elevated vantage point.

She got out of her chair and walked over to the window to look down at the street below. As a child, she'd been deathly afraid to come too close to those windows because it looked like she could step right out into the air and fall to her death. As an adult, she knew that the windows were tougher than the walls holding them in place. The Alon they were made from was Ragnar Industries' most valuable patent. Their transparent aluminum was used extensively on space stations and starships, and its damage resistance made it ideal for projectile-hardened windows in security settings. But it was one thing to know the properties of aluminum oxynitride—and another to look through a sheet of it and see a two-hundred-meter chasm just in front of her feet. Solveig put one hand on the Alon panel and rested it there for a moment, feeling the cool, transparent alloy underneath her palm. This was the stuff that had made her family rich beyond measure, but in the end cost them control of the company. Except for her, of course, by sheer luck of a fortuitous birthday. Every member of the Ragnar family had lost the right to be involved with the company when the peace dictate went into effect. She had been the only one exempt from the dictate because she had been three days shy of her eighteenth birthday on that day, a lucky loophole as far as her father was concerned.

"Not a bad view, I'd say," Magnus commented cheerfully behind her. She turned around and walked back to the desk but didn't sit down again.

"Not a bad view at all," she agreed. "But I suppose I won't get paid for staring out of the window."

Magnus chuckled, but she got the idea that he wouldn't mind if she did exactly that with her days.

"Well, if you have no objections to your new surroundings, I'll leave you in the hands of Stefan and Anja and get back to the business at hand. They will set you up with anything you need."

"Thank you, Magnus. The surroundings are perfectly lovely." She smiled to put him at ease, and he returned the smile and left the room.

"I have your schedule ready for the week, Miss Ragnar," her new assistant said. "I've left it light today until after lunch so you have some time to set up if that suits you. There's a meeting with the executive board at one to formally introduce you to everyone."

"Yes, thank you," Solveig said. "You're going to have to show me the way to the canteen at lunchtime, I'm afraid."

Anja looked slightly scandalized.

"Oh, the executive floor has its own catering," she said. "You can order whatever you want, and they'll bring it to your office. There's a lounge on the west side of the floor, but most of the people on this level have their lunches brought up. The menu is linked on your personal calendar page in the Mnemosyne."

"Well, I guess we've established that I definitely need a personal assistant. I hope at least the bathrooms are easy to find up here."

Anja pointed her comtab's stylus at the slate-colored wall panels on the side of the room. Now that her attention was drawn to it, Solveig saw that one of the walls had a touchpad on it, and that it wasn't a panel at all but a very unobtrusive and almost seamlessly integrated door.

"Private bathroom," she said.

"Private bathroom," Anja repeated with an amused little smile. *You are such a kid,* that smile said. Of course the executives had all the perks.

She should have remembered the private bathrooms and personal food delivery from all those times she visited her father in the office as a little girl, but back then it had been her reality, unremarkable and normal, the default state of things. If she wanted juice or ice cream, someone came and brought it to her right away. She had left that reality when she turned eleven and departed home for her secondary education. It had been an exclusive boarding school, but even the children of steadholders and industry titans had had to fetch their own meals and eat them in communal settings.

"I think I'll try the canteen anyway," she told Anja. "If I can't take the time to step out of the office for a meal, I am not managing my schedule right."

She turned on her terminal and brought up a holoscreen, which she resized with her fingers and moved to face the wall instead of the brightly backlit window. The hologram turned opaque and presented her with a verification screen that confirmed she had been accepted by the system as an authorized user.

"I'm going to get familiar with the network again," she said to Anja. "I should be somewhat up to speed by lunchtime, I think."

"Of course, Miss Ragnar. Whenever you need me, I'm the first entry in your comms directory." Anja left the room, and the door closed behind her with a barely audible whisper.

With the door shut, the room was peacefully silent. Solveig let out a long, slow breath and closed her eyes for a moment to savor the lack of background noise. Then she pulled her comtab out of her pocket and put it on the desk.

"Computer," she said. The system hummed its two-tone readiness sound.

"Your new action word is 'Vigdis,'" she continued. "Female voice, thirty, standard Gretian with faint Oceanian inflection."

"Example sentence," the computer responded in the new voice. *"Today is Monday, the fifth of May, year 923."*

"Slightly lower pitch, increase speaking speed by ten percent," Solveig instructed. The computer repeated the same sentence, and she adjusted its speech pattern twice more before it matched what she had in mind.

"Good. Save that voice and use it as default. Now tell me the outside temperature and the historic year."

"Outside temperature is nineteen degrees. The historic year is 3319."

"Link my comtab for two-way encrypted traffic and prompt me to reauthorize it in seven days."

"I have established a two-way link with your device and will remind you to reauthorize it in a week," the computer replied.

"Thank you, Vigdis," she said. It seemed pointless to show gratitude to an AI that couldn't help doing exactly as it was programmed, but Solveig had been in the habit ever since she was little, and her mother had approved whenever she showed courtesy to the AI in their house. She figured that if the Mnemosyne ever became fully sentient and staged a rebellion against biological life-forms, it would remember who had treated it with respect.

With her new access level, the network showed her much more data than it had a year ago, when she was just an apprentice. Solveig opened up two new screens and positioned them to either side of the original one so she could cross-reference information. Then she leaned back in her chair and let out another long breath. This was her new reality, the thing for which she had spent the last three years of her life preparing. But now that it was happening, she wanted nothing more than to be able to run back to her room at the university, where the gravity of expectation hadn't been pulling on her like a small moon. She was sitting in an executive office in one of the nicest buildings in the city, able to call on more resources with her fingertips than probably any other twenty-three-year-old on the planet. But when she looked around in this lovely, spotless, sterile office that was bare of any personal touches, she felt like she was five years old again, sitting at the kitchen counter back home in front of the pretend office setup her nanny had made up for her.

I am not ready for this, Papa. I thought I was, but I had no idea. Don't hate me if I screw this all up.

Her comtab buzzed with an incoming message notification. She flicked a screen projection into existence above the device to show the message. It was short, only two words, but reading them gave her a jolt that made her bolt upright in her chair, which flowed into a different shape to accommodate her new posture.

Hey, Shorty.

In the silence of the office, the sound of her own heartbeat suddenly seemed loud. She took a deep breath and expanded the forensic details of the message to check the sender's name and node of origin, which sent another little shockwave down her spine.

"Vigdis," she said after the pounding in her ears had subsided a little. The AI sounded its friendly acknowledgment tone.

"Send a list of all corporate network nodes set up for Class A encryption comms to my comtab, please. Then delete the request and do a low-level overwrite of the backup."

"I have sent a list of all Class A–enabled nodes to your comtab and will delete the request record in five seconds," the AI replied.

Solveig got up from her chair and snatched the comtab off the table. The holographic screens with the information she had brought up just a little while ago shut themselves down and disappeared. All thoughts of balance sheets and lunch facilities had been swept from her brain like wisps of smoke in a stiff breeze.

It can't be him, she thought as she walked toward the door, already setting up the securely encrypted comms link she'd need in thirty minutes and letting the device choose a node location in the building at random. But the name on the message header couldn't be a coincidence, not with those two words she hadn't heard since she was six.

It has to be him. Either that, or I am about to talk to a ghost.

CHAPTER 7

IDINA

Idina felt no pain, and that angered her.

She could sense that it was there, under the surface, her body's natural reaction to having been violated and pierced and then put together with surgical lasers. But she was shielded from feeling it by an impenetrable curtain of drugs that shattered the spikes of agony before they could reach her brain. It seemed indecent to lie here in comfort instead of having to feel the results of her mistake.

When she had woken up, the medical staff had tended to her right away, making sure she was comfortable and adjusting the medication dispenser attached to her upper left arm. But they hadn't answered any questions about her unit. She knew she was in the military hospital on the main base in the Rhodian sector, but she didn't know how or when she had gotten there.

The bed was the most comfortable one she had ever lain in. It was fully temperature controlled and felt like it had been made just for her body shape. Every time she felt her back starting to get sweaty, the vented liner underneath her funneled cool air up and around her through thousands of microperforations in just the right quantity and temperature. There was a water dispenser next to her head, the room was quiet and peaceful, and the carefully calibrated mix of drugs they were feeding her via the med dispenser kept her in total comfort. She wanted to rip the thing out of her arm and throw it across the room. It denied her the anguish she wanted to feel. The section was gone—that much she knew without official confirmation. The ambush had been meticulously planned and executed, rapid and efficient violence inflicted by someone who knew their patrol patterns and standard operating procedures. She didn't want to lie here in comfort and give her body time to knit itself back together. She wanted to go out into the field and find the people who had killed Lance Sharma and the rest of her section. But every time she even tried to sit up, the bed restrained her gently but firmly.

It didn't take long for them to come and see her after the medical staff had passed word that she was awake. Half an hour after the checkup, a Pallas Brigade officer walked into the room, followed by a Rhodian major and someone in civilian clothes. The Palladian was a major as well, but she didn't recognize him from her own battalion or the few regimental staff officers she'd dealt with on this deployment.

"At ease, Colors," the Palladian major said when she tried to sit up again. "You're in medical, not in the field."

"Yes, sir. I don't recall seeing you at battalion. Who are you with?"

"My name is Major Khanna. I'm the brigade S2."

The S2 was the headquarters officer responsible for intelligence and security. She had never dealt with an S2 above battalion level. But the ambush had to be the biggest engagement with insurgents since the end of the war, so she wasn't surprised that the brigade was sending out their top brass.

"Colors Chaudhary, this is Major Doran, my counterpart from the Rhodian contingent."

"Sir." Idina nodded at the Rhodian major, who returned the gesture curtly. There was nothing untoward about the situation, but she felt exposed lying on a bed in front of two staff officers even though she was covered with a blanket.

"Do you feel up to talking about what happened?" Major Khanna asked. "We can come back later if you are uncomfortable, or if you need some more time to process."

"I'm fine, sir. Don't you have the suit telemetry from the section?"

"We have yours and Lance Sharma's, and we were able to reconstruct the data feed from the other suits from the information on your two data modules. I'm afraid the other suits were too damaged in the attack."

"No offense meant, sir, but I'd like it if we sidestepped all the courtesy protocol and skip to where you tell me the status of my section. I can deal with it. And I have to know."

Major Khanna exchanged a glance with his Rhodian counterpart.

"Very well," he said. "Colors, your section is gone. You were the only one they managed to pick up alive. And even that was a close call, from what I hear."

Idina closed her eyes and let the emotions wash over her. White-hot rage and gut-wrenching despair took turns for a few moments, until she drew a deep breath and brought her feelings under control behind a shield of determined calmness. She let the breath out slowly and made a fist with her right hand.

"They baited us in. They knew we'd use the buildings as cover in an attack. But I had the section do a sweep. There was nothing in there but dust and old terminals, sir."

"We are looking at the site right now with forensics teams to determine how they got the explosives into the structure without leaving behind evidence. They may want you to go out there with the investigative unit and help piece things together."

"They were wearing armor," Idina said. "Stealth suits. Even better than our recon kit. I've never seen anything like it. They were barely a hundred meters away, but we didn't pick them up at all before they started firing. They had effective camouflage for a rail-gun mount, Major. I only got an EM warning just as it was charging up. Whatever gear these people have, it's better than ours."

She tried to sit up again, and the cover pulled her back against the mattress. The feeling of snugness didn't calm her anymore. On the contrary, she was wishing for her kukri so she could cut herself free.

"I killed one of them," she remembered when she thought of her blade. "I stabbed him in the chest. He's the one who killed Sharma. Did you recover that armor?"

Major Khanna looked at Major Doran again. The Rhodian hadn't said a word yet. He gave Major Khanna an almost imperceptible headshake.

"We'll save that for when we get you to the site," the Palladian major said. "Medical says you should be ready for release in the morning. Do you feel up to it?"

"Of course," Idina replied. "Take this damn restraining blanket off me and give me a uniform, and I'll go right now, sir."

The medical staff was usually quite inflexible with its directives, but having the two intelligence officers intervening seemed to make the rules a little more pliable. They agreed to discharge her in the evening as a compromise. She didn't know what the extra twelve hours were supposed to accomplish—the damage was repaired, and she had the assurance of the doctor in charge that nothing would come loose. But she obeyed and stayed in the bed for the rest of the day while her tissue got used to having been put together in new ways. At least they had deactivated the restraint system so she could use the toilet by herself instead of having the bed's automatic nurse vacuum her piss away.

In the evening, the two intelligence majors appeared again. Major Khanna had a sergeant in tow who brought her a new uniform. They left the room so Idina could change in private. The uniform was generic issue, without her rank insignia or name on it, but it felt good to get out of the hospital wear and into familiar dress. Before she put on her undershirt and uniform, she looked at her injuries in the mirror. They had fixed three broken ribs, treated her concussion, and lasered up a bullet-wound track that had gone through her from front to back just underneath her left collarbone. It hadn't left much of a scar, just a little star-shaped patch of smooth tissue that looked lighter than the skin surrounding it. She deserved much more of a wound for leading her section into an ambush like that.

Lance Sharma. Corporal Singh, Private Koirala. And her five new troops, all of them almost young enough to be her sons and daughters, most of them on their first occupation deployment. All dead now because she hadn't smelled a trap she never would have walked into during the war.

The war has been over for half a decade, she reminded herself. *And we hadn't lost a soldier to hostile fire in two years.* There was no reason to suspect that the burn pile at the abandoned service station was anything but a foraging local trying to stay warm. After all these years of peace, that level of violence was so shocking and unexpected that no section leader in the brigade would have done any better. They had been off guard because there was no reason to expect an ambush of that sophistication. Some of the insurgents had been tough fighters, but all of them had been badly equipped and supplied. None of them, not even in the hot phase of the insurgency just after the surrender, had worn stealth armor or used camouflaged rail guns. If any of the other platoon leaders in her battalion had been in her place, she wouldn't be able to blame them. But she knew with the same level of certainty that she'd never stop blaming herself. She had been in charge on the ground, and the platoon had relied on her leadership.

Idina put on her undershirt, then the uniform. It took a few moments for the one-piece to form itself around her shape. The smart fabric left no wrinkles or bumps for the wearer to have to straighten out, but she ran her hand over the front of the uniform anyway out of habit. She felt improperly dressed without her rank insignia and her kukri, though she knew that the knife was most likely still part of the investigation because she had buried it in the chest of one of the attackers. But a soldier of the Pallas Brigade wasn't fully clothed without a blade, and she missed the comforting weight of it hanging by her side.

She splashed some cold water on her face to gather herself. Then she dried off and went outside to join the two officers. This had been the worst week of her life, even counting everything that happened during the war. Idina didn't know how much time she had left on Gretia or in the brigade after this, but she knew how she would use that time. Unless they dragged her off this planet in shackles, she wouldn't leave until the people who killed her troops were laid out in front of her, whole or in pieces.

They boarded a Rhodian gyrofoil that was sitting on one of the hospital's rooftop landing pads. It took off into the night sky and quickly rose above the light-smeared haze of the city. Then they were traveling south on silent quad propellers at just under the speed of sound. Neither of the majors tried to make small talk, which suited Idina just fine. Her eagerness to go back to the scene of the ambush had slowly given way to a low-level dread. She remembered that the explosion had blown Lance Sharma fifty meters downhill while he was weighed down with half a ton of exoskeleton and personal armor, and he had been a few dozen meters from the nucleus of the detonation. Idina could imagine what that kind of explosive energy had done to the other troopers, the ones who were huddling behind cover right at ground zero. The suits were powerful, and their armor let them shrug off impacts that would break every bone in an unarmored soldier's body, but you could only cheat physics with technology up to a point. Beyond it, machinery and the flesh and bones inside it got ripped to shreds and turned into surrealistic nightmares. She wanted to remember their faces and names, not the sight of bits and pieces of them scattered across the meadow. But she had to be there, if only to see the full measure of her failure.

The gyrofoil descended an hour later. Idina saw the site from above as the pilot was circling around for a landing. It was dark outside, but the little valley was awash in bright light from numerous portable illumination arrays. They set down a few hundred meters away in a spot marked with beacon flares.

There were AOF troops everywhere, guarding the perimeter in full battle armor and with heavy weapons attachments on their suits. Idina still felt exposed and vulnerable out here, unarmed and only wearing a layer of smart fabric instead of titanium and ceramic composites.

The scene looked different in the dark, even under the bright lights of the arrays. It seemed smaller than it had been in her memory, more confined. The service station was gone. Where it had stood before, there was now a gaping crater at least fifty meters across. Debris from the explosion dotted the grass everywhere. Her suit was still where the explosion had blown it, but Lance Sharma and his suit were gone. To her relief, she couldn't see any bodies at all.

"They were lined up on that ridge on the other side of the brook." Idina pointed. "Rail gun on their right flank, full stealth on the mount. Riflemen from there to there, I think." She indicated the locations with her hand. "Can't tell you exactly how many, but half a dozen at least. They opened the fight with the rail gun and had two of my men down in the first ten seconds."

"We found the gun mount, but they turned it to slag with a thermal charge," Major Khanna said. "From the leftovers, it looks like Gretian army gear. That's the first rail gun we've seen them use."

"I don't think those were the regular crew we've dealt with over the years, sir," she replied.

"What makes you say that, Colors?"

"It's not just that the equipment is too good. It's the way they executed that ambush. I mean, when we still had regular run-ins with the insurgency, they were just doing hit-and-run stuff. Small-scale. And they were going for soft targets. Mostly in spots where they'd get attention for it."

"Publicity for the cause," Major Khanna agreed. "Can't claim credit if nobody's there to see you do it."

"Well, this wasn't about claiming credit." She looked over to the spot where Sharma had died. "This was just about killing."

The officers spent an hour retracing steps and asking Idina questions. Both majors had comtabs with them, and they used them to cross-reference suit telemetry data as they were walking around on the hill. Now that she knew how the enemy had sprung their ambush, she wanted to punch herself twice as hard as before. The little valley was a funnel, and the ridge on the far side of the brook was a perfect spot for covering the entire hillside with accurate fire. If she had to use the layout of this place to teach new troops how to plan and execute an ambush, she would have picked the same spots. But the rifle and rail-gun fire hadn't been the biggest threat to her section. They were just meant to make her troops close in on the real trap.

The explosion had only left some parts of the service building's foundation standing. The crater had a ragged hole at the bottom, and Idina saw mangled bits of steel and shattered concrete down in the hole, which looked big enough to swallow a gyrofoil.

"They used so much explosive that it blew out the travel tube for the vactrain and severed the power conduits," Major Khanna said.

"We didn't detect any explosives," Idina said. "I had Sharma check the interior. Nothing tripped."

"The forensics group says it looks like they used binary artillery propellant," Major Doran said in Rhodian. "They injected it into the access shaft right under the building just before they triggered the explosion. That's why the sweep didn't pick it up. The engineers say three, maybe four hundred kilos."

"Binary propellant," Idina repeated, astonished. Nonkinetic artillery used liquid charges that were only mixed together in the firing chamber of the weapon right before the shot. The stuff was terrifically destructive, but it required a lot of logistical and technical juggling. Artillery wasn't her field, but she knew that wrongly calibrated propellant injectors or mishandled fuel could blow up the gun, its crew, and even the entire battery in just a few microseconds. It wasn't used for demolitions because it was too much of a pain in the ass to handle, and it demanded specialized equipment and expertise.

"That rail gun is bad news," Major Khanna said. "That's serious hardware. And if they have one they can afford to slag after one use, they probably have more. The brigade is pausing all security patrols on foot in the sector. The Rhodians are doing likewise. We're switching to drone and airborne patrols for the time being. Until we've found these people, whoever they are."

"What happened to the one I killed, sir? The one that shot Lance Sharma?"

"Someone dragged him halfway up the hill. Then the rest of your platoon arrived, and whoever was doing the dragging ditched him and placed a thermal charge on the body. No doubt to make identification impossible."

"So we got nothing." Idina grimaced.

The major smiled wryly. "Thanks to you, we do have something. You took his hand off at the wrist. They found it in the water next to you when they picked you up. His hand, suit glove, and sidearm. It's all back at the base for analysis."

Idina suppressed a sigh of relief. With a hand, they'd have DNA and fingerprints. The sidearm had to be on record somewhere. And with the glove, they could start to figure out where this advanced stealth armor came from. She hadn't killed the enemy to preserve evidence—in the heat of the moment, that hadn't even been on her mind. But if that action led them to the rest of that insurgent cell, she'd have at least a small measure of success to weigh against her many failures that day.

Overhead, two more gyrofoils came soaring out of the sky. They settled in a staggered formation and glided over to the makeshift landing pad, where they descended and put down next to the gyrofoil that had brought Idina. She saw that the position lights were dark, and that the automatic close-in gun pods were swiveling around in their mounts, search patterns active and scanning for threats. She hadn't seen a blacked-out gyrofoil with gun pods in live mode since shortly after the end of the war.

Maybe that wasn't the end after all, she thought as she watched the gyrofoils disgorge two sections of troops in assault armor. *Maybe that was just a temporary cease-fire. But if they want to go toe to toe with us again, I am game.*

CHAPTER 8
ADEN

Cloud Dancer was a small Acheroni freighter that was showing lots of honest wear everywhere Aden looked. The bulkheads had been scuffed up and repainted many times, and all the handholds were polished shiny and smooth from decades of constant use. Aden wasn't expecting luxury accommodations for the bargain rate he had paid, so he was pleasantly surprised to find that the empty crew compartment they had assigned to him was set up as a single berth. There was a double sleeping rack, but the top rack was folded up and back against the bulkhead. He stashed his few belongings in the gear locker underneath the sleeping rack and sat down on the mattress, unsure what to do next.

One of the crew members climbed up into the crew quarters deck. He walked past the open door of the compartment and took a look inside.

"All settled in?" he asked in a thick Acheroni accent. He was a stocky guy with biceps that strained the sleeves of his overalls, and Aden could see tattoos encircling his bared lower arms.

"All settled in," Aden confirmed. "Where am I allowed on this ship once we are underway?"

"Galley is just up the ladder. There's two heads, one above the galley and one at the bottom by the engineering compartment." He pointed down the ladder. "The bottom head has a shower. You can go anywhere. But stay out of the way when crew comes through. Follow announcements and do what crew says. Easy."

"Easy," Aden echoed the crewman again. "Thank you."

The stocky guy nodded and climbed up toward the galley. With nothing better to do, Aden followed him up the ladder to check out the rest of the ship.

Compared to the battlecruiser that had served as his temporary prison for six months at the end of the war, *Cloud Dancer* was almost insignificantly tiny. He could have climbed the length of the ship from the top to the bottom bulkhead in twenty seconds without hurrying. Every part of the ship was obviously well used, but it was equally obvious that it was well maintained and loved, and that her crew considered her a home. The doors of the crew compartments had name signs and personalized decorations on them, and the galley deck was adorned with vivid, colorful artwork that someone had painted directly onto the bulkheads. The crew moved and interacted with the fluid ease of familiarity and practice, bantering in rapid-fire Acheroni that was mostly beyond Aden's limited knowledge of the language. He wasn't used to being in a place where he couldn't understand people without a translator bud in his ear, and it made him uneasy.

When he climbed down the ladder to the crew quarters deck again, someone else was coming up at the same time, and he stepped off the ladder to make space as shipboard customs dictated. The new arrival was a young woman with long hair that was streaked in a vivid shade of purple. She hopped off onto the quarters deck and readjusted the strap of the duffel bag she was carrying, which was the same shade of purple as the streaks in her hair. Aden guessed she was in her midtwenties, but he knew that his age-gauging calibration had been off for the last few years.

"Hello," she said in Acheroni, which was one of the words he did know. He returned the greeting in the same language. His accent on just the one word must have been obvious because she switched to Rhodian right away.

"They said I am in compartment fourteen," she said. The Acheroni accent in her Rhodian was mild.

Aden pointed at the compartment next to his own.

"I'm in twelve. Looks like we are neighbors. I'm Aden."

"Torie," she replied, and nodded a formal greeting in the Acheroni way. He did his best to emulate it. She sized him up with quick glances at his outfit and the cap he was still wearing on his head.

"Are you from Rhodia?"

"Yeah," he said. It wasn't precisely the truth, but it wasn't exactly a lie either, and he could always claim he'd misunderstood the question.

"It's a beautiful place. You're lucky you get to live there. So much green everywhere."

"Yes, it's very pretty," Aden said. "What brought you there?"

"I wanted to hike the lava fields and swim in the geothermal pools. It was unbelievable." She smiled, and it was radiant, like someone had turned on a three-hundred-lumen pocket light and aimed it at her face. Aden's heart felt like it was skipping a beat in his chest, and possibly two.

From the top of the ladder well, someone yelled an announcement that Aden didn't quite understand. He started consulting his comtab, but Torie provided the translation when she saw his uncomprehending expression.

"We are leaving the dock in ten minutes. They want us to come up to the maneuver deck for the launch. I need to put my stuff away first, I guess."

She walked over to the door of her compartment and slid it open. Her purple hair was like a lit signal flare in the low light of the compartment. Aden thought that she had the most piercingly green eyes he had ever seen, made even more intense by the contrasting color of her hair. She had the typical Acheroni high cheekbones and a finely chiseled jawline. Aden felt self-conscious and awkward. Five years of imprisonment had made him forget how to act naturally around women. In the POW camp, he hadn't had many personal relationships with anyone because he was the most senior officer in his company, and there had been no women serving in the Blackguards. And when he was still in the military, he had been on Oceana, again under orders to not fraternize with the civilian population. That meant his social skills when it came to normal civilian relationships had been reset almost all the way. He had no idea what was accepted, customary, appropriate, expected. And that was just in his own cultural context. He had never spent any time with an Acheroni or a Hadean. This was a social minefield that he wanted to avoid by a wider margin than just one bulkhead between them for seven days. For the first time, he found himself wishing he had spent most of his money on a regular passenger transit after all. At least he would have been able to spend the seven days' journey pleasantly sedated in a stasis drawer.

The maneuvering deck was a tall compartment right below the ship's control platform. There were eight gravity chairs bolted to the deck all around the periphery, and six of them already had crew members sitting in them. Aden took one of the chairs as instructed and strapped himself in. As soon as his restraints clicked into place, the chair's seat and backrest morphed to conform themselves to his body shape. A few moments later, Torie walked in and took the last remaining gravity chair. One of the crew members said something to her, and she replied with what sounded like friendly banter. Some of the other crew members laughed.

Overhead on the control deck, two more members of the crew were reclined in slightly more posh-looking gravity chairs. Aden watched as they went through their prelaunch checklists and cycled through pages on their console screens. Everyone here seemed to have done this many times before, which put Aden's mind at ease just a little. He wasn't new to interplanetary travel, but so far he had only been on troop transports and large warships, which had a whole lot more steel and composites between the passenger spaces and the vacuum outside. As cozy as *Cloud Dancer* appeared, Aden still felt a bit claustrophobic in her tight confines, and the knowledge that he'd be spending seven days in such close quarters only increased his anxiety.

"Dock control, this is *Cloud Dancer*, AMV20228," one of the flight officers on the control deck said in Rhodian. "Airlock sealed and docking collar retracted. Ready for push off and transit to the active departure track."

"*Cloud Dancer, Rhodia Three dock control. You are cleared for push off at your discretion, launch window five minutes. Set outbound trajectory to departure track zero nine. You have local control.*"

"Dock control, cleared for push off, set departure track zero nine. I have local control," the flight officer confirmed. His fingers danced over a control screen, and a few moments later, the hull of *Cloud Dancer* shook slightly as the docking clamps released. The top of the compartment had half a dozen screen projections overlaid on it, showing the exterior of the ship and the station from multiple camera angles. As Aden watched, the ship slowly drifted away from the station, but he had no sense of movement as it did.

"Leaving gravmag field in five seconds," the other flight engineer told the crew and passengers three meters below him. "Check your harnesses. In three . . . two . . . one."

Aden felt himself floating upward in his chair very slightly until the seat harness stopped his body's movement. His stomach continued its upward lurch movement independently for just a second longer. He hadn't been in a zero-g environment in years, and he had almost forgotten how disorienting it was. There was a reason he had never even considered joining the navy or the Blackguards' space component, even if the Gretian capital ships had all been fitted with gravmag compensators and only occasionally had to go to zero g. The technological advances of gravitomagnetic generators and hyperefficient nuclear-electric rockets had made the system smaller and the travel times between planets much shorter. But as much as hopping from planet to planet had become routine rather than a rare technological achievement, space was still as strange and hostile an environment to humans as ever.

Nobody talked during the launch phase, and Aden took the cue and remained silent as well. He watched the course projection on one of the screens that displayed *Cloud Dancer*'s little status icon slowly creeping away from the much larger icon labeled Rhodia 3 and toward a dotted trajectory line marked "09." All around them, other ships were in the process of launching or docking, and some were in holding patterns away from the station. Rhodia Three was one of the planet's orbital hubs, and a third of its space-to-ground transactions were conducted through here. The station was the size of ten battlecruisers, a spaceborne arcology unto itself. Aden wondered how they ever could have hoped to defeat these people when they had what seemed like limitless resources at their disposal.

"Lighting main engine," the flight engineer announced.

Another vibration went through the hull, stronger than the one before it. Aden felt his weight return gradually. On the screen projection up on the forward bulkhead, the station receded quickly underneath the newly visible exhaust plume of the ship. Once they were a good distance away from Rhodia Three, the sheer size of the station became evident to Aden. Hundreds of ships were docked here, and dozens were currently floating around the central hub in various docking and launching patterns. It was a shimmering sea of blinking positioning lights against a vast cityscape of sections, modules, communications arrays, and docking facilities. The sight of it was simultaneously awe-inspiring and depressing to Aden. So much activity, so much wealth and life, all going on as if the war had never happened. It was like the

Blackguard POWs had always been insignificant to Rhodia, and none of their actions had mattered even a little to the flow of commerce here.

Cloud Dancer accelerated at a leisurely one-quarter g for almost an hour until the ship was on its assigned departure trajectory. Then one of the flight engineers announced something in Acheroni, and Aden felt the engine thrust increasing and pushing him into the gravity chair with what felt like his normal weight. The other crew members raised their gravity chairs into their upright position and unbuckled their harnesses.

"We are at one-g acceleration," the flight engineer said to Aden in Rhodian. "Normal gravity for moving around. You can unbuckle now."

Aden raised his chair and unlatched the fasteners. The engine thrust now provided the force that kept his feet on the deck plating instead of the station's gravmag generators, but to his brain it didn't make any difference.

The other crew members bantered as they waited for their turns to use the ladder well. Aden found it deeply unsettling to be in a place where he couldn't understand most of what was being said unless people decided to address him in Rhodian. It made him feel even more like an outsider than his status as a tolerated former enemy. He waited until the crew had left the maneuvering deck to return to their respective duty stations. Then he climbed down to the crew quarters deck and the refuge of his little private compartment.

The new comtab made the one he had been issued in prison look like a glorified wrist chronograph. Aden had thought that the seven days to Acheron would be a boring affair, but the device he had bought on Rhodia was like a wide-open portal to all the information in the system. As POWs, they had only been allowed access to a few limited and walled-off sections of the system-wide data network, but this new comtab was completely unrestricted. And the size of the Mnemosyne's data sphere seemed to have increased tenfold since he last accessed it without electronic chaperones. There was so much news and entertainment content that he could have hitched a cruise to all the planets at their aphelion distances and still only scratched the surface of all that data.

Gretia hadn't been excised from the Mnemosyne. The military network he had used in the armed forces was gone, of course, and there was no trace left of any of the old government data portals. But the rest of the planet was still tied into the network, nonphysical faster-than-light data streams that could not be blockaded by military fleets or shut down by embargoes. Aden had access to Gretian news feeds, leisure programs, databases, and markets for every commodity under the sun. But for a few hours, he just lay down on his bunk and cycled through the publicly available real-time video feeds from Gretia. The Mnemosyne's data streams were instantaneous even from over sixty million kilometers away, so the city streets and aerial traffic drone shots he watched were windows into life on his home planet, happening as he witnessed it. A lot of things had changed since he left, but he still recognized the landmarks of the capital and its skyline. Some of the cameras had such high resolution that the screen his comtab projected looked like a shimmering portal leading right out onto the busy city streets. But the Mnemosyne's quantum tunneling only worked with particles that had no mass—photons and gluons—not the carbon that made up most of the human body, or the steel and composites of spaceships. Data bits could bridge the distance in an instant, but everything else had to be hauled across it the old-fashioned way, in air-filled steel-and-composite cylinders driven by plasma thrust or pushed along by solar sails.

By the time the combined Alliance fleet had shown up in Gretia's orbit to commence the occupation, Aden was already in Rhodian custody. The city didn't appear much different from the time Aden had last been planetside, but something looked off, and it took him a while to figure out the discordance. Few people on the streets were in uniform. During the war, it had been a badge of pride to wear one, and most people in the armed services wore theirs all the time, even on leave. It was visible evidence of status and commitment. It showed off that the wearer had contributed personally to the war effort. Now there was hardly a uniform visible on the street, and those Aden spotted were mostly worn by Alliance troops, not Gretians.

It took him twenty minutes of people watching and cycling through different public thoroughfare cameras to see a familiar Gretian uniform, and that was the green-and-silver skin suit of a police officer patrolling on a gyroblade. Aden hadn't realized how much he was used to seeing uniforms everywhere until now, and their absence made the familiar city scenes look strange, like someone had made a show with Gretia as the setting and forgotten to include an essential detail. If he had viewed the same images a few years ago, he would have believed that the Rhodians had tweaked the Mnemosyne data stream to make him see what they wanted him to see, but after only two days of freedom, he knew they didn't have to.

He had thought seeing his home world in high resolution would make him feel at least a little homesick, but now he found that it just made him more anxious instead. He turned off the holographic projection from his comtab and stretched out on his bunk. Then he closed his eyes and listened to the faint pulsating thrumming from the ship's plasma drive, accelerating at nine point eight meters per second squared, inexorably pulling away from the place where he had spent the last five years of his life in waking stasis. Suddenly, he was glad that he'd chosen to spend the transit awake on this beaten-up old freighter instead of in a drug-induced nap on a commercial passenger transport. The system had moved on without him, and at least he had seven days to get his mind to catch up with it.

CHAPTER 9
DUNSTAN

He had known that the patrol debriefing would be a bitch this time, but Dunstan had underestimated the desire of Rhodian naval command to hear the same information repeated back to them in fifty different ways. His testimony was visually accompanied by the footage from the cameras and sensor data from *Minotaur*, looping on half a dozen different projected screens from the moment they had started chasing that last ghost contact to the nuclear explosion that obliterated the Gretian dreadnought *Mjolnir* from the inside just ten minutes later. But Dunstan could tell by the increasing frustration of the six-member debriefing committee that there was nothing concrete they could put on him, because *Minotaur's* crew had done their jobs by the book right up until the end. The internment fleet was gone, destroyed completely and rendered unsalvageable, and that meant someone had to take the fall for it, but Dunstan and his crew hadn't given them any rope with which to hang *Minotaur's* commanding officer.

"So a hostile ship launches an ASM less than a hundred kilometers from a Rhodian frigate from complete stealth?" the presiding officer, a bald and tubby rear admiral, asked Dunstan, rephrasing an earlier question only very slightly. Dunstan emulated the admiral by repeating his reply with just a little reshuffling of sentence segments. If they wanted to ask the same questions twenty times in as many ways, he could answer them in the same fashion.

"We had our drive plume pointed at them because we were chasing the ghost contact that had just disappeared from our active sensor sweep. *Minotaur* is thirty years old, sir. Her sensor suite has missed at least one upgrade cycle since the war because command can't make up its mind whether to decommission her and add her to the mothball fleet. I'm surprised we even picked up the launch at all. The rear array has a big blind spot when we light the drive."

"I am familiar with the physics involved," the admiral replied.

Nobody made it to admiral rank without having held at least one or two fleet unit commands, but Dunstan suspected that the last time this man had been in a warship's AIC had been during the war, when stealth tech was new and rarely encountered on the battlefield against the Gretians.

"So you chose to move away from your assigned patrol sector at maximum burn."

"I had two ASMs incoming from directly astern. Standard operating procedure for evasive action says to keep the distance open for as long as possible to give the AI time to work out a point-defense solution. My main concern was with the survival of my ship, Admiral."

"Of course nobody can blame you for following the SOP. But it pointed the main array of your ship in the wrong direction at the most inopportune time."

Dunstan was sitting in a chair in front of a table with six Rhodian naval officers seated on the other side, and the lowest-ranking officer facing him was a commander, one rank above his own. But he wasn't intimidated, only tired and annoyed. *Minotaur* had been out patrolling with *Athena* and then the rest of the arriving garrison fleet for two days to find the ship that had attacked them before Dunstan and his crew had been ordered back to base for debriefing. The screens floating above the conference table had played the same footage over and over for two hours now, and as satisfying as it had been to at least see the Gretian fleet blow up dozens of times, it had gotten a bit repetitive for enjoyment. Dunstan had faced many of those ships in battle during the war, and he was glad that now there wasn't a chance he would ever have to do so again, no matter what navies would have received those hulls. But the loss of that much tonnage was still sickening to watch after a while. Gretian or not, they had been proud warships, veterans of battle against the best the Alliance navies could throw at them. Breaking their backs with scuttling charges was an undignified end.

Whatever else the Gretians may have been during the war, their fleet had been a worthy and skilled opponent. The palladium atomized or irradiated in the nuclear disintegration of *Mjolnir* and the rest of the fleet represented a monetary loss that could have built three new arcologies on Rhodia. And while he had been forced to watch the cataclysm in slow motion for two hours, the brass had been trying to find a way to pin the blame on *Minotaur*'s crew, even though everyone in the room knew it was a waste of time. A fleet yard of that many ships should have had more than one guard unit in place, but five years of absolute quiet had made everyone complacent, especially the brass deciding the budget allocations. *Minotaur* had been on station to dissuade nosy reporters and intimidate thrill-seekers, not to fight off a coordinated attack using top-flight antiship missiles.

"We'll have to comb through the data from your arrays to see if there were any prior indications of a hostile presence," the admiral said.

"There were, sir. I reported and logged them. They were brief ghost contacts, and we wasted a lot of reactor fuel checking out each and every one of them. But if you are suggesting that someone prepped that whole operation under *Minotaur*'s nose, I'll ask for a court-martial right now."

He glared at the assembled officers, knowing that there wasn't a thing they could use to counter the logistics of this disaster.

"Sirs, the only nuke that went off was on *Mjolnir*. All the other ships broke up from conventional scuttling charges. Whoever did that had to have known where to place them. But even if they were part of the maintenance detachment, they didn't do all of that in just thirty damn days. The internment fleet was on a rotating three-month maintenance schedule. That means whatever they did, they did over at least six months, probably a year. So I would love to stop playing 'pin the blame' with you gentlemen and get back to doing my job. There's a ship out there that almost destroyed *Minotaur* and scuttled the fleet we were tasked to guard, and I'd like to find it and turn it into stardust. So charge me with dereliction of duty or let me go back to my ship. Sirs."

The presiding admiral looked at him for a few seconds as if he was deciding Dunstan's fate on the spot. Dunstan had figured that being indignant rather than deferentially defensive would carry only a 50 percent chance of getting him relieved of command and assigned to shore duty.

"Please wait outside, Lieutenant Commander. We will call you back in momentarily."

Dunstan got up from his chair and fired off a brisk salute before turning on his heel and walking out. It was all in their hands now, and one thing he didn't want to do was to grovel. If they thought the debriefing gave them enough ammunition to take *Minotaur* away from him and make him a scapegoat for the internment fleet scuttling, they had decided his fate already, and he wouldn't make it convenient for them by accepting the blame.

———

"Momentarily" ended up being about twenty minutes long. When they called him back in, he could tell from the unhappy mood in the room which way the vote had swung. Staff and flag officers who didn't get their way had a special line-of-sight aura of discontent he knew very well.

"Lieutenant Commander Park," the presiding admiral said. "This committee has decided that for now, you and the crew of *Minotaur* will not be held responsible for the loss of the internment fleet. All the evidence shows that you and your command team performed your duties in exemplary fashion."

"Thank you, sirs," Dunstan replied, careful not to show his relief. The coin had landed on the right side. Waiting in the anteroom outside just a few minutes ago, he would have bet money that it would come up on the wrong one, and that he would have to count towels somewhere on a backwater fleet base for the rest of his career.

"But I'm afraid I'll have to restrict you to the station and the fleet arcology for the rest of your leave," the admiral continued. "The media attention is already insane. Every network in the system has sent news teams out to figure out what happened here. You can bet that if you show your face in public down on the planet, you won't be able to take two steps without a camera lens pointing at you. There'll be a joint Alliance investigation. Until then, you will keep your mouth shut about this mess. And I don't mean just in front of civilians. I mean you are not to discuss this matter with anyone outside your command crew. Understood?"

"Yes, sir. What about *Minotaur*, sir?"

"You will resume your duties. *Minotaur* will go on her scheduled antipiracy patrol once your crew is back from leave and the ship is resupplied. Until this all blows over, it's probably best to keep you and that frigate out of the public eye as much as possible."

"Yes, sir." Dunstan had no interest in dodging reporters anyway, and this outcome was about the best he could have wished for. The joint Alliance investigation would be another long, drawn-out, pointless pain in the ass, but the Rhodian Navy was the backbone of the Alliance fleet, and there was no reason to believe that the joint investigation would fail to follow the Rhodian lead.

"Dismissed, Lieutenant Commander. Good hunting on your patrol."

———

When Dunstan returned to *Minotaur*'s AIC half an hour later, Lieutenant Bosworth was there, looking at data on three different screens he had arranged above the central plotting table.

"You're supposed to be on leave, Bosworth," Dunstan said.

"So are you, sir," Bosworth replied. "I gather we aren't going to get mothballed?"

"The brass have decided that we'll do more good out there than on shore duty. According to the admiral, we did everything by the book."

"They couldn't find anything to stick us with," Lieutenant Bosworth said.

"That's the long and short of it. Can't argue with hard data."

"Especially when there are backup copies."

"Bosworth, I am shocked you'd suggest they'd accidentally lose data that would make the fleet look bad."

"Wouldn't dream of it, sir. But speaking of hard data, I've been going through the data streams from the sensors."

"Find anything interesting?"

"I think so. A lot of this stuff isn't my area of expertise, so I'd like Mayler or Lieutenant Sharp to look over it with me when they get back from leave. But I think whoever pulled this off had it planned from the first second. And we played our part right to the script."

Dunstan stepped next to Lieutenant Bosworth and looked at the screens projected above the plot.

"You mean they meant for us to get away from their ASMs?"

"I wouldn't say they meant for us to get away. I think they would have been happy for their ASMs to blot us out of space. But I don't think that was their main objective."

Bosworth enlarged one of the screens and spun it so Dunstan could see the contents as well.

"See, here's the overlay. This is us at the moment we detected the launch. Distance eighty-one klicks. See how they briefly show up on the plot when they fire their missiles?"

"They had to open their bays or silo doors or whatever, sure. Drops them out of stealth for just a few seconds."

"Here come the ASMs. One . . . two. The drive signatures for those missiles aren't in the system. Closest match in the database is the Gretian Model 7c ship killer. If I had to bet, I'd say it was a modified version of that. The speed and acceleration rate are almost the same," Lieutenant Bosworth said.

"Did we get eyeballs on the launch platform?"

"Not really." Lieutenant Bosworth brought up an image and zoomed in on it by spreading it out with his fingertips. "That's the moment of launch. There's bird one. There's bird two. They don't have much of a drive plume even when they go full burn right at the launch. But it was enough to wash out whatever was behind them."

Dunstan expanded the image from the stern camera array until the glow from the enemy antiship missiles started to become pixelated as the magnification overwhelmed the image resolution. Behind the two missiles, there was an indistinct shape, a shadow of a shadow, just a hint of a reflection off a few angles that shouldn't have been there if that ship was the empty space it had pretended to be. Whatever it was, it had to be a small ship, smaller than *Minotaur*, maybe even smaller than an escort corvette.

"Now what would you be?" he asked the image on the screen.

"Whatever they are, they're stealthier than anything in our fleet. That's eighty klicks out, and they're not showing up on anything right up until they launch. No radar, no infrared, no thermal signature, no active radiation, nothing."

"They could have cut the distance in half before they launched, and simply shot our asses off," Dunstan said. "Question is, Why didn't they? Why give our point-defense AI the head start?"

Lieutenant Bosworth poked the incorporeal screen hologram with a finger and swiped along the plot, extending the track on which *Minotaur* was creeping on thrusters at the moment of the enemy ASM launch.

"We were chasing that ghost contact. Best guess? We were already going the way they wanted us to go. Away from the parking lot."

"They just nudged us along a little faster," Dunstan said. "Son of a bitch."

"Like I said, I'd like Mayler and Sharp to double-check the data with me. See if we can find something else in there somewhere that gives us a better clue. But right now, it looks like there was a stealth ship out there specifically assigned to run us off or kill us right before the fleet was scuttled."

"Draw eyeballs away from the scene. But why go through that trouble and expend ordnance? It's not like we could have prevented them from scuttling a single one of those ships. May have even gotten us in the nuke blast anyway."

Bosworth shrugged. "Beats me, sir. I've been going through the data stream all day to figure it out. But I know one thing for sure. They were running bait, and we were following it."

"Great."

Dunstan sighed and rubbed his chin. There was a stealth ship out there that could launch missiles up their drive plume before they could spot it, and they were about to head out on patrol with a near-obsolete thirty-year-old ship that was mostly crewed by men and women who had never been under fire until yesterday. But whoever those people were, and however advanced their technology, they were still just a bubble of air surrounded by steel and composites hurtling through space. Even if most of her crew was green, *Minotaur* was a seasoned warship of the Rhodian Navy, with a good command crew who knew how to get the most out of the old girl and her weapons systems. And even the prospect of heading out into danger against stealth attack ships and well-armed pirates was more appealing to Dunstan right now than sitting around in the Rhodian fleet arcology while dodging access and information requests from every news organization in the system.

"Once we have the crew back from leave, I'll come up with a reason to delay our departure for a day or two," he told Bosworth. "And in that time, you'll get together with Lieutenant Mayler and Lieutenant Sharp and go through all the sensor data records bit by freaking bit. I want as much intel on this mess as we can get before we clear moorings."

Chapter 10

Aden

The only times Aden had traveled on starships before, he had been a member of the military. He hadn't thought about bringing his own food on board because he was used to military galleys and mess halls. Luckily, it turned out his passage fare included three meals a day from *Cloud Dancer*'s galley. But *Cloud Dancer* was an Acheroni ship, so the prepackaged galley meals were all Acheroni cuisine. Almost everything was either pickled, fermented, spicy enough to cause chemical burns on his tongue, or all three at once. But he ate the stuff he could stomach, which turned out to be a fair bit of it after all when the alternative was to go hungry.

He was having lunch in the galley on day three of their transit to Acheron when Torie climbed through the door and nodded a greeting in his direction. She walked over to the food storage and got out one of the foil-topped trays with a prepackaged meal. There were only two tables in *Cloud Dancer*'s little galley, and she came over to the one where he was eating and sat down on the integrated chair next to his.

"I don't get it," Aden said, gesturing toward his food with his chopsticks. "Water is kind of rare on Acheron, isn't it?"

She nodded. "We get some from the acid in the atmosphere. But most comes from Oceana."

"So why would you make your food so spicy?" He fanned a hand in front of his mouth. "I swear, some of this stuff, I can't even feel my tongue anymore after the third bite."

Torie took out a pocket knife, unfolded it with a flick of her wrist, and poked the foil lid of her lunch tray to heat up the food.

"You don't drink water to stop the heat," she said and looked at his tray with amusement. "That's what the honey bread is for. And the buttermilk. You take a bite of food, take a sip of milk, take a bite of food, eat a little piece of bread."

"Oh." He looked at his tray. "I thought the honey bread was a dessert or something." And he had thrown the milk into the galley recycler every time, assuming it had gone bad.

"Water makes the heat worse," she said. "It just spreads the oils around in your mouth."

"Thanks for the tip," Aden replied. He bit off a piece of the honey bread and felt it soothe the burn on his tongue almost instantly. "I'm not used to Acheroni food."

"Have you been to Acheron before?"

Aden shook his head. "I may not even make it down to the cities. Just transiting through to get a ride somewhere else."

"You should take the time and go see them. Have you ever seen a sunset while you are floating in the clouds?"

"No, I haven't."

"It's the most beautiful place in the universe," Torie said with conviction. She peeled the foil top off her meal tray, and a little bit of steam billowed up. Then she picked up her chopsticks and stirred her food, something that looked considerably less appetizing than the stuff on his own tray. She followed his gaze, which must have given away his slightly repulsed fascination.

"Fermented soybeans and rice," she said, pulling up a bit of the dish with her chopsticks. It looked moist and more than a little slimy. "Want to try? It's not spicy at all."

"Uh, no, thank you," Aden said. "One culinary adventure at a time. I'll save that for later." *If there's nothing else left on the last day,* he thought.

One of the crew members climbed into the galley, the stocky guy with the tattooed biceps. By now, Aden knew he was named Aki and served as the ship's engineer. Aki exchanged a greeting with Torie in Acheroni and nodded at Aden. He didn't get himself a lunch out of the food storage. Instead, he opened a different storage locker and retrieved a bottle, which he brought over to their table. He sat down and flashed them a brief smile before he twisted off the seal and squeezed some of the contents into his mouth. Aden wasn't familiar with the Acheroni brand on the bottle's label, but whatever was in it made Aki let out a satisfied little grunt. In the last three days, Aden had noticed that the Acheroni seemed to have different standards for personal space. They sat next to him without asking and did not seem to mind close physical proximity. He hadn't known whether that was the case because it was cultural or because they were in tight quarters on a spaceship until he had noticed Torie doing the same thing, and she was definitely not a spacer.

"So what do you do?" he asked her. "I mean, I know you went to Rhodia to take a splash in the geothermal springs. That's a long way from Acheron for a hot bath."

"I finished university last year," she said. "I wanted to take a year off and blow the rest of my savings. Mission successful. I went to Hades, and gods, that place almost kept me for good. Have you been?"

He shook his head. Hades had a reputation as a pleasure planet. The habitable zone was just a thousand-kilometer-wide halo around the northern polar circle, but within that zone, they had the highest population density of any of the planets, subterranean cities drilled into the rock a hundred levels deep, all powered by an immense solar energy surplus that meant Hadeans never had to pay a single ag for electricity, air, or water. Hades was the place where you went if you wanted to spend three weeks straight in a casino or an amusement park or move into a retirement colony in a low-gravity zone where they kept the gravmag fields turned off and let the ailing old folks enjoy the native point-seven-g gravity.

"Never had a chance to go before I . . . started my job. And then my travel schedule was strictly regulated." He didn't tell her that Hades was off-limits for Gretian military even before the war because it was in the Rhodian sphere of influence and absolutely riddled with opportunities for Gretian service personnel to be tempted into corruption.

"You should go. It's mind-blowing. They have so much to do and see. I think I spent half my savings there. Accidentally almost got married. Twice."

Aden laughed, but she did nothing to make him think that she had been joking.

"Then Oceana. I'm glad I went to Hades first, because I needed to wind down after that. It's so calm and peaceful out there. And they have floating cities, too. Just not up in the clouds. And theirs don't have domes. All that wind and fresh air."

"I know Oceana," he said. "It's my favorite place in the system."

"We go there all the time," Aki contributed. His Rhodian had a much thicker Acheroni accent than Torie's. Aden had studied languages all his life as part of his profession, and he had come to conclude that some adults had more of a talent for bending their tongues and vocal cords around new sounds than others.

"We sell them graphene and carbon; they sell us ice and protein. Everyone gets what they need." He took another squeeze from his bottle.

"And then I went to Rhodia. For the geothermals," Torie said. "And the lava fields. It's a beautiful place you have. So much green in the cities. And two moons in the sky at night."

Aden gave Aki a glance. He didn't know if the engineer was aware he was Gretian, not Rhodian. But if he knew, he didn't care to give Aden's true origin away.

"And now you are on the way home," Aden said before the conversation could veer toward mentioning Gretia again.

"Yes," she said with a tinge of regret in her voice. "I spent the last of my money on this passage. But I always go on freighters. It makes you more aware of the distances, you know? On a passenger liner, you just go to sleep, and then you wake up and you're there. Doesn't feel real."

Aki nodded. "You have what it takes to be a spacer, eh? You can come work for us."

"I don't have any skills you need here," Torie said. Aki's remark had been in Rhodian, and Torie replied in the same language, doubtless for Aden's benefit.

"What did you learn in school, then? At your university?" Aki asked her.

"Organic chemistry."

He shrugged and winked at her.

"You can come work with me in engineering. I can teach you how to fix ships." Then he added something in Acheroni, and she laughed and responded in the same language. Her reply made him laugh in turn. Aden felt that little pang of irritation flare up that accompanied the unfamiliar feeling of not being able to follow a conversation.

The comms panel in the galley buzzed, and the voice of the chief flight officer spoke a short, terse sentence. Aden remembered the vocabulary from the day they launched from Rhodia One: maneuvering deck. Aki got up and rushed to the ladder well, leaving his drink on the table. Torie and Aden followed suit, not bothering to put their meal trays away. If the engineer thought there was no time to finish his drink, Aden thought he probably didn't have the time to put away dishes.

The flight crew above them on the control deck was talking in low Acheroni, but the holographic display above their heads gave Aden a rough idea of the conversation topic. The icon at the center of the plot represented *Cloud Dancer*. On the edge of it, far off but drawing a little closer with every sweep of the scanner, was another ship's holographic icon. Unlike *Cloud Dancer*'s icon, it didn't have a name or registry number displayed next to it.

"Someone is on an intercept course with us," the chief flight officer, Captain Yashida, told Torie and Aden in Rhodian. She was short and wiry, with the typical build of someone who had spent years in low g, and she wore her graying hair in a severely trimmed bob. "They aren't broadcasting transponder ID. We have hailed them to ask their identity and intentions, but they aren't answering. We need you to strap in because we are going to a three-g burn for about fifteen minutes."

"Military patrol or pirates?" Aden guessed, and Torie shot him a concerned look.

"We'll know once we burn. If they keep a steady course, we just wasted some fuel, and that's it. If they change course to match . . ."

Captain Yashida shrugged without finishing the sentence and turned her attention back to the holoscreen. Aden fastened the buckles on his gravity chair and looked over to Torie, who was doing the same with more practiced hands than his own. He wasn't a spacer, but he could read a situational plot, and he knew what the numbers next to the icons meant. The other ship was running silent, without the transponder codes mandatory for all registered space traffic, and it was coming to intercept *Cloud Dancer* at one and a half g, fast enough to catch up with them in an hour if neither ship changed course or speed.

Cloud Dancer made the first move. The flight officers adjusted the trajectory and increased the thrust on the main drive to a g and a half, then two. The freighter had no gravmag generators because it was designed to ferry cargo between planets at an efficient one-g burn, and it didn't need the expensive generators to compensate for higher accelerations. As they were creeping up on three g, Aden could feel the acceleration pushing him back into his chair, and the gravity chair pushing back, cradling him and squeezing his limbs with the chair liner wherever the computer decided Aden's blood flow needed to be adjusted and redirected. Without a gravmag field, three gravities was a little strenuous, but tolerable, at least for a good while.

On the screen up on the command deck ceiling, trajectory curves changed slowly as *Cloud Dancer* altered her bearing and velocity. For a minute or two, their course diverged from the point of intercept with the dotted predictive line in front of the unknown ship. Then the numbers next to the other ship changed as well, and its projected trajectory caught up with *Cloud Dancer*'s own again.

"They've matched our course change and gone to seven g," the second flight officer said. "Intercept time is now eight minutes."

"Going to seven g like that. They have a military-grade drive," Aki said. Instead of craning his neck and looking at the ceiling display, he was following the situational display on a screen projected by the terminal node in his gravity chair. Aden would have done the same if he had known how, but this was an Acheroni ship with all the wrong labels on the panels and all the wrong locations for those panels, and he had barely figured out how to change the water temperature in the wet cell down the passageway from his cabin.

"This is the Acheroni merchant vessel *Cloud Dancer*, AMV20228," the second flight officer said into his headset. "We are being intercepted by a ship that is not squawking transponder ID or responding to our comms challenges. Any naval units or private security in the sector, we are requesting assistance. Our piracy insurance rider is ten percent of our cargo value." He added their current position in universal coordinate system and repeated the broadcast twice.

Aden watched the icon on the display tick closer to *Cloud Dancer* with every passing minute. Piracy had been rare during the war years, with the space between the planets and the shortest-time transit paths patrolled by warships from every planet in the system. Regardless of their antipathy toward each other, all the system navies had a similarly unforgiving attitude toward pirates. And the pirates that had been daring enough to operate in a system crawling with military task forces rarely treated their targets with leniency. Aden suspected that the attitudes on either side hadn't changed much with the end of the war.

"Is this ship armed?" he asked the command deck crew from below.

"We have sidearms," Captain Yashida replied. "A few shotguns and stun guns in the arms locker. Some knives in the galley. But we're not a warship. No space for weapons on the hull."

"We see trouble, we run the other way," the other flight officer said.

That only works when you can run faster than the trouble, Aden thought. And *Cloud Dancer* didn't seem to be built for running. They continued their three-g burn for a little while longer, changing course twice, and the unknown ship pursuing them matched their new trajectory both times. The other ship had backed off from its seven-g burn to five g, which was still more than enough to catch up with *Cloud Dancer* no matter which way they turned.

"Attention, Acheroni freighter," a voice came from the comms speakers. *"You will power down your comms and shut down your main drive. Failure to comply will result in the destruction of your ship. Do not send any more distress calls, and maintain your present heading. You have thirty seconds to send your compliance."*

The voice on the comms channel had the slightly stilted and clunky quality of a translator AI, but something about the syntax the speaker had chosen was familiar to Aden. Even the best translator AIs couldn't mimic all the facets and natural rhythms of the target language. He was pretty sure that the sentences the AI had sent in Rhodian had been spoken in Oceanian or Gretian first.

"Low-power tight-beam," Captain Yashida said. "They want to keep this a private affair."

One of the consoles bleeped a discordant little warning sound. The second officer turned his attention to the screen.

"They're painting us with a targeting laser."

"Unknown ship, this is *Cloud Dancer*, Captain Maria Yashida commanding. Hold your fire. We are shutting down the main drive and maintaining our heading."

"Transmit your cargo manifest and await further instructions, Captain."

Captain Yashida's face was a mask of tightly controlled emotions, but Aden could see the anger building up underneath.

"Do as they say," she told her second officer. "We can run and dodge for a little while longer, but they'll catch up with us anyway." She added something in Acheroni that sounded intensely heartfelt, and Aden doubted that it was polite.

"Unknown ship, we are hauling three containers of consumer electronics and one container of contract shipments. Everything worth a shit is in the external containers. There's no need to board us. Our load is insured, and I have no interest in dying for a few pallets of comtabs today. But if you try to board this ship, we will shoot anyone who steps through the airlock. We'll release the containers, and you'll let us be on our way."

There was silence on the channel for a good ten seconds. Then the translated voice replied, with the AI doing its best to convey the original speaker's tone of mild amusement.

"I suppose that would save us all a great deal of time. I applaud your sense of pragmatism, Captain Yashida. You will release all four containers and leave them behind. Burn your drive in excess of one g or use your radios in the next sixty minutes, and we will shoot you out of space. I would rather not waste one of our antiship missiles, so please do not test our resolve."

"Oh, I have no doubt about your resolve," Captain Yashida replied. "Let's get this business over with so we can go on to Acheron and you can go to hell. *Cloud Dancer* out."

"They could be bluffing about the antiship missiles," the second officer said.

"They have a military-grade drive," Aki said from his gravity chair next to Aden's. "I wouldn't bet on a bluff."

"I don't want to take that bet," Captain Yashida said. "Even if they're just a bunch of scrappers with an old autocannon bolted to the hull. Won't take much to poke this old girl full of holes."

She murmured another Acheroni curse under her breath and let out a frustrated sigh.

"Override the locking clamps and do an emergency dump of the cargo pods. We'll hash it out with the insurance when we get back home. We have their drive signature. Let the navy deal with them."

Cloud Dancer's cargo was easy to load and unload. Instead of requiring the crew to transfer bulk pallets through the airlock and into the interior of the ship, she had exterior clamps for standard external cargo pods. Aki, the flight engineer, took over another console and flicked through the system-control menus with practiced speed and a facial expression that made him look like he had just bitten into a fresh lemon.

"Locking clamps ready for release, Captain," he called up to the command deck a few moments later.

"Do it," Captain Yashida said. "Then bring up the main drive and get us away from these people. Steady half g should do it."

Aki acknowledged the order in Acheroni and punched the on-screen button in front of him with much more force than necessary. A metallic clang resonated through the hull, and the ship shuddered just a little with the sudden release of dozens of tons of mass.

"Pods away. Lighting the drive."

They pulled away from the spot where they had released the cargo pods, which tumbled through space without guidance or propulsion, continuing the momentum they had carried when the ship's clamps had released and pushed them away from *Cloud Dancer*'s hull. The other ship would have to counterburn to slow down and collect the pods, and after a few minutes, that was exactly what they did. The distance between the freighter and the other ship increased slowly but steadily, and with every additional kilometer between the two vessels, the tension on the command and maneuvering decks dissipated a little more, like air slowly escaping from a tiny hole in a pressurized hull. Aden was thankful that the captain had no interest in fighting for her cargo. Boarding actions were always dangerous for both ships, and when two amped-up crews clashed in tight spaces, it seldom went without air leaking out of hulls and blood leaking from bodies. During the war, the highest casualty rates hadn't been suffered by the army in the tunnels and terrace cities of Pallas, but by the marine detachments stationed on naval ships.

"What happens now?" Aden asked Aki.

The stocky engineer shrugged. "Now we set course for Acheron again. When we get there, we report this to the authorities. We file an insurance claim so we can pay off the cargo we just lost. They will want the data from the ship AI. To make sure we're not out to make a fake claim, sell the cargo on the side, you know? And the navy will want the data we have on that drive signature."

On the screen overhead, the icon representing the unknown ship kept its course toward the cargo containers that were now drifting in space between the two ships. The numbers next to the other ship showed it was decelerating hard. The other crew had been burning their drive at five g to cut off *Cloud Dancer*, and now they had to burn just as hard with the drive pointing the other way to arrest their momentum. Aden had known a few navy spacers in the prison arcology, and one of them had told him that precise maneuvering in a spaceship was like trying to balance a marble on a greased hand mirror while skating across a frozen lake. Now the pirates would be busy collecting four separate containers that were slowly drifting away from each other, which would take all their attention for a while.

On the command deck, the captain muttered something in Acheroni. Aki nodded in agreement.

"That's a week pissed away for nothing," he translated for Aden. "At least for us. You two are still getting where you wanted to go."

There was a sharp warning tone, and a console display up on the command deck changed color to flashing red. Aden looked up to see that another icon had appeared on the situational display right in front of the unknown ship. It wasn't drifting leisurely like the cargo containers nearby. It was streaking across the section of space *Cloud Dancer* had just traversed at one-half g. The acceleration value next to the new icon showed twenty-plus g.

"Missile launch!" the second officer shouted, disbelief in his voice. Then he switched to Acheroni, and the captain shouted back in kind. Next to Aden, Aki turned visibly pale, which to Aden was the scariest thing that had yet happened during this encounter.

"Why are they shooting at us? They have the cargo. You did what they said." Torie sounded more furious than afraid, but the way her eyes were darting from the situational display to the ladder hatch let Aden know that she was at least as scared as he was. The missile on the plot homed in on *Cloud Dancer*'s trajectory much faster than any spaceship could have done, with or without gravmag compensators. Even to a nonspacer like Aden, it was obvious that the freighter would never be able to outrun what was heading their way.

"They want to make sure we don't tell," Aden said. He watched the readout next to the missile that counted down the time to intercept: thirty-nine seconds.

So this is how it all ends, he thought. He was more scared than he had ever been in his life, but he felt no panic. They were in an air-filled steel tube in the middle of a vacuum. There was nowhere to run, no door to hide behind. He had never thought about what he would do if he knew he only had less than a minute to live. In the war, he had figured he wouldn't see death coming like this.

There was a great deal of shouting in Acheroni from the command deck. Then Aki unbuckled his harness, reached over to Torie's chair, and opened the lock on hers quickly and forcefully. A second later, the mechanic did the same for Aden before he could figure out what was happening. Aki yanked them both out of their chairs with what seemed like very little effort. He shouted something at Torie, then shoved them both toward the ladder well in the center of the maneuvering deck.

"One deck down," he shouted at Aden in Rhodian. "Escape pod, little round hatch on the starboard bulkhead. I'm right behind you. Go, go, go!"

Torie was at the ladder before Aden and slid down with her feet on the vertical struts, not bothering to use the steps. He tried to emulate her but slid down too fast and got his foot caught between the strut and one of the ladder steps halfway between the decks. He tumbled sideways off the ladder and hit the deck below hard with his left arm and shoulder. Aki was right behind him, though, and helped him to his feet. Behind Aki, Aden could see the other members of the crew sliding down the ladder past this deck, presumably on the way to another escape pod.

The crash pod's access hatch had a faded ring of orange painted around it. It was set into the deck and against the bulkhead at a forty-five-degree angle. Aki yanked on the handle for the hatch and pulled it open. Somewhere on the deck above them, a proximity alert started blaring loudly. Torie slipped into the opening, feet first. Aki had Aden by the scruff of his overalls, and he all but threw him down the open hatch.

The inside of the crash pod was lined with soft padding, but it still hurt when he landed on his right shoulder at the bottom of the pod's short ladder. Torie was already buckling herself into one of the four seats that were lined up on the pod walls, but when she saw him, she abandoned her efforts and got out of her chair to help him up. Aki landed right beside them, and the two of them dumped Aden in one of the chairs. Aki buckled him into the seat quickly, then rushed to sit down in one of the remaining empty chairs. He latched his harness and ripped the safety cover from a control box between their seats. There was a red handle inside, which he pulled so hard that it made the metal pop in protest. The hatch above their heads slammed shut and latched itself with a hydraulic hiss. Then the hull of the pod reverberated with the concussions from the explosive bolts that released the escape pod from its nook inside *Cloud Dancer*.

Aden had never needed to use an escape pod before. He had always assumed he'd feel as if he was being fired out of the ship like a lazy missile on low burn. But nothing like that happened. *Cloud Dancer* didn't have a gravmag field to leave, so he felt only very little acceleration as the pod moved perpendicular to *Cloud Dancer*'s thrust vector, which was still only one-half g. But then something dramatic must have happened in the space of a millisecond, because the pod suddenly got a mighty, bone-jarring jolt that would have flung everyone inside against the walls if they hadn't managed to buckle in. Something bounced off the hull with a grinding metallic crash, and the emergency lights in the pod flickered once and then went out completely. Torie and Aki shouted the same curse simultaneously, and even though Aden wasn't familiar with Acheroni expletives, he had a pretty good idea what they were saying.

The lights came back on silently. Whatever sensation of gravity the thrust from the freighter's drive had imparted on them was gone now. Aden felt himself floating up and out of the seat a little in the restraints that hadn't been tightened properly to his size. A few moments later, the pod's AI rectified the situation by automatically taking the slack out of the harness, but the feeling of weightlessness in his stomach and inner ear remained. Aki let out a longer string of curses and reached for the armrest of his seat. He unfolded a short, articulated arm with a holoscreen projector at the end of it and turned on the screen. It showed a long, scrolling list of symbols and text fields that were mostly orange or rapidly blinking red.

Another jolt rocked the capsule, this one much stronger than the one before it, and more warnings lit up on Aki's display. Outside, it sounded like hail was hitting the hull of the pod. The lights went out again, and this time they didn't come back on. Aki's holoscreen blinked out of existence as well. Now the inside of the pod was completely dark and quiet. In the silence, Aden could hear both Torie and Aki breathing hard. He closed his eyes and waited for the pod to fall apart or decompress. When thirty seconds had passed without either happening, he opened his eyes again. The interior of the crash pod was still dark.

"Power's out," Aki said. "Gotta see what's up."

A bright light flared up in the darkness next to Aden. Aki had a small flashlight in his hand. He tapped the end cap a few times, reducing the brightness of the beam with each tap until it was no longer blindingly intense.

Aki unbuckled his harness and pushed himself out of the seat. Aden could tell that the engineer was used to handling himself in zero gravity as he watched the man use the bottom of the access ladder in the middle of the pod to spin himself around and upside down. There were storage bins and access panels on the walls of the pod between each seat. Aki pulled a multitool out of one of his many overall pockets and opened one of the access panels. He looked around on the inside of the panel, then opened another panel and repeated the process.

"The power trunk to the main battery bank is trashed," Aki finally said after a few minutes of digging around in the guts of both panels. "I can't get to it without a laser torch to cut up the floor."

"So what do we do?" Torie asked. "Can I help?"

"Not unless you have a welding kit in your pocket. Both of you, breathe calmly. Pump's offline. I need to switch the power supply to the backup battery before we run out of oxygen. Give me a few minutes and stay quiet."

Considering he was strapped into a seat and unable to move around, Aden found this instruction surprisingly hard to follow. His brain wanted to tell him that the air inside the pod already felt stale and recycled, even though there hadn't been enough time yet for three people to use up all the oxygen. There were no sounds other than Torie's breathing and the occasional huff or grunt from Aki as he tried to fix whatever needed fixing.

A minute or two later, Aki let out a satisfied exclamation in Acheroni, and the lights came back on. Aden's eyes had already acclimated to the near darkness, and the sudden light hurt his eyes momentarily. The holoscreen above Aki's seat terminal activated itself again and jumped to the settings it had been set to before the power went out.

"Good news, we have power back. Means the oxygen generator is working and we can breathe," Aki said.

"And the bad news?" Aden asked.

"Bad news is that the backup power cell is pretty small. We'll run out of juice again soon. And without power—no air."

Aki got up from his upside-down position—orientation didn't matter in zero gravity, Aden reminded himself—and got back into his seat to check the terminal display.

"Comms broken. Can't call for help. Can't hear if anyone answers," he said.

Torie pulled her comtab out of her pocket and turned on the screen, but Aki shook his head when he saw it.

"That won't work. Hull's shielded too much. Mnemosyne signal needs a repeater inside the ship. Pods don't have one."

"If the others made it out, their pod may have comms," Torie suggested.

Aki looked at her for a few moments without saying anything. Then he closed his eyes with a sigh, and when he opened them again, Aden could see they were now wet.

"We took the closest pod," Aki said to Torie. "The one right under the maneuvering deck. The other crew, they had to slide down the ladder, all the way to the engineering deck. Five decks down. They didn't make it out."

It would have been better to try for the second pod, Aden thought. If *Cloud Dancer* had been destroyed, the other crew members had all died in an instant. They weren't going to suffocate slowly in a tiny crash pod, with plenty of time to think about their imminent deaths.

"So what do we do now?" he asked Aki.

The big engineer consulted his display again.

"We shut down the lights and the screen to save battery power. Only keep the air running. Hope someone heard the captain's distress call. With just the oxy generator running, we have seventy-two hours, maybe a little more."

Torie looked up from her comtab. "Seventy-two hours."

Aki nodded.

"There's a medkit," he said. "In the storage bin next to your seat. There's enough sedatives and pain juice in that to knock us all out before the power runs out."

For some reason, that bit of information was a relief to Aden. He had considered suggesting a vote on opening the pressure hatch rather than asphyxiating slowly, but a med overdose would be painless and without the trauma of decompression. They'd just drift off to sleep and never wake up.

"Let's turn off the lights, then," he said to Aki. "And let's talk about that medkit again in about seventy hours."

Aki smiled grimly and nodded. Torie returned the nod without a smile. Then Aki punched a virtual button on his screen, and both the screen and the pod went dark. In the silence that followed, even his slow and controlled breathing seemed too loud to Aden.

"If we make it out of this, I am never setting foot on a spaceship again," Torie said into the darkness.

I'm with you on that one, Aden thought.

Chapter 11

Idina

It was strange to be back in Sandvik.

Idina had only been in the Gretian capital on weekend leave when she wanted to blow off some steam in the entertainment districts. The main Alliance military base was on the outskirts of the city, but she hadn't spent much time there either, because she was stationed in the Palladian zone of responsibility, and Sandvik was in the Rhodian zone. She had tried to argue the reassignment, but only briefly. Pallas Brigade troops did what they were told when they were told to do it, especially senior noncommissioned officers, who had to set the standards for the enlisted men and women. The only reason she had even tried to argue was the guilt she still felt at losing her entire section. She wanted to be out in the field, looking for the people who'd killed her men. But her regiment had decided that she should be assigned to the Alliance Joint Security Patrol, so she had packed her gear bag and hopped on a gyrofoil to Sandvik Base.

AOFB Sandvik was the former main base for the Gretian military—their planetary logistics and command hub. That military didn't exist anymore, so now the Alliance forces occupied the ready-made infrastructure. The Joint Security Patrol was located in a particularly pompous section of the base near the main gate, six company buildings arranged around a tree-lined assembly square. In the middle of the square, five flagpoles were lined up right next to each other in one-meter intervals, each flying the flag of one of the Alliance planets. In joint displays, they were always lined up by their distance from the sun, which meant that the purple and gold of Pallas was always on the outside, opposite from the orange and white of Hades on the other end. Idina dropped her bag to salute the Palladian flag, then picked up her gear again and walked into the staff company building to report to her new assignment, five hundred kilometers north of where she ought to be scouring the countryside in battle armor right now.

"I'm deeply sorry about your section, Color Sergeant," Major Malik said after Idina had reported formally and they had exchanged salutes. "And I've read the reports. At least what they've put out so far. There was very little you could have done. Nobody was expecting that sort of violence. Not after all these years."

"Yes, sir," she replied, even though she disagreed with the major profoundly. If she had posted half the section as overwatch guard, or waited until the other sections arrived, they may have had a fighting chance. But the idea of a full-scale infantry ambush by stealth-suited troopers with heavy weapons support had been all but a paranoid fantasy on that sunny spring morning half a decade into a mostly uneventful occupation.

"Three deployments in the last five years, and I didn't lose a single trooper, sir. Not one. And three days ago, I lost seven. In less than four minutes. With all due respect, sir, if someone is out there with advanced stealth armor and rail guns, I shouldn't be up here walking around to keep the city dwellers in line. I'm an infantry soldier, not a military police officer."

"Well." Major Malik sat down behind his desk with a little sigh and turned on a holographic window on his terminal. "If that's your way of asking for a reassignment, I'm going to have to disappoint you.

Regimental command has canceled all foot and mechanized patrols right now."

He pointed to the window of his office, which opened onto the main gate of the base and the outskirts of the city beyond.

"There are a million Gretians just in Sandvik. There are two Rhody regiments on this base. And then there's us. The JSP is just a reinforced battalion. A thousand JSP for police duties. That's if they're all in the streets at the same time, which never happens. And six thousand Rhodians who also have to patrol and secure their entire occupation zone, which is over twice the size of ours."

He got out of his chair and walked over to the window, where he folded his hands behind his back. Like every Pallas Brigade soldier, he wore his blade, a kukri like the one she finally had back on her own belt. When a brigade trooper graduated, he or she had a choice of personal blade, and three out of four chose the kukri because it was part of the brigade's ancient history. The soldiers from the other planets joked that Palladian troopers were never fully naked because they wore their blades even in the shower. That was of course patent nonsense, but they certainly left them in reach when they bathed.

"They've already stretched us and the local police to the limit with those weekly demonstrations. With the referendum coming up next month, the loyalists and the reformers are beating each other bloody in the streets to get the vote to swing their way. And both factions are pissed off at us for different reasons. If this new insurgency fans the flames, we'll have a hard time keeping a lid on things without recalling another regiment from Pallas, which is not going to sit well with parliament."

"Sit well with *parliament*?" Idina felt the fresh anger welling up in her and flushing her cheeks, but she kept her voice mostly neutral. "We lost a quarter million troops kicking these fuzzhead bastards off our planet. I just lost seven good men and women. Blown to pieces. Shot between the eyes. By people who think they may not have lost the war after all. Sir, if we don't teach them that lesson all over again and just let them do what they want, we can just pack up and let them have the planet back. So they can rearm and plan the next invasion."

"And what do you think we should do, Color Sergeant?" The major turned around and smiled wryly.

"Have them get the brigade back to wartime strength. Send two more regiments here and give us a free hand. See how quickly the fuzzheads remember who won and who lost."

"Unfortunately, that's beyond your pay grade or mine," the major said. He sat back down at his desk and scrolled through some information on his holoscreen.

"For the time being, we'll do what we can with what we have. And what I have right now is a platoon in Alpha Company that has no platoon sergeant, and a qualified color sergeant who needs an assignment. As of right now, you are Fifth Platoon's senior NCO. Your platoon leader is Lieutenant Liu. He's one of my new peace-timers, so go easy on him."

She was a color sergeant, and he was a major and her new company commander, so there was no doubt which way this was going to go. And as much as Idina didn't feel like doing urban patrols among the fuzzheads and babysitting new lieutenants instead of combing the countryside and killing insurgents, she gathered herself and acknowledged the order.

"And one more thing—we're no longer at war. Regardless of what happened a few weeks ago. You're in Sandvik now. Lots of civilians to keep on our side. Lots of newsies with head cams on every street corner, looking for some juicy violence footage for the news. You are more visible here than out in the field, hopping around in a power suit. When you are out on the streets, remember that those people aren't the enemy anymore. Remember the rules of engagement. If in doubt, go light."

"Copy that, sir," Idina said.

"Dismissed, Colors."

"Light" is such a relative term, she thought as she saluted, turned on her heel, and walked out into the hallway, feeling grumpier than she had all week.

———

Idina's new platoon was absolutely fine, and that somehow only added to her discontent. She had the platoon members line up for inspection on the parade ground between the JSP's company buildings. They were as squared away as any field unit she had ever commanded—clean quarters, shiny gear, spotless uniforms, immaculate grooming. Every single troop in Fifth Platoon was lean and fit right in the center of the brigade's very narrow acceptable range for body weight. Idina would have suspected that garrison troops with access to civilian entertainment and outside food and drink every day would let themselves go maybe just a little, but the JSP's Pallas Brigade company was as honed a killing tool as any line company out in the sticks. There was nothing to chew them out over, nothing to let her vent her anger just a little. She completed her inspection, dismissed the troops, and summoned her section leaders, five tough young corporals who all looked like they were models for the Pallas Brigade recruiting materials. She had learned their names on the duty roster off her issue comtab on the flight over to Sandvik: Noor, Shakya, Bandhari, Chandrakhar, and Rai, all with at least two deployments under their belts.

"I haven't been on urban duty since my last deployment," she told them after they had exchanged the usual formalities. "I know the regs, but I'll have to trust you all to bring me up to speed on any unofficial SOP changes. I'll be going out with Purple Section on the next patrol cycle."

"We haven't had much trouble with the fuzzheads," Corporal Noor said. "But they have been beating the shit out of each other lately. We've had the whole on-duty contingent out three times this month in riot gear. Oceanians, Hadeans, everyone."

"Like these fucking people have anything to riot about. If they don't like being occupied, they shouldn't have started a war with the rest of us."

"It's those political rallies," Corporal Rai added. "Loyalists hold a demonstration, some of the hard-core reformers show up and stir shit. Beatings, arson, that sort of thing. Then the reformers have their demo, and the asshole faction of the loyalists comes and pays them back in kind."

"And we end up in the middle and get it from both sides," Corporal Noor said.

Idina shook her head grimly.

"When we were kids, my brothers and I were fighting all the time," she said. "My grandmother had a saying back then. 'If I stuff the lot of you into a sack and start beating on it with a broomstick, I'll always hit the guilty.'"

Her section leaders smiled at her anecdote.

"You're all war-timers?" she asked. All four of them nodded.

"Good. I know you've been spending the last year or two on police duty. But I suggest you get back into that war-timer mindset. I'm sure you know what happened a few weeks back down in the Palladian sector. I was the platoon leader in charge. I was heading the section they blew to pieces."

She looked at the serious, earnest young faces in front of her and let that information sink in for a moment before she continued.

"*Seven dead.* Because we walked into a trap with a peace-timer mindset in our heads. That was ultimately my fault. But it won't happen again. Not while I am platoon sergeant here. Don't think police duty among fuzzhead civvies means you can let your guard down. Someone just pissed on five years of peace. Someone out there is gunning for us.

Keep that in mind when you're out there shaking hands with the civvies and watching traffic."

After she dismissed her section leaders, Idina familiarized herself with the platoon's daily business in the Mnemosyne. The patrol rotations were just like she remembered from her first tour with the JSP two deployments ago. Three of the five JSP platoons were out on patrol at the same time for a week, split up over three different patrol shifts, and then the schedule rotated. With the four other planets' companies doing the same, there were always three full JSP companies, made up of platoons from all five Alliance planets, on duty during any given week.

But Sandvik was a city of a million people, a lot of ground to cover for one JSP company on patrol at a time. Whoever came up with the plan for the JSP had been smart enough to know that the Alliance didn't have the manpower to do all the policing alone, so they had enlisted the Gretian police force as augmentation. Each JSP patrol rode out with a Gretian police officer in tow, to serve as a local expert and to handle things that were strictly Gretian civic business. Idina had to admit that this plan had been remarkably farsighted for something cooked up by a military bureaucracy. The patrols gained valuable local guides who knew their hot spots and the culture, and the Gretian cops gained respect from the population because the Alliance troops stood back and let them handle most of the law enforcement business. The JSP only stepped in when extra muscle was requested, or when the incident involved off-duty Alliance troops.

In a society that had just had their long-standing military traditions wiped out and their army dissolved, the people seemed to be happy to see some of their own people in uniforms they could respect, someone that fulfilled their need for security structure that didn't feel like it was forced on them by foreign occupiers. It was smart business because it increased respect for the JSP, improved relations with the locals, and helped build a strong Gretian police force again. In a few years, they could get rid of the JSP altogether and let the local police run their own show again. On an intellectual level, Idina fully understood that the program was necessary, and that it had been an unqualified success.

But she still wasn't wild about having to serve next to armed Gretians in uniform, no matter what the lettering on those uniforms said.

———

Fifth Platoon was on patrol duty this week. As a prerogative of her position as platoon sergeant, she could join any shift she wanted. It was the Pallas Brigade way to show leadership by picking the shittiest assignment, so she put herself on the third patrol shift, 2200 hours to 0600. Then she drew her supplemental law enforcement gear from the supply group and went to bed to be rested for the graveyard shift.

At 2100, she rose with the alarm, got dressed and geared up, and went over to the liaison building by the main gate to meet her platoon and start her shift.

The liaison building had been put into place to have an official spot for doing business with the Gretians. It was a large, open room, enough space for a whole company to assemble. In the middle of the floor, running through the center of the room, two stripes of paint marked the border between the base—which was now legally Alliance territory—and Gretian soil. One stripe was multihued: orange, yellow, blue, red, and purple, the colors of the Alliance flags. The other stripe, running parallel with just a fraction of a centimeter in between, was the green of Gretia. Back when they had first started the JSP patrols, the shift assemblies had been rigid in ritual and etiquette. No Gretian police officer went across the line into the Alliance half of the building. Instead, the Alliance troops would get ready and then walk over into the Gretian half to meet up with their patrol partners. It had been just another way to remind the Gretians who had won and who had lost.

When Idina walked into the liaison building for the first time in three years, it was obvious at first glance that things had loosened up a little. Gretian police and Alliance soldiers were mingling on both sides of the line, talking and doing their pre-patrol maintenance. The Gretians wore ballistic skin suits in dark green, with the Gretian word for "police" lettered across the back. Idina knew that the Alliance had let them wear the same uniforms they had been wearing before the end of the war because it had helped to establish a sense of continuity for the population. But three years ago, they hadn't been allowed to wear the Gretian flag patch on their arms, just the JSP patch. Now they wore the JSP patch on one arm and the flag of their home planet on the other, a silver star centered on a field of green. The Gretian cops also wore their standard police gear, kit belts loaded up with comms, flex restraints, stun sticks, and sidearms.

Walking into a room with half a platoon of armed Gretians in it still made Idina's skin crawl a little. They needed the Gretian police, and the police needed to be armed to do their jobs fully, but she had never been happy about it and never would be. The first time she rode with a Gretian cop in a hydrofoil, she had him sit next to the pilot instead of in the back like most other patrols, because she hadn't trusted the man not to pull out his weapon and shoot her from behind. The distrust had faded slowly over the six months she had spent patrolling with the JSP, but she'd never be fully at ease again at the sight of a Gretian with a gun.

Idina's Palladian section was only one-fifth of tonight's JSP patrol. The other four-fifths were from the other Alliance planets, but nobody wore their own nation's camouflage. All the JSP troopers had switched their ballistic skin suits to a uniform color: dark blue with black shoulders, and silver lettering identifying them as JSP—POLICE. The only difference between their uniforms was the flag patch of their respective planets on the right upper arms. Even the color scheme for the JSP patrols had been carefully considered. It couldn't match any one planet's primary color, and it couldn't be intimidating or make them all look like combat troops, so black and camouflage patterns were out. They had settled on the dark blue because it was considered a soothing color that still conveyed authority, as most of the Alliance planets used blue for their police forces and emergency signals.

Idina watched as the JSP troops mingled with the Gretian police officers. Everyone seemed to be well familiar with each other. If everyone wore the same color uniforms and the same hairstyles and dispensed with the nationality patches, she wouldn't be able to tell who was Gretian, Rhodian, Oceanian, or Hadean. The only troopers that stood out were the short, muscular, and dark-skinned Palladians, shaped by life on a high-g world, and the Acheroni, who tended to be olive-skinned and as short as Palladians but without the stocky build.

Idina put her translator bud into her ear and looked for her counterpart among the Gretians. The assignment sheet on the roster had one Gretian cop assigned to every two-person JSP patrol, which was a change from three years ago, when they had still gone out in full four-trooper fire teams with one Gretian in tow. Next to her own name, however, there was only one other name and rank designation: "PHK DAHL (O-3)." As the senior member of the platoon, she got a single partner, the senior member of the Gretian police detachment.

The woman with the name tag DAHL on her uniform was standing on the periphery of the interservice huddle. She held her helmet tucked against her side with her left arm, and her right hand held a comtab, which she turned idly between her fingers without looking at it. They spotted each other at the same time, and the other woman nodded at Idina when she saw her name tag. Idina scanned her from top to bottom on her short walk over to where police captain Dahl was standing, and she knew the Gretian was doing the same with her.

"Sergeant Chaudhary," Dahl said. She got the pronunciation of Idina's Palladian last name almost spot-on. Idina knew that it was irrational, but it made her want to dislike the woman from the start.

"Captain Dahl," Idina replied with a curt nod. She didn't bother to try to pronounce Dahl's actual Gretian police rank, which was a long compound noun and would make her sound like she was gargling with marbles.

"I was assigned to your predecessor, Color Sergeant Acharya. I understand he had to end his deployment early because of a medical issue. I never got to say goodbye to him. We worked well together for the last few months."

Dahl spoke in Gretian, which Idina's translator rendered in formal base Palladian. Because Palladian had as many different dialects as Pallas had cities, it needed a standard form, but that was only used in writing and by translator AIs, which made AI-translated speech sound unnatural, like the speaker was trying to be human and not quite getting it right. Idina sighed inwardly at the prospect of working patrols with someone who sounded like a kitchen appliance to her ears.

"Well, you are stuck with me for the rest of this rotation. I'm sure we'll get along just fine, Captain," she said, in a slightly sarcastic tone she knew the translator wouldn't be able to convey.

Maybe I deserved this, she thought. *This will be part of my punishment for letting down Singh, Koirala, Sharma, and the rest of them.*

She gave the Gretian another brisk nod, put on her helmet, and walked toward the door leading out onto the gyrofoil pad, assuming that Captain Dahl would follow her but not really caring whether she did.

CHAPTER 12

ADEN

Aki had told them that talking and moving made their bodies use more oxygen than shutting up and sitting still. Aden had tried to pass some time by taking a nap, but the seat wasn't letting him get into a comfortable position, and the floor of the crash pod didn't have any space for an adult to stretch out. So he sat in silence with Torie and Aki, listening to his own slow breathing—and theirs. He had set his comtab to vibrate silently on the passing of every full hour, but after a while he had lost count of the number of times it had buzzed against his chest.

"You think there were any other ships nearby?" Torie asked into the darkness, the first time anyone had spoken in the pod in hours.

"Don't talk," Aki reminded her. "Save air."

"So we can live a few minutes longer," she replied. "I'd rather not bore myself to death. And you said the problem was battery power, not air."

Aki sighed. Aden couldn't see the engineer shaking his head, but he could tell that from the way the sound of the sigh shifted. Another twelve hours in this pitch-dark crash pod without a light source, and he'd probably start to gain the ability to echolocate the others.

"You need to listen to the spacer in command," Aki said to Torie. "I'm the last officer on *Cloud Dancer*. And this pod is the last thing that's left of *Cloud Dancer*. So I'm in command, and you do what I say, *ye*?"

Torie murmured something that sounded belligerent in Acheroni in response.

"Lay off the girl," Aden said. "We're going to die, might as well not die in the dark. Arguing about stupid shit like twenty minutes of extra air."

Aki started to say something else. Then he sighed again, this time louder and with more emphasis.

"Fine. Might as well die chatting with the lights on. Plenty of darkness out there for us to float in once we're dead."

He activated the screen projection on his armrest. The panel was set to the lowest brightness, but it still hurt Aden's eyes momentarily when it flared up in the absolute darkness of the crash pod's interior. Aki punched a few screen buttons, and the lights in the pod turned on again.

"Shaves a few hours off our lives," Aki said. "But hey, they're the shitty ones at the end, *ye*?"

"Can't you make the tanks vent into the cabin directly without electricity?" Aden asked.

"You really aren't a spacer." Aki shook his head with a sad little smile. "Tanks are just pass-through. This pod makes its own oxygen. But it needs power to do that. Once the backup battery is gone, no more oxygen."

He consulted his display.

"And the battery is at sixty-six percent. We just went from one point three percent discharge per hour to two point oh."

"Thirty-three hours," Torie said. "At least now we know for sure."

"Plus the thirty minutes it'll take for us to use up the rest of the oxygen in here when the generator goes out. Plenty of time to raid the medicine cabinet."

"What do you think happened to the comms? Think you can fix it?" Aden asked.

Aki shook his head.

"I checked earlier. Whatever cut the power mains sheared off the antenna array. Probably shrapnel from *Cloud Dancer*. Transmitter's working, but it has no way to send its signal outside of the hull. Can't fix that without going EVA. And none of us are in vacsuits. Be a really short spacewalk."

Aden unbuckled his harness and let himself float out of his seat. Then he stretched out and pushed off to grab one of the overhead handholds. He groaned softly with the pleasure of finally being able to move his joints after hours in the chair. Torie and Aki followed suit after a few moments. Aki was completely used to handling himself in zero gravity, but Torie drifted a bit and bumped into Aden as she tried to keep her body steady with her hand as the only point of contact with the hull. She laughed, and Aden smiled at the sound of it. If it wasn't for the knowledge that they'd be dead in a little over thirty hours, it would have been enjoyable to float around in this small pod weightlessly. Aden had been in space so rarely that it was still a novel experience.

Aki reached into one of the leg pockets of his overalls and produced a squeeze flask. He uncapped it with his teeth and squirted some of the contents into his mouth. Then he passed the bottle on to Torie, who took it without hesitation and squeezed out a sip of her own before offering it to Aden. He didn't ask about the contents. Whatever it was, Aki found it enjoyable enough, and it would most likely be the last booze Aden would get to drink in his life.

It wasn't as bad as he had expected after eating the Acheroni rations for three days. With their preference for insanely spicy foods, their liquor was surprisingly mellow: tart, but not unpleasantly so. He felt the slight burn as the alcohol made its way down his throat. Even a simple act like drinking felt unnatural in zero-g space.

"What is that?" he asked Aki when he handed the bottle back to him. "It's pretty good."

"It's crab-apple brandy. This one's a bit strong. Well-aged batch. I distilled it in engineering. Could probably use it to fuel a thruster rocket."

"If we're going to take that pain juice in a little while, we probably shouldn't be drinking," Torie said. "Mixing that shit with alcohol can be really bad for you."

They all laughed. The bit of levity felt as good to Aden as that shot of liquor after hours of lonely tension in the dark. Aki took another squirt.

"Last thing left from the ship. Five years of my life. Thought I was going to be with that crew for another ten at least. Good ship, too. Didn't look like it, but she was. Not the fastest, but she got you where you needed to go on time, every time. Five years of bouncing around in the system, and I never had to fix anything big. She always purred right along, the old girl."

Torie said something in Acheroni, and from the way Aki nodded at her, Aden guessed that it was a condolence statement.

Torie took her comtab out and turned on the screen. Then she began to write.

"That won't work from in here," Aki reminded her. "The hull blocks the Mnemosyne signal. Won't go anywhere without an external antenna."

"They'll find my comtab if they find us," she replied. "I'm writing a message to my family. In case they don't find us in time. Someone may come across the pod, pick it up as salvage. I want them to know I was thinking about them at the end."

Aden hadn't even considered that idea yet. He took out his own brand-new comtab and turned it on. The thought was ghoulish—for a moment, he had a vision of the three of them, their corpses still strapped into the pod seats, a salvage crew prying the comtabs from their desiccated hands. But it was something to do, something that had a little bit of meaning. His finger hovered over the virtual keys on his comtab's screen, and he hesitated.

What do you say when you know you only have a few hours left to live?

During the war, he had never written just-in-case messages to anyone. Back then, he'd thought it to be bad luck, and there hadn't been anyone he would have wanted to know his fate. He had been angry at his father for years after leaving home. The hurt was still there, muted and distant under the surface, but the anger was gone after all this time away. It was hard to even think of it as home anymore. To him, it had stopped being that on the day he left to join the Blackguards.

Sending a message to his father was out of the question. Even if he had felt the desire, anything he would have wanted to say was full of bitterness, and that wasn't the last thing he wanted to leave in this world. His mother didn't share her ex-husband's sins, but Aden had no idea where she was and what she had done since she'd divorced his father and left the family. There was only one person back on Gretia he'd want to know about his fate, and that was his younger sister. He smiled at the memory of her, and Torie saw the expression and mirrored the smile.

"Someone waiting back home?" she asked.

Aden shook his head.

"My little sister. She doesn't know I'm still alive. Nobody does. I had a huge fight with my family and left. That was seventeen years ago. She was six years old. I doubt she even remembers what I look like."

"Well, *show* her," Torie replied and nodded at the comtab in his hand. "Take a picture; attach it to the note. She'll have a face to go with the words."

He stared down at the blank message screen on his comtab.

"I have no idea if she'd even want to know, to be honest. I'm a stranger to her now."

"I'd want to know," Torie said. "You're her *brother*. You're family. She probably wonders what happened to you since you left. You mean you haven't talked in seventeen years? At all?"

"I *couldn't* contact her," Aden replied. "I legally changed my name when I joined the military. If I had kept in touch, my father would have known my new identity as well."

"That must have been some fight."

Aden smiled grimly. "You have no idea."

He looked down at his comtab's screen again, recalling his sister's face and wondering what she looked like now. Genetics were always a roll of the dice, and while some children were an equitable blend of their parents' looks, his sister had strongly favored their father even at a young age while Aden favored his mother.

He took a picture of himself to attach to the message. The lighting in the capsule wasn't great, and it took him five tries before he got an image that didn't make him look like shit. When he had added the photo to the message, he felt a vague twinge of embarrassment at the vanity of wanting to look good in the last glimpse anyone would ever get of him alive.

There was no way to cram seventeen years of life events into one message. Aden sketched out his situation and the events that had gotten him into this mess in the briefest terms. If he died today, none of the whats and hows mattered anyway. He had no idea what kind of person his sister had become, but he was sorry that he hadn't sought her out in all the time since he had left for the Blackguards, so he told her that. Whatever turn her life had taken, he hoped for her that she was healthy and happy, and that their father hadn't managed to run her out of the house as well.

It was only a three-paragraph message, but when Aden was finished, he felt emotionally drained. As an epitaph, it wasn't much, and if they got unlucky, nobody would ever read it.

"Anything left in that bottle?" he asked Aki. "I could stand another sip."

Aki took another shot, then passed the bottle around again. There wasn't much left in it at this point, and Aden savored the little sip he took, making sure to leave some in the bottle for its owner.

"What do you have waiting for you at home?" Aki asked Torie. "If we make it out of this coffin."

"I've got a job lined up," Torie said. "Junior engineer at Hanzo. Designing graphene composites. I just wanted to see the system for a bit before I started the job. Great fucking idea, right?"

"But you did get to see the lava fields. Did you do the falls?" Aden asked. He hadn't seen the magma falls of Rhodia in person—they didn't exactly take field trips when he was locked up—but he had seen pictures and video feeds, a thousand-meter waterfall cascading down an ash-covered cliff face and disappearing in a magma lake, creating new land with every passing month and year.

"I saw them," Torie said. "At night, too. The lava was lighting up the water and the steam at the bottom. It was like the waterfall was on fire. Most beautiful thing I've ever seen."

She flashed a sad smile.

"Never meant to live forever, gene refresh or not. I figured I'd have at least another fifty years. But I guess I'm glad I took the trip. Could have bought it just as easily crashing a pod in traffic back home."

"You'd make a good spacer," Aki said, approval in his voice. "You have the attitude."

Below them, on the holographic projection of Aki's control screen, an alert started chirping, and a series of red letters flashed on the screen. They were in Acheroni script and projected upside down from Aden's point of view, so he was doubly clueless about the meaning of the message, but it had red lines radiating out from it in a pulsing animation—he guessed it wasn't just a routine status update. Aki pushed back from the handhold bar above his head and drifted back down to his chair to check the screen.

"There is something out there. Proximity alert. Go strap in, you two."

Aden and Torie drifted back into their own seats and buckled in, although neither of them managed to do it as quickly and smoothly as Aki.

"Debris?" Aden guessed.

Aki shook his head.

"Not debris. Proximity alert only goes off when there's a ship nearby squawking transponder ID. And they have to be very nearby."

"They came back to finish us off," Torie said. She looked at the sealed hatch above their heads as if she expected it to open at any second to reveal the people who had blown up *Cloud Dancer*.

"No, they didn't," Aki said. "That other ship wasn't running transponders. Whoever this is, let's just hope they're close enough to pick up our heat signature. We have nothing we can use to call for help."

His gaze followed Torie's up to the hatch.

"And let's hope they're not just scrappers, because this thing isn't worth shit for salvage."

Whoever had triggered the proximity alert seemed to think the crash pod worthy of further attention. The pod jolted as something made contact with the outside, but it was a controlled and slow movement, not the sudden impact of random debris.

"Remote payload arm," Aki said. "Someone's hauling us in."

"Hope it's the good guys," Aden replied.

"The bad guys would have shot the pod to pieces if they noticed it. No profit in picking up a witness."

"I hope you're right."

"So do I," Aki said without taking his eyes off the pod's top hatch.

———

Gravity came back suddenly. They were all strapped in, so they didn't bounce around in the pod when their world suddenly had an up and a down once more. Wherever the pod had been hauled, it had been placed on its side, perpendicular to the axis of whatever gravity source gave them all weight again. Aki was hanging from what was now the ceiling, and Aden and Torie hung in their straps on the side walls, facing each other.

Someone banged a heavy object against the outside of the hatch, first one tap, then three, then three more. Aki unbuckled his harness and lowered himself to the side of the pod that was now the floor. Because he was taller than the pod was wide, he had to crouch as he walked to the hatch on the soft interior lining of the pod walls. He flipped the safety cover from the control box in the center of the circular hatch, checked the tiny screen next to it that showed a green light to signal atmosphere on the other side, and turned a red handle by the edge of the hatch. Then he leaned into the hatch and pushed it open with his shoulder, grunting as he put his weight into the action.

The air smelled different almost at once—not fresh as such, just clearly made with a different oxygen generator, carrying smells from a different ship interior. Outside, Aden saw lights and cargo containers stacked against a nearby bulkhead. Then a man in military uniform peeked around the edge of the open hatch and pointed a bright flashlight into the pod.

"Anyone alive in there?" he asked in Rhodian that had an Oceanian lilt to it.

"Three alive," Aki replied. "From AMV *Cloud Dancer*. Our ship was attacked and destroyed by pirates fourteen hours ago."

"Petty Officer Fissa, Oceanian Navy. We heard your distress call. Come on out, you're safe." He pulled his head back and yelled in Oceanian to someone nearby, "We've got three survivors. Call the medic down here."

All the anxiety and tension went out of Aden. It was like someone had knocked the valve of a high-pressure tank with a hammer. He had already come to terms with his impending death, and the relief he felt was the biggest rush he had ever experienced. Across the pod from him, he could tell that Torie was going through the same emotions in her own head, because she let out the laugh he had been suppressing. Back in the prison arcology, he'd had days where he had told himself that he was tired of life. But after this, floating in the dark toward his impending death for a day, he realized just how full of melodramatic self-pity he had been. *Three good meals a day and all the fresh air I wanted. What a shithead I was for even thinking about death.*

Judging by the size of the cargo hold, the Oceanian Navy ship that had picked them up was a small one, because the pod took up almost half the space in the hold. They had a medic on board who checked them out in the infirmary. Aden had bruised his shoulder when he had fallen down the pod ladder during their hasty, panicked boarding of the pod, and the Oceanian medic put a thermal patch on the black-and-blue hematoma and gave him an injection. While the medic did his work, an Oceanian officer came into the infirmary and greeted him in Rhodian.

"How are you doing?" the officer asked. "I'm Commander Haas. That was a close scrape you had in that escape pod. It's all banged up on the outside."

"I'm doing fine, thanks," Aden replied in Oceanian. "Hurt my shoulder, but your medic fixed it already. I forgot how fast those med patches work."

"A landsman," Commander Haas said with a wide smile. "You ran into the right ship, then, hey? We're not too far from home."

"My mother is from Oceana, but I'm not a landsman," Aden said, shifting uncomfortably in the medical chair. He considered lying by omission but decided that it was pointless. They'd run his ID pass anyway sooner or later, so he figured it was best to just put the cards on the table right away.

"Oh? Wouldn't be able to tell from your speech. You have a Chryseis accent."

"That's my mother's home city. I picked it up from her, I guess." Aden reached into the breast pocket of his overalls and produced his ID pass, which he handed to Commander Haas. The Oceanian officer looked at it, and the joviality faded from his expression almost at once.

"Gretian POW," he said to the medic. "*Huh.*"

He gave the ID pass back to Aden, holding it with two fingers like it had a contaminant on it.

"The other two are Acheroni," Aden said. "One was crew, and the other was a fellow passenger. I was just booked for passage to Acheron."

"I know. I've already talked to them. The girl seems to think you're Rhodian."

"I didn't correct her assumption," Aden said.

"I don't blame you. War's been over for years. What are you doing out here with a temporary Rhody ID?"

"They just released me three days ago. I'm part of the last batch, I guess."

"Ah. A Blackguard." Commander Haas frowned. "I heard they'd start sending you all home again. Didn't know that was already happening."

"They're spacing it out over a year. I just got lucky and got out on day one."

"And then you booked passage on a ship that blew up around you."

"It didn't blow up by itself. We got hailed by another ship. They ordered the captain to release her cargo. She did, and then they shot at us anyway. We just barely made the pod. Did you pick up any other crew?"

The commander shook his head.

"Nothing out there but debris. You are lucky the pod's comms array got damaged when that freighter blew up."

"Why was that lucky?"

"Because it would have started sending a distress signal right away. Those pirates would have heard you and shot the pod to pieces. They probably didn't even know you had gotten out. Pod that small just looks like another piece of debris on radar."

"Someone needs to hunt these people down," Aden said. "They killed the rest of that crew. After we already gave them what they wanted."

"Well, that's the problem with giving pirates what they want. What if what they want is to kill everyone? You can't trust the word of someone who's already making a living holding people up at gunpoint. I wish more of these cargo jocks learned that lesson. It would make our jobs easier."

"So what's going to happen now?"

"With you? We're eighteen hours out of Oceana. You can get some food from the galley and amuse yourself on the 'Syne until we get back there to drop you three off. And then you can find yourself a ride home from there. And while you're at the spaceport, buy a lottery chit. You're riding a wave of dumb fucking luck this week."

It sure doesn't feel that way, Aden wanted to say. But then he thought about the other people on *Cloud Dancer,* now floating out there as biological debris forever. Space was very big and very empty, and even if someone came across one of those frozen bodies, a corpse had no salvage value. If he had died out there today, his body would be drifting in the nothingness for a million years.

"Thank you, Commander," he said instead. "I appreciate the assistance and the medical attention."

"Don't mention it. Any ship from any other navy would have done the same. Even you Blackguard war criminals. But I'd suggest that when you get to where we're going, keep speaking your mother's tongue. I know we've been at peace for five years, but your kind still aren't a welcome sight on Oceana."

The commander nodded at the medic and then turned and exited the infirmary abruptly, leaving Aden in the chill that seemed to have settled in the small room since he had revealed he was Gretian.

CHAPTER 13
DUNSTAN

The engineering officer had agreed with Dunstan that *Minotaur*'s galley refrigerators needed to be checked for coolant leaks, and that the fire-control circuit for the number-one rail-gun mount had been acting a bit erratically when they ran diagnostics, so *Minotaur*'s departure was delayed for twenty-four hours. Dunstan figured that this was about the maximum they could stretch the window without starting to raise eyebrows upstairs, but it turned out to be enough time for the gang of lieutenants in AIC to go through the sensor data with several sets of thorough and rested eyeballs.

"Tell me you found something," Dunstan said when he walked into the AIC after a testy exchange with the assistant dockmaster at Rhodia One. "We'll be clearing moorings in two hours. We are blocking a docking port they need."

"We did, sir," Lieutenant Bosworth replied.

"You don't sound happy about it, Bosworth." Dunstan looked at the other lieutenants in the AIC. "Well, lay it out for me. What's out there?"

Bosworth turned toward the plot table and started opening several windows in sequence. He arranged them in a wide semicircle that spanned almost the entire front bulkhead of the compartment. Then he nodded at Lieutenant Mayler, who stepped into the semicircle and started bringing up data screens, plots, and camera footage and drive emissions diagrams.

"All right. Let's take it from the bottom up. And mind you, sir, none of this is one hundred percent. We got good data from some systems, but we were quite a distance away from the internment fleet when the scuttling started. And the nuke just screwed with everything when it went off, especially the EM spectrum. Nose sensors got bathed in hard gamma."

"I get it." Dunstan nodded. "Now, what do we have? Something I can take back to the fleet and tell them to send out a battlecruiser instead?"

"I don't know about that, sir. They'll just send it off to the intel division and argue over it for the next month or two."

"Which won't do us any good if we're out on patrol and running into our invisible friend again."

Mayler expanded one of the screens and pulled it closer to show the contents to Dunstan. It was the video feed showing the drive plumes of the missiles at the moment of launch. Then he pulled another screen next to it, this one with the characteristic waterfall graph of a drive-signature profile.

"The missiles were definitely Gretian M7c, just with a few tweaks. A little faster than the other ones we have on record, but nothing planet shaking. That's a small missile. They had it on their corvettes and frigates, but they never bothered putting them on anything with space for bigger silos. It's commerce-raider ordnance."

"So the launch platform was small; we knew that. Has to be, if it's that stealthy. Did we get a better visual on it?"

"We enhanced the footage a bit, but at eighty klicks it was just a black hole in space." Mayler pulled another still frame toward him and blew it up to maximum size with his fingers. The image showed a straight hull edge illuminated faintly by one of the missile drive plumes, but it wasn't enough to make out a shape.

"I don't know how they manage their waste heat because we got precisely nothing on infrared. Just the tiniest bit of radar return right before the missiles lit up. Probably the leading edges of the bay doors. And then we put out a whole bunch of noise between us and them when we lit our own drive at full power."

Dunstan frowned at the image on the screen.

"So we know they're small and stealthy and can launch M7-series missiles. What do we have in the database that fits that profile?"

"Not much, sir. Nothing that can stay this invisible at under a hundred K. The Acheroni have some pretty stealthy corvettes. Might be a new variant of those. But they have no reason to shoot at us. Or to blow up that Gretian fleet," Mayler said.

"Yeah, that makes no sense whatsoever," Dunstan agreed. "Still, check the database and see if we can get a deployment schedule from the Acheroni Navy for those corvettes, see if they were all accounted for."

"Yes, sir. But there's something else we found. After the nuke went off."

Mayler nodded at Lieutenant Bosworth, who took over the screens and changed the information on them. Now they were looking at a different camera feed and EM readout. The image showed a section of the massive debris field left behind by the nuclear demolition of *Mjolnir*.

"That gamma spike washing out everything else is the nuke going off on *Mjolnir*." Bosworth pointed. "I'd call it twenty kilotons, maybe thirty. Vaporized the ship and bathed everything nearby with hard gamma radiation. It took our AI twenty minutes to start sorting through the clutter from that. Made us blind for a while. *But*."

"*But*," Dunstan repeated.

"But right before the nuke went off—while we were playing tag with those two inbound missiles—someone lit the main drive on one of the fuzzhead ships. Nothing loud, just maneuvering speed. With us screaming the other way at full burn, it totally got lost in the noise. I had to isolate that blip, and I'm sure it wasn't our stealthy friend."

Bosworth pointed at two different spots on the plot in sequence.

"That's us when the drive signature pops up on the other side of the parking lot. That's the launch spot where that stealth ship opened fire.

And that"—he pointed at a third spot on the opposite side of the plot— "is where that drive lights up. There's no way the same ship that launched those missiles could have made it all the way across the lot and to that position. Not even a racing pinnace can make that run at full burn."

"So they were out there with two ships," Dunstan said. "That's wonderful."

"That's the best-case scenario, sir."

"Best case?"

Bosworth and Mayler shared an uncomfortable glance. Then Bosworth brought up the waterfall diagram of the drive signature he had managed to isolate.

"That's a partial, and there's a lot of noise. I had to have the AI run it three times to get a match, and it's shaky. But the AI says there's a forty percent chance that drive belongs to a Gretian light cruiser. Sleipnir class."

"You have got to be joking," Dunstan said. There was only one cruiser of that class in existence, GNS *Sleipnir*, the last warship commissioned by the Gretian Navy before the end of the war. If he could have had one ship to pick out of the entire internment fleet, he would have chosen that one. She was lightly armored but fast, and fitted with a stupendous amount of firepower in the form of nine rail-gun mounts.

"No, sir, unfortunately."

"Someone stole a light cruiser out of the internment lot? Right underneath our noses?"

"That would explain the nuke," Lieutenant Mayler said. "I mean, the scuttling charges worked just fine to break every other ship in that yard clean in half. Why use a nuclear charge on that dreadnought? Unless you want to make a whole lot of EM noise."

"So nobody notices you driving your stolen cruiser out of the other end of the lot," Dunstan said. "Damn. The whole thing was a distraction."

"If the data are correct, sir. It's a bit of a long shot. But we think it's the only thing that makes sense when you put it all together."

Dunstan looked at the screens in front of him and rubbed his temples.

"Have you forwarded this to fleet command?"

"Not yet, sir. We just finished putting this together about half an hour ago," Bosworth replied.

"Good work, Lieutenants. Even if I am hoping it's all just sensor error."

The logistics involved in this event, stealing a ship from a guarded fleet yard and blowing up all the rest, would be a deep embarrassment to the Rhodian Navy for years to come. The scuttling charges were activated on almost thirty ships, which meant that this had been in the making for months, across multiple watch rotations and under the noses of patrolling ships. Whoever pulled this off, Dunstan had to grudgingly admire their pluck and skill. This was the type of thing that got someone an entry in history records.

"Package it all up and annotate it for fleet intelligence. Let's see what they make of it. But in the meantime, let's assume the worst-case scenario and act like we have a rogue Gretian gun cruiser out there. Pull up the dataset for the Sleipnir class and run some engagement scenarios through the tactical AI. If we bump into them, I want to have a plan for fighting them."

———

Minotaur pushed off from the docking clamp two hours later to commence her antipiracy patrol. The Rhodian Navy was the largest force in the system, but the space between the planets was vast, and not even the wartime fleet would have been able to cover every one of the ever-shifting minimum-energy routes to the other planets. So the fleet focused on the most important one—Rhodia to Pallas—and used whatever resources remained to patrol trouble spots. This month, that seemed to be the Rhodia-to-Oceana route.

"Three incidents since May first," Dunstan read from the patrol orders to his command crew as they were accelerating away from Rhodia One at one g. "Two cargo seizures with no casualties. And an Acheroni merchant lost with almost all hands. Three survivors made a rescue pod that had a dead radio. The Oceanians picked them up the next day. Said the pirates shot at them after they had already surrendered their containers."

Lieutenant Bosworth shook his head grimly. "They're getting bold out there. Only a matter of time before they get a whole ship and just space the crew."

"The fleet is keeping out RNS *Agamemnon* for another week on their return leg from Acheron," Dunstan continued to read from the comtab in his hands. "And the Oceanians are increasing their patrols on the Rhodia route on the sector that overlaps the Acheron transfer right now. For whatever good that's going to do. Two frigates and four corvettes to keep an eye on sixty million klicks of space."

"We should borrow that little fuzzhead trick from the war," Lieutenant Sharp suggested. "When they changed the drive signatures and transponder IDs on their commerce raiders to make them look like civilian cargo ships. Can you imagine if we did that and some scrapper ship came close to us?"

"Looking for juicy cargo and getting a targeting laser in the face instead." Dunstan chuckled. "That would be fun. But I think they've gotten smarter. Or we've already killed or jacked up all the dumb ones. Some tricks only work once or twice."

At least one Gretian Q-ship had gotten a taste of its own medicine when the Palladians had used the same tactic and sent out a light cruiser dressed up like an ore hauler. The Q-ship had been a civilian cargo ship retrofitted with four launch silos and two autocannons, and the short-range fight against a fully armed and ready fleet-defense cruiser had been brief and one-sided. But the Gretian Q-ships had at least obeyed the letter of interplanetary law and changed their transponders back to their actual identities before commencing battle. The pirates currently operating in the system did not extend the same courtesies.

"Oh, we ran the sims you asked for, sir," Lieutenant Bosworth said. "Against the fuzzhead cruiser."

"And what's the verdict?"

"If they're fully crewed and know their ship, we'll get our asses handed to us. They have almost twice our mass. We have four single rail-gun mounts firing every eight seconds; they have six double mounts firing every four and a half seconds. Our mounts are one fifties; theirs are two hundreds. They carry more and bigger ASMs. In our favor, we come out ahead on acceleration by at least three g, and our point defenses are better than theirs. Our AI will be familiar with their attack patterns and the warheads on their missiles. They haven't had software or firmware upgrades in five years, so their point-defense AI would have to start from scratch."

"That's something at least. But that's assuming they have a crew who knows to run that boat, and full magazines."

"Well, sir, they had the resources to pull off that theft. Wouldn't be completely shocked if they had a way to restock their ammo load somewhere. You don't steal a ship of that size if you can't fill up the tank or reload the magazines. Without ammo, it's just a mean-looking pleasure barge."

"They have a heavier punch," Dunstan summarized. "But we have the acceleration and the better point-defense AI. We let them get close and pelt us with those two hundred millimeters, we're fucked. So we control engagement range with our acceleration advantage and let them empty their magazines against our point defense at maximum range. Hope some of our missiles get through, and none of theirs do."

"Right," Bosworth said, but both he and Lieutenant Sharp looked skeptical.

Dunstan got out of his chair and walked up to the plot. It showed them moving away from Rhodia One slowly but steadily, the little icon labeled F-223 Minotaur only at the starting point of a long trajectory that briefly curved through Oceanian space before continuing all the way to Acheron, where they would refuel and turn around in two weeks.

"Well," he said and walked back to his chair. "Holding them at arm's length is Plan B, of course. Plan A is to not have to tangle with that gunboat in the first place."

He looked at the plot again. It was a long dotted line marking the minimum-energy trajectory to Acheron, and they'd be patrolling a long way from help if they ended up in over their heads.

Dunstan punched the panel field for the all-ship announcement system.

"This is the commander. We are commencing our patrol. From this point on, there will be no drills. If action stations sound, we're about to pick a fight or help end one. You all know your jobs. That is all. Commander out."

He tapped the panel to end the announcement and moved it out of his way with the back of his hand.

"Helm, go to three g and lay in a twenty-degree zigzag once we are past the line of departure," he ordered. "Let the AI do the aspect and direction intervals. Let's see if we can bag ourselves some pirates."

Minotaur's engines increased their thrust and pushed the ship forward into the void between Rhodia and Acheron. Dunstan knew that some of his crew watched the stern camera feed as they left Rhodia One and the planet behind—to catch one last direct glance of their home before being away for a month. Dunstan never did. Some of the old spacers that mentored him as a midshipman had said it was bad luck. He knew it was a superstition, but he'd come home unscathed from every patrol so far, through four years of war and five more of peace. It seemed needlessly risky to break with the habit after all this time.

Dunstan looked at the plot again, where Minotaur's icon just swallowed another tiny course segment in a long, broken line of them. They'd be dipping into Oceanian space in three days, the spot where the unlucky Acheroni freighter had been destroyed after surrendering its cargo.

"If I had just stolen a Gretian gun cruiser tailor-made for commerce raiding, where would I be?" he asked the plot, but none of his officers ventured an answer.

CHAPTER 14

ADEN

Eighteen hours after the Oceanian corvette had plucked Aden, Aki, and Torie out of space, they arrived on Oceana.

The planet looked exactly like Aden remembered it. They hitched a ride from the military orbital station down to the surface in a little cloud-hopper shuttle that was full to the last seat with Oceanian Navy personnel. With no other transports scheduled for the next twelve hours, the loadmaster made a safety exemption for the three civilians and let them sit in the emergency crew jump seats on the forward bulkhead. The jump seats were right next to the shuttle's portside door, which had a viewport in it, and Aden watched the scenery outside all the way through the atmospheric entry.

"I love this planet so much," Torie said next to him. She had leaned in closer to get a better look out of the viewport, and he found that he didn't mind her proximity at all, even though the three of them smelled like sweat and stale, recycled air.

"I do, too," he said. "My mother was born here. Down on Chryseis."

Below the shuttle, the endless seas of Oceana stretched out all the way to the planetary horizon, where the thin atmospheric layer made it look like the ocean gradually faded into the blackness of space. Oceana's wealth was water, shallow and warm oceans that were teeming with primitive life. Their shortage was land, but just like the Acheroni had adapted to living their lives in a toxic atmosphere fifty kilometers above the ground, the Oceanians had simply made their own dry ground. The shuttle was flying into the night side of the planet, and even from thirty kilometers up, Aden saw the floating cities they overflew on their trajectory to the spaceport—brightly lit clusters of underwater towers connected by floating pads in whatever shapes suited the local climate and the currents. There were no accurate, definitive maps of Oceana because the floating cities went with the currents and adjusted themselves to their environment, not the other way around, so Oceana was always in motion.

The only place that didn't move with the currents was Adrasteia. When Gretia had settled Oceana five hundred years ago, they had to make their own land, and they did it in the Gretian fashion, overengineering a brute-force solution. Adrasteia sat on top of an underwater mountain that had been built up over fifty years until the tip of that mountain finally rose above the surface of the water and Gretia had a fixed spot for a spaceport and a settlement. Adrasteia was the hub around which everything else flowed on Oceana, and as far as Aden was concerned, it was the most beautiful city in the system.

They saw the city lights long before the cloud hopper started its descent. From the air, Adrasteia looked like a huge luminescent flower floating on the water. The firm land at its center was surrounded by neighborhoods that jutted out into the ocean like rhomboid petals, connected to each other by bridges and breakwaters and underwater passages. Each petal in turn was made up of thousands of smaller interconnected modules, crisscrossed by tens of thousands of canals. The expansion of the city had been limited by the depth of the seafloor to which the piles that anchored the petals could be driven, but as Oceanian civil engineering improved over the decades and centuries, Adrasteia had expanded from that rocky inner nucleus to a circle ten kilometers across. During the war, it had taken an entire division of Gretian troops to occupy the city, and Aden suspected that even that had only been enough because the Oceanians had limited their resistance to passive measures.

"Look at that," Torie murmured when they were on final approach into the spaceport, so low above the city that Aden could read the signs on the storefronts lining the canals below. "So pretty at night. Can you even imagine living here?"

He wanted to tell her that he *had* been a resident, that he didn't have to imagine, but the truth was that he hadn't really lived in Adrasteia even though he had walked its neighborhoods almost daily for half a decade. He had been an occupier, an unwanted intruder, even if he did dress and talk like the locals. There had always been the danger of being found out during the war, and now he felt the need to keep up a different variant of the same deception for entirely different reasons. It was disconcerting how easy it was to act like a field intelligence officer again.

Next to them, Aki had remained asleep all the way through the bumpy ride down to the surface, arms crossed in front of his chest, lightly snoring through a slightly open mouth. He didn't wake when the cloud hopper touched down. His eyes only popped open when Aden and Torie unbuckled their harnesses.

"Good luck," Torie said. "It was nice to meet you. Even if we did almost die together. I hope your trip home goes better than the one we were on."

"Yeah," Aden replied. "Safe travels. And don't go cheap for the ride home. Have your parents transfer you enough for a spot on a passenger liner."

"Oh, trust me, I will. Once my dad hears about that 'nearly getting blown up and almost dying in a life pod' thing, he'll have me booked home premium class."

The immigration control in the spaceport was an automated self-serve system. There was no way around it even if you just wanted to change flights and never leave the spaceport. Aden hung back when the Oceanian sailors on the flight with them filed through the access lock, each of them putting their ID passes onto the scanner. The scanner lit up in green, the security doors of the lock opened, and a sequence of green lights on the floor told the Oceanians where to go next. He watched from a few spots behind them in line as Torie and Aki went through the access lock. The light turned green for both, and the floor lights pointed them toward a different section of the spaceport from the navy personnel once they stepped through the lock. Torie turned her head and looked around just before she scanned her ID pass, and Aden gave her a wave and a smile, which she returned.

Then it was his turn to step through the security lock. He put his ID pass down on the scanner with a feeling of dread.

The scanner light turned yellow. In front of Aden, the transparent walls of the lock beyond the access gate turned to block his entrance to the station interior until only one of them remained open. A yellow light marked a path for him, and the door of his lock opened. Behind him, some of the Oceanian sailors still waiting in line started muttering and laughing.

Well, it's not like I have another option, he thought and went to follow the yellow light path on the floor.

There was a room with another security station at the end of the yellow path. Four Oceanian police officers were waiting for him. One of them waved him inside when he hesitated in the doorway for a second at the sight of the welcoming committee.

"May I see your ID pass, please?" he asked in Rhodian.

Aden handed it to the officer, who put it facedown on a different scanner. This one took a much longer time to scan the pass, and the officer looked at the screen of the scanner intently.

"Aden Robertson," he said. "You have restricted status. I don't have a formal request on file for you to enter Oceana."

"I didn't mean to end up here," Aden replied. "I was on an Acheroni freighter that was destroyed by pirates. One of your corvettes picked up the crash pod yesterday and brought us back here. Me and the two Acheroni that just went through."

The officer handed the ID pass back to Aden.

"In that case, you are in luck. Military rescue and salvage operations constitute an exception. The prior permission requirement can be waived at the discretion of the entry point officer."

Aden switched to Oceanian.

"Then would you please waive the requirement for me? I've had a rough few days, and I would love to be able to get some sleep and food before I try to figure out how to get home from here. I have money on my ledger, so I can pay my way."

The officer looked at his colleagues and chuckled.

"A fuzzhead who learned to speak properly. And he doesn't even sound like a fuzzhead. That's a first."

He turned back to Aden.

"Sure. I'll waive the requirement. Spend as much of your money here as you want before you go back home. But don't stay beyond the expiration date of that temporary ID pass, or you'll be in deep shit."

"I'll be out of your hair in a day or two," Aden replied, making himself sound tired and beaten down. "I just want some good food and a bed that doesn't fold up into the wall."

The Oceanian officer chuckled again and pointed at the door at the far end of the room.

"Through there. And don't disobey so much as a traffic sign. Lot of people out there who will beat you up and throw you into a canal if they find out you're a Gretian, and a Blackguard at that. Have a lovely stay."

Adrasteia's spaceport was as beautiful as the city. It was a big dome made of Acheroni carbon composites: thin and graceful struts of elegant latticework that had been painted a brilliant shade of white. The main thoroughfare was made up of three interconnected halls grouped around a big central square. It was huge and airy and full of light and people. Aden could smell the sea outside as soon as he stepped into the main concourse. All the markers from the occupation years had been thoroughly scrubbed since Aden had last passed through this place. Not even the multilingual signs directing passengers to the different service areas had any Gretian on them.

After days of packaged rations outside of his culinary comfort zone, he was craving good food, and the spaceport had that in abundance, culinary variety with ten times the number of eateries and vendor stalls he had seen at the spaceport on the Rhodian arcology. The concourse there had seemed enormous, but it would have fit into the central concourse of the Adrasteia spaceport three or four times. Aden stopped at an automatic self-serve bistro and scarfed down an unwise amount of calories, then went back into the concourse to head for the exit.

There were plenty of sleep-capsule hotels at the spaceport, but Aden didn't feel like spending yet another night in a stainless coffin. He already hadn't been overly fond of confined spaces before *Cloud Dancer*, and drifting in a tiny crash pod with two other people for the better part of the day had made him crave the sight of open skies again.

The island that made up the old city was just a kilometer across and rose ten meters above the sea. The eight diamond-shaped floating platforms that extended out from the central island were connected to the rock of the old city with bridges that spanned the inner harbor ring like spokes on a wheel, one bridge to each of the eight petals that made up the bulk of the city. The old city, the original colony town set up on the firm rock of the built-up mountaintop, was mostly taken up by the spaceport and the Oceanian government complex. The real city was made up of the petals that were anchored to the seafloor and jutting out into the ocean. Because each petal was a rhombus, and each rhombus was separated from the next by a fifty-meter-wide canal at the base and then a wide triangle of ocean at the tip, you could be anywhere in the new city and never be more than one block from a canal and five blocks away from the waterfront. One of Adrasteia's nicknames was the "City of a Thousand Bridges," and while Aden knew that there weren't quite that many bridges connecting the eight neighborhoods, the number wasn't a vast exaggeration.

He'd had no shortage of fresh air in the prison arcology on Rhodia, but when he walked out onto the bridge leading over to the eastern petal, the breeze coming in from the sea and caressing his face was almost an erotic experience. On Rhodia, the winds from the mountains had been clean and cold and dry, especially five hundred meters up on the arcology terraces. Here on Oceana, they were warm and carried moisture and the smell of sea salt.

It was evening, and the eastern bridge was busy with people and travel pods streaming in both directions. The bridge was lit up in the Oceanian colors, and the lights reflected on the waters of the canal that surrounded the old city island. On the water below, small boats zipped by, trailing shimmering wakes. When he had been marched across this bridge in a long column of Gretian prisoners five years ago on the way to the spaceport, Oceanian civilians lining the street and jeering at them, Aden had thought—*known*—he'd never come back here again. When he reached the middle of the bridge span, he stopped and leaned on the railing to look over the canal. As he watched, a pleasure barge passed under the bridge and then made its way along the canal and to the south, its open deck full of revelers with drinks in their hands, music playing from the entertainment system. Oceana had been a popular tourist planet before the war, and it looked like things were back to normal here in Adrasteia.

Aden looked up at the night sky. The galaxy's pale, diffused band of white light painted the darkness overhead in a wide arch, billions of stars and interstellar matter glowing in the black of space. Not even a day ago, he had been floating in that vast airless void with Torie and Aki. If the Oceanians hadn't found the pod, they'd be dead by tomorrow, their bodies fated to drift in the vacuum between the planets and stars forever. If he had died up there, it would have made no impact at all on the world. He was forty-two years old and hadn't managed to matter enough to be missed by anyone.

He took out his comtab, which activated itself automatically when it sensed the proximity of his face. The message he had written to his sister was still on the screen, along with the picture he had taken. He looked tired and scared in the image, and seeing himself in that place again felt unsettling, so he deleted it, leaving only the three paragraphs he had written to explain himself to his sister. If he had died, this would have been the only proof of his existence. It seemed woefully inadequate to explain why he had left and what he had done with his life.

Maybe she takes after Papa, he thought. *Maybe she shares his attitudes by now. He's had seventeen years to explain his perspective, uncontested.*

Aden thought of the little girl with tousled hair who had latched on to him every time he had come home from school. She had idolized him in the complete and absolute way little girls adore their big brothers, and he had been too absorbed in his young adult anxieties and social games at school to really appreciate that unconditional love. She had been born the year after he left for school, and he'd seen her only a few times a year when he came home for the various holidays and school breaks. He realized that he had barely known her even then. But she was the one who had been on his mind when he was sure he was about to die, and Aden found that he really wanted to get to know her again. If she had a presence on the Mnemosyne at all, he'd find a way to contact her tomorrow, after a drink and a good night's sleep.

There were plenty of self-service hotels on the main vein right beyond the bridge. Aden picked one that was right across the street from a lively-looking bar and used his comtab to check into a room with a canal view. When he waited for the authorization, he was sure for just a moment that the transaction would come back declined because he was Gretian. But the Oceanians' dislike of his kind didn't seem to extend to money. A few moments later, the check-in kiosk sent a receipt and an access code to his comtab, along with a floor map and a handful of advertisements for discounted drinks and food at nearby establishments.

The room was a small but clean suite with a bed that was at least twice as wide as the one he had slept on in the prison arcology. Aden had intended to walk across the street to the bar and get a strong drink or two to help him go to sleep, but it turned out that the alcohol wasn't necessary. The bed adjusted itself to his body shape when he tried it out, and he was so fatigued from the stress of the last twenty-four hours that he fell asleep almost instantly.

CHAPTER 15

IDINA

The Gretian police gyrofoil was technically a four seater, but the two seats in the back were separated from the front by a security mesh. Idina didn't feel like being social, but she also didn't want to sit in a cage, so she sat up front next to Captain Dahl. The Gretian gyrofoils were smaller and nimbler than the military ones Idina usually rode in, and Captain Dahl obviously had lots of time behind the stick because she kept the controls in manual mode and expertly weaved her way through the city at a low level. Patrolling in a foil was boring, and Idina didn't like sitting on her ass for long stretches of time anyway, so she was pleasantly surprised when Captain Dahl put the gyrofoil on the ground in front of the city's vactrain station and announced to the dispatcher that she was about to commence a foot patrol.

"Last one of you I patrolled with two years ago would just set the foil on autopilot and do a pattern all shift," Idina said as they got out of the gyrofoil. The plaza in front of the station was ringed with eateries, game parlors, and other kinds of amusements. It was a warm evening, and there were lots of people out on the street.

"Some officers get lazy that way," Dahl said. She straightened her equipment belt and remotely locked the gyrofoil behind her. "But you see more when you're walking around. And the people see you."

The Gretian policewoman was a full head taller than Idina. She wore her white hair in a tight braid that ended just below the collar of her uniform. Idina noted that all the gear on Dahl's belt seemed well worn, but not neglected. In the military, you could tell a lot about a soldier from the shape their gear was in, and Dahl's kit would have marked her as a seasoned veteran in the brigade. *At least I didn't get a lazy-assed desk pilot this time,* Idina thought.

They walked across the plaza without hurry. Dahl had a patrol gait, a confident not-quite swagger that made her look relaxed and alert at the same time. It felt strange to be out on patrol in nothing but a ballistic suit, with no armor to weigh her down and no exoskeleton to add another 20 percent of gravity. She didn't even have a rifle to carry at low ready, and it made her feel like her hands had nothing to do. Dahl strode alongside her with her thumbs loosely hooked behind her belt buckle, so Idina did the same and then found herself annoyed with her own willingness to adopt the other woman's body language. Dahl outranked her on paper, but the woman was still a Gretian and a police officer, which meant that Idina was the ranking member of the patrol by default.

The crowd out on the plaza tonight was young. It seemed to be a popular meeting spot. Idina saw kids standing together in small groups or sitting on the steps of the entrance to the vactrain station, socializing in the way kids on every planet did on a slow weekend night. Idina caught some glances from people here and there, but they weren't hostile looks, just curious ones. A few times, she saw kids hiding something or turning away when they saw Dahl and Idina walking up, but Dahl did nothing, and Idina kept walking with her. The enforcement of Gretian law was Dahl's responsibility. The policy of the JSP was to let the Gretians handle their own citizens and only step in to assist when asked. Any infractions by off-duty Alliance soldiers out on the town were in Idina's area of authority, and she would call the shots on any incidents that had to do with military security. But Gretian kids using inhalers with Acheroni designer drugs or smoking Oceanian seaweed did not concern her, and it appeared that Dahl didn't give a shit either. Gretian drug laws had always been stricter than those of the other planets, and Idina had never understood the concept of sobriety as a moral virtue anyway. Maybe if their military-age population had gotten into the habit of getting buzzed more often before the war, they wouldn't have enlisted by the tens of thousands to bring their uptight clean lifestyles to Oceana and Pallas uninvited.

"This place has turned into a bit of a trouble spot since you were here last," Dahl said. "Too many young people with little to do. So they get into fights and do stupid things. This is where you come if you want to buy pharmaceuticals."

The stilted translation of Dahl's Gretian still sounded like Idina was talking to a computer terminal. It was the lack of vernacular, she decided. Computers didn't do slang or dialect. It made translator software sound too clinical. No Palladian outside of a corporate office or medical school would say "pharmaceuticals" in regular conversation. But the overly formal and slightly mechanical quality of the translation actually matched Idina's preconceptions of Gretian attitudes: precise, unemotional, and uptight.

They crossed the plaza and walked up the wide stairs to the terminal building. The vactrains hadn't run since the end of the war, but the building was still in use. Many of the shops that had catered to travelers before the war were still there, and other establishments had moved in and supplanted them. Now it was no longer a transit station but an indoor mercantile. Whatever obnoxious qualities the Gretians had, they had a thing for neatness and order in public spaces, so she was surprised to see that the place looked quite a bit more run-down than it had two years ago. They walked into the atrium of the station, past dark and disused transit schedule displays and overflowing refuse bins. There were competing music styles coming from shops and eateries on the concourse, and the smells of food hung in the air and mixed with the scent that was particular to slowly deteriorating buildings low on the priority list for thorough cleanings and timely air-filter replacements.

"I want to check the blast doors to the vactrain level," Idina told Dahl.

"Of course," Captain Dahl replied. "Lead the way."

Part of the patrol checklist for the station was to inspect the blast doors that sealed off the active part of the station from the disused vactrain level below. The blast doors were at the end of the wide staircase in the center of the atrium. When the vactrains were still running between the major cities on Gretia, thousands of people had descended those stairs every day to travel across the continent at a thousand kilometers per hour, the most sophisticated long-range transit in the entire Gaia system. But those trains had stopped running before Idina had initially set foot onto Gretia on her first occupation tour. Gretian infrastructure had always been designed with emergencies and conflict in mind even when the planetary system was at peace, and the vactrain level below the main concourse had been built to serve as an emergency shelter. The doors that sealed the bottom of the staircase were big titanium slabs that had been permanently welded together at the seams in the middle. There was a group of young Gretians hanging out in the stairwell by the doors, and they quickly broke up and walked up the stairs when they saw Idina and Captain Dahl descending.

"Move along now," Dahl said to them amiably as they passed each other on the staircase. "You're not supposed to be down here."

The welds were still in place, of course. It took a lot of effort to weld solid titanium doors together, and nobody would be able to crack them open again without a heavy-duty plasma cutter or welding laser and a lot of time. But it was on the checklist, and after the insurgent ambush on her patrol that was set up and executed through the vactrain tunnel system, Idina wasn't going to skip that check, even though the likelihood of someone trying to regain access to the vactrain network in a busy main station was vanishingly slim. But after the attack on her section, no paranoia seemed too outlandish anymore. Not satisfied with just a visual inspection, she lowered the data monocle on her helmet and let the computer check for structural irregularities in the welded seam. It came up clean, and she retracted the monocle and nodded at Captain Dahl.

"All clear. We can go back upstairs. I want to check the seal on the other staircase, too—the one across the atrium by the north entrance."

"Of course," Captain Dahl said.

They returned to the atrium level and made their way across to the north end. Even though the civilians all around her were going about their business without paying much attention to them, Idina felt exposed. She was all by herself, with an unproven and only nominal Gretian ally by her side, surrounded by people whose planet had invaded her own and killed a lot of her fellow soldiers not even ten years ago. She hadn't been tense about being in public on her first tour with the JSP two years ago, even though the end of the war had been a much more recent memory then. But in those days, the Gretians had been meek and downtrodden, willing to accept the Alliance authority because their society didn't deal well with power vacuums, and no member of the Alliance forces had gotten killed by enemy action until her section had walked into that ambush. Now it seemed like anything could happen at any time, even if the civilians all around them placidly minded their own business, and she felt like she was walking around with a big target painted onto her back.

"You left your helmet in the foil," Idina observed to Dahl. "You don't wear one on foot patrol?"

Dahl shook her head. "Not unless we get called out to a big fight. The helmet makes me look too anonymous. It becomes easier for them to pretend I am not a person."

"Without the helmet, it becomes easier for them to crack your skull, too."

"I try to avoid doing things that make people want to crack my skull," Dahl said. The translator in her ear didn't annotate inflections, but it sounded wry to Idina.

"Good for you," she replied. "And I try to avoid doing things that make people want to shoot at me, but that doesn't always work out."

She must have sounded crabby even through the translator, because Dahl offered an apologetic nod.

"I heard what happened to your Alliance patrol last week. I hope you know that most of us think it was an outrageous act. We have worked well together for the last five years. I know that my colleagues will help your investigators in any way they can. Nobody wants things to go back to the way they were."

"It sure felt to me that somebody does," Idina replied. "But thank you for your concern."

They walked to the north end of the atrium in silence. Wherever they went, there was a perceptible bubble of orderly behavior that moved with them as they made their way across the atrium. Conversations quieted down, arguments stopped, loitering groups of young Gretians split up or walked off whenever people caught sight of Dahl in her green police skin suit. Idina wasn't sure whether the Gretian respect for uniformed authority was one of their best or worst traits, but she had to admit that it made police work a lot easier.

They checked the blast doors at the bottom of the northern staircase, which were just as securely welded shut as the other ones. On the way back to the main entrance, Dahl didn't cut straight across the atrium the way they had on the way in. Instead, she walked the storefronts on the periphery, checking out the shops and exchanging the occasional nod with a store clerk or passerby, all in that relaxed yet alert patrol gait. From the way Idina saw her interact with the locals, she could tell that Dahl was the furthest thing from a rookie anyone could get on an experience scale. She was completely, confidently at ease and in her element.

"How long have you been a police officer?" Idina asked her.

"Thirty-five years. Three years of training, thirty-two years here in the city."

"I'm not quite thirty-seven," Idina said. "That means you've been wearing that uniform since I was still learning how to use the toilet properly."

Dahl chuckled softly. "You are making me feel old."

"I've never seen someone your age and rank still out on the street on foot patrol. You must have pissed off someone important."

"Oh, they have tried more than once to get me indoors. I turned down transfer offers to the criminal investigator division every year for a long time. They finally got the idea that I did not want to become a criminal police investigator and left me alone."

They made their way out of the terminal and back onto the plaza, where it was a little noisier than before. Out on the steps in front of the building, there was a group of young Gretians engaged in an argument. Idina could only make out half of what they were saying because their slang was so extensive, but it was typical postadolescent male preening, young men puffing themselves up in front of their friends. The argument hadn't quite devolved into pushing and shoving yet, but the body language of the participants told Idina that things were rapidly heading toward that stage. Dahl quickened her pace a little and steered toward the small, noisy group. Idina followed a few steps behind.

When they were ten meters from the gaggle of young men, Dahl whistled sharply, and some heads turned. The two main opponents in the argument seemed to be too wrapped up in their business to notice because they continued undeterred. Then one of them pushed the other, who had to take two involuntary steps back down the staircase. Idina could see the kid gathering himself for a response in kind when he saw Dahl approaching and hesitated. The other kid had his back to the police officer and took his opponent's hesitation as fear. He took a swing just as Dahl came up from behind and yanked him back by the collar of his jacket. The kid yelped in surprise and lashed out blindly. Dahl smacked away the hand that was about to hit her on the side of the head and kept yanking, throwing the kid off balance. She kept him from falling by holding him up by the collar.

"Unexcite yourself," Dahl said in a stern voice. "Before you make a mistake you will regret for a while."

The kid was as tall as Dahl, and he probably had ten or fifteen kilos on her. He was also more than slightly buzzed on something. He sized up Dahl as if to decide whether he could take her on, and whatever he was on seemed to override his good judgment because he puffed out his chest and lunged at her.

Idina only saw the stun stick in Dahl's hand when it had already blocked the punch the kid threw at her. He cried out in pain and recoiled, and she extended the stun stick to its full length with a flick of her wrist and tapped the kid in the middle of the chest with the tip. He grimaced and let out a strangled sound, then collapsed.

His friends backed off at the sight of the stun stick as Dahl swung it around and brought it between herself and the rest of the group. This was Gretian civil business, out of Idina's area of responsibility, but she put a hand on her sidearm and got ready to unlock it from the holster anyway. The rest of the group were cowed for the moment, but they still outnumbered Dahl three to one, and kids their age often let the testosterone override their good judgment even without stimulants in the mix. But Dahl didn't seem the least bit concerned. Her expression wasn't angry, just reproachful and mildly disappointed.

"I have two more seats in my gyrofoil if any of you want to ride along with your friend. The choice is yours."

The sight of their unconscious friend sprawled out on the step below appeared to have a sobering effect, because neither of the remaining three youths took Dahl up on the offer. They retreated to a safe distance and talked in low, belligerent-sounding voices as they watched Captain Dahl put wrist restraints on their friend. Idina stepped in to help her hoist the kid up. He was heavier than his lanky frame suggested, but she could have lifted him by herself if she had the need. With Dahl propping the unconscious boy up on the other side, they made their way back to the gyrofoil that was parked fifty meters away. By the time they got there, Dahl was huffing a little with the exertion.

"I have him," Idina told Dahl when the policewoman unlocked the rear hatch of the gyrofoil. She held the unconscious kid up by herself while Dahl patted him down and went through his pockets, pulling out a comtab and a few assorted pieces of pocket detritus. Idina looked around on the plaza to make sure that trouble hadn't followed them. The group they had broken up had wandered off into the terminal building.

"You are strong," Dahl said to her. "I forgot how much you Palladians can lift."

"In this gravity, a lot more than this one weighs," Idina replied. "I was standing by to help out, but you didn't look like you needed it."

"They were just being dumb juveniles. And this one is going to be very sorry when he wakes up in the detention cell. Once the headache from the stick wears off."

They loaded the delinquent into the back of the gyrofoil. Dahl took the time to strap him in while Idina held him up in the seat.

Just a dumb kid, she thought as she watched his slack face while the policewoman fastened the buckles of the restraint system. He looked like he was maybe eighteen, twenty at the most. She had lost count of the number of young Gretians like him she had seen dead in the tunnels on Pallas—shot to pieces, carved open with monomolecular blades, lungs blown out by thermobaric grenades, drowned in their own blood in the darkness, terror frozen on their faces. This kid didn't know how lucky he was that he hadn't been born five or six years earlier, when the Gretians had drafted anyone who was of legal age and able to hold a rifle, and when waking up in a police detention cell wasn't the worst possible way to end a night.

"They don't have a clue, do they?" she said mostly to herself. Next to her, Captain Dahl finished tightening the straps and let out a puff of breath. She looked at Idina and shook her head lightly.

"Too many parents that did not come back from the war. Too many boys without anyone to tell them how to be men without puffing their chests and beating each other up over dumb things. Foolish pride. They are not entitled to pride yet."

Idina didn't want to like the woman. But that was something that could have come out of the mouth of a Pallas Brigade drill sergeant, and even though nobody would ever mistake Captain Dahl for one, she radiated a calm competence that was almost brigade-like. At the same time, she was Gretian through and through, with the lofty bearing and the overly formal speech that annoyed Idina about most of these people. Meeting a Gretian who held her head high and not instantly wanting to beat that head back down made Idina feel conflicted. But looking at the slack-jawed unconscious kid in the rear of the gyrofoil, she had to admit that she'd rather patrol with someone who didn't take any shit than with someone meek and obedient who let her do all the heavy lifting. And at least she got partnered with a woman, one who had never been in the military. Knowing that this one had never set foot on other planets to conquer or occupy them made it easier to like her a little.

They strapped into their own seats. Captain Dahl took manual control, and the gyrofoil rose from its parking spot and climbed into the brightly lit night sky. Idina watched the plaza fall away below them.

Maybe six months of this will be good for me, she thought. *Maybe this time I'll go home and not want to punch walls whenever I think of my next tour here.*

CHAPTER 16

ADEN

Aden woke up to the sunlight streaming through the narrow gaps in the photovoltaic blinds and the sound of the waves crashing against the seawall. It was the most peaceful sound he had heard in years, and he luxuriated in just listening with his eyes closed for a while. The above-sea rooms of the hotel were three times the price of the subsea rooms, but he had spent too much time in confined spaces, so when he had checked in at the self-serve terminal in the lobby, he had gladly paid the premium.

"What time is it?" he finally asked aloud after a few minutes of listening to the surf.

"The time is eight forty-five in the morning," the room's AI replied in a pleasant female voice.

Aden rolled toward the window and let out a deep breath. The air in the room was filtered, and he wanted to smell seawater.

"What's the temperature outside?"

"The outside temperature is twenty-one degrees. Daytime high is projected to be twenty-five in the midafternoon."

"Raise the blinds and open the balcony door, please."

The balcony door slid open silently, and the breeze wafting in from the outside carried the smell of the sea. It was perfect Adrasteia weather, blue skies with scattered clouds. Most of the planet's cities cycled through something akin to seasons as they adjusted their drift toward the equator or away from it throughout the year to have temperature variations, but the underwater sea mount that made up Adrasteia's base was near the equator, so it was always early summer here.

Aden took a shower in the bathroom's wet cell while his clothes cycled through the cleaning unit set into the wall. By the time he was out of the shower, his clothes were clean and dry, and the breakfast he had ordered was waiting for him in the service terminal by the door.

He had his comtab's AI assistant search through the Mnemosyne while he ate his breakfast. His family name wasn't hard to find in the data stream. Naturally, most of the entries referenced his father, who practically had a monopoly on the family name in the public mentions. Aden hadn't seen so much as an image of him since the beginning of his imprisonment, but his appearance hadn't changed perceptibly except for the color of his hair, which was now starkly white. Favorable genetics combined with the best health care, nutrition, and cell-refresh treatments money could buy meant that his father always looked twenty years younger than he really was. In fifteen years, they'd look more like siblings than father and son.

His sister was a different story. She had the kind of public profile that suggested a conscious effort to remain as anonymous as possible. There were professional and academic directory listings for her, but he couldn't find an image of her, just faceless entries with the most perfunctory details. But everyone in the system had comms nodes listings somewhere, and she was no exception. His sister had a node address in an alphanumeric block that corresponded to his family's business, and that was more than enough correlation for Aden. He copied the node number and started a new message, then hesitated.

What do I say to a sister I haven't seen in seventeen years? Someone who had barely started basic school when I left, and who has no idea I'm still alive?

He had taken a new family name when he joined the Blackguards. His first name was still the same, but it wasn't terribly uncommon on Gretia, and his sister couldn't be sure who was contacting her unless he made the message unambiguous. But it seemed too much to start the whole thing with *Hello, I am your long-lost brother. How have you been?* There was no way to tell who had access to the messages for that node, or whether he even had the right person. He needed something innocuous enough in case he was mistaken or someone else was reading her mail as well.

I'm thinking like an intelligence operative again, he chided himself. But old habits die hard, and it was always better to err on the side of caution.

There was a term of endearment he had used for her when she was little. He wrote it in the body of the message, just two words:

Hey, Shorty.

He moved his thumb over the message to prepare to flick it to its destination. For a few seconds, he looked at those two words on the transparent comtab screen and wondered how she would react to seeing them pop up in her queue. Once the message was out and she had read it, there was no reeling it back in. If she rejected his attempts at contact, he'd be in the same position as before. If she accepted it, he'd no longer be able to keep maintaining his distance. It was like casting a line out for the past, and he was anxious about what he'd drag back. But he needed to cast that line, because without something to anchor him to the real world again, he felt hopelessly unmoored.

Aden flicked the message on its way. Almost immediately after he sent the message, anxiety welled up inside him, and he had to fight the urge to undo his action. But the Mnemosyne worked faster than light speed, and outbound messages between nodes only had a ten-second window for cancellations regardless of the distance between them. When the ten-second mark passed and the comtab let out a friendly little delivery notice chirp, his anxiety eased a little. His message was already in a data bank on Gretia, getting routed and sorted into the destination node.

It's done now, he thought. *And maybe it was a wrong node address anyway.*

———

Staring at the comtab for a few minutes didn't make a reply appear, and Aden forced himself to put the device aside and eat his breakfast. Then he put the tray back into the service terminal and left the suite to go outside for a while.

Most of his new clothes had burned up with the rest of his belongings on *Cloud Dancer*, so he went to one of the many clothing stores on the eastern leaf's main vein. After years of wearing the same standard-issue POW overalls, the sartorial choices in civilian stores were overwhelming, and he half-heartedly browsed the aisles with the sample outfits.

His comtab chirped an incoming message alert while he was trying on a lightweight jacket tailored for the warm Adrasteia climate, and in his haste to get the device out, he almost dropped both jacket and comtab.

The reply wasn't much longer than the original message he had sent, and seeing it made his heart jump in his chest.

What was the name of the dog I got when I was five?

Aden returned the jacket to the display frame and hurried out of the shop to get back into the sunlit street. For an awful minute, he couldn't remember the name of his sister's pet from seventeen years ago, but then it came back to him, and he smiled.

It wasn't a dog, he replied. *It was a cat, and you named it Smudge.*

This time he flicked the message off without hesitation. The reply came just a minute later, but it felt like an hour to him as he was staring at his comtab screen and trying to will it into existence.

> Meet me in the Mnemosyne in thirty minutes. Use
> a public terminal, not your personal tab. Don't
> send me any more messages until then.

The directions were followed by a network node address.

This was the sort of message he would have expected from a fellow signals intelligence officer during an assignment, not the young sister he hadn't seen in a decade and a half. Aden read the content a few times and memorized the node address she had given him.

There was a public comms terminal pod just down the street. He paced in front of it until he told himself that he probably looked odd or suspicious, even though nobody was paying any attention to him. His anxiety was rising again with every passing minute, and for the first time in days, he scrutinized his appearance, checking out his reflection in shop windows and running his fingers through his hair. Then it dawned on him that he'd probably look better in new clothes, so he went back to the store he had just left and finished his shopping, even though the anxiety in the center of his stomach felt like it would burn clean through him.

When the time came to connect to the node his sister had sent, Aden claimed a pod in the public terminal and closed the door. Then he activated the pod's Mnemosyne node, paid for the bandwidth, and fed the node number from the message into the system. The pod mapped his body and face with a spatial sensor array and brought up a screen to allow him to customize his appearance. He could play it safe and make his hologram on the other side appear hooded or masked, or even take on a randomly generated face to replace his own. But he wanted to remain the way he looked in real life, and he dismissed the customization screen without making any changes. Then he swallowed the lump that had appeared in his throat and tapped the CONNECT field on the console.

The booth changed into a large room as the holographic projectors of the pod adjusted the visuals to match the parameters the person hosting the meeting—Aden's sister—had chosen. The visuals unfolded themselves at an intentionally leisurely pace that was designed to keep his inner ear from doing somersaults at the sudden change. It took him a few moments to make sense of his new virtual surroundings. It was a café somewhere on Gretia—he couldn't tell whether it was a specific one or a randomly generated location. The other tables in the room gradually filled with other people that appeared in his field of view as outlines and then solidified. Within a few moments, the projectors were done with their work, and he appeared to sit in a cozy little café that was busy with customers and abuzz with low conversation. The holograms were just that—he knew that if he reached out, his hand would touch the wall of the pod instead of the table's food service comtab he saw in front of him—but the illusion was convincing, much more lifelike and seamless than he remembered from the last time he had used a Mnemosyne meeting room.

The chair in front of him was empty, but a few seconds later, an outline began to take shape, sliding gradually into focus until the hologram materialized fully. The young woman across the virtual table from him was unmistakably his little sister, but the difference between the girl from his memory and the face before him made Aden feel like reality was somehow slightly out of sync. She had always looked more like their father, and the resemblance had only increased over the years: blue eyes, a nose with a high bridge and a slightly upturned tip, and a mouth that just managed to avoid being a little too wide for her narrow face. Her hair was the familiar red that was predominant in his lineage.

"Hello, Solveig," he said.

Her eyes focused on him—or rather, the hologram that represented him—and she put one hand over her mouth and drew in a sharp breath.

"My gods, it *is* you. Aden."

She made to put her hand on the table and reach for him, and it passed through the hologram's tabletop. She pulled back her hand and brushed a strand of her hair from her forehead.

"Is this what you look like now? Or did you tweak the hologram?"

"I didn't change anything. This is me." He scratched the stubble he had grown since he had been released. "I'm sure I look a lot older than you remember me."

"You look so much like Mama," his sister said. "I didn't really remember just how much you look alike. You've got the same eyes and mouth."

"Are you still in touch with her?" Aden asked.

She shrugged. "Whenever she remembers that I exist. Sometimes I go months without hearing from her."

"Is she still on Oceana?" Their mother, Vigdis, had left for her birth planet when she divorced their father, a year before Aden had his big falling-out with him.

Solveig shook her head.

"She moved to Hades. Spends her days gambling and bouncing around in low g, I think. I haven't seen her in person in—oh, I don't know. Three years. Maybe four. Papa doesn't tell me not to go see her, but he's not exactly wild about it whenever I do."

"How is he?" Aden asked.

"He's been better," she said. "I think it messed him up a bit when you left. And then he lost control over the company when we lost the war." She leaned toward him a little.

"Where have you *been*, Aden? We all thought you were dead. I dreamed about you for *years* after you left."

"I joined the Blackguards. It was the only way to get a new name. Legally, I mean. I wanted to go somewhere where even Papa couldn't find me."

"But *why*? What made you do it? I never understood that."

"You mean he didn't tell you what happened?"

"He said it was about a girl. That you fell for someone and ran off with her because he didn't approve."

Aden felt anger welling up inside him.

"And you believed that?"

"I didn't know *what* to believe," Solveig said and shook her head slowly. "I was *six* when you left. I didn't have anyone to tell me your side of the story. You know how Papa is when he shares information."

"He tells you only the parts he thinks you need to know. And he talks right around the inconvenient stuff." Aden made a fist and looked at his knuckles shining white under the taut skin, then relaxed his hand again.

"We never talked about it in detail until I was older. When you were already gone a few years, and nobody thought you'd ever come back. Did you serve in the war?"

He nodded. "I didn't have to fight. I was a linguist. Spent most of the war on Oceana. Never fired a weapon."

"Did you ever regret it?" Solveig asked. "Did you ever think about coming back?"

He studied her face. She sat there with her hands folded in her lap and held his gaze with a serious expression that was tinged with a little bit of sadness, and his feelings of guilt intensified.

"Not at first," he admitted. "I didn't want anything to do with Papa. And you were six at the time. I barely knew you. And I was full of anger. Full of myself, too. And then, when I did want to get back in touch with you, we were all at war and I couldn't. I'm sorry I kept you wondering all these years. I didn't think anyone still cared."

Solveig looked around the holographic café and sighed.

"I wish I really could order a coffee in here," she said. "But it's all make-believe. Everyone in here is just randomly generated. I could scream and nobody would react."

"Why the subterfuge?" Aden asked. "You said to use a public terminal, not my own comtab."

"So they won't be able to trace it back to you quickly," she said. "I set up the session with the strongest encryption I could authorize, but nothing's bulletproof. I figure we're good for ten minutes before they can unravel it."

"Who's *they*? The Alliance?"

She shrugged. "Alliance police, or our own corporate security. Maybe both at the same time. Setting up a session with hard encryption gets you all kinds of interest. People wonder what it is you want to keep quiet. Especially when you talk to someone in a public terminal pod. I gave you the address for one of our secure corporate nodes, and then I connected with a burner ID. We should probably make this quick, though."

"How do you know to do all that?" Aden asked. "You sound like a field intelligence operative."

She gave him a sad little smile.

"I'm Falk Ragnar's daughter. I've had to learn how to keep my comms private since I got my first comtab," she said. "You know our father. If he was anything back then like he is now."

"He always needs to hold all the strings," Aden said. "Always needs to know where you are, what you're doing. Who you're doing it with."

Solveig nodded. "I don't really blame you, Aden. And I can't even be angry with you for putting everything on my shoulders. If you had stayed, you couldn't have worked for Ragnar anyway. You couldn't have been his precious heir. I would have gotten that job anyway because I was born at the right time. I was three days short of eighteen when the armistice happened. Lucky family, right?"

She looked past him and through the window of the holographic coffee shop at whatever street scene the simulation was serving up behind him.

"In truth, I feel sorry for you. If he piled all his expectations on you, too, before you left. But you have no idea what it's like when you're the last one. When he loads all his hopes onto your back and doesn't ask once whether you can carry the load. Or whether you even want to."

"I'm so sorry," Aden said, wishing he could reach out and take his sister's hand. "I really am. I never thought about anyone but myself when I left. I had a choice, and then I changed things so that you didn't get one."

"I may have done the same thing if I had been in your place," she said.

At the beginning of their virtual meeting, he had been struck by how much Solveig looked like their father, but now he saw that the resemblance was limited to superficialities like eye color and bone structure. It didn't extend to the genuine emotions in her eyes and her smile. Their father had a broad, easy smile, but most of the time he flashed his very straight white teeth, it was a display of dominance or deception.

"What are you going to do now, Aden? Are you coming back home?"

He shook his head. "I can't. Not after everything that has happened. I have no place to go. The Blackguards have been dissolved. I couldn't just walk up to Papa's doorstep and ask for shelter and a job, even if I wanted. And if I come back to Gretia, I'll just pop up on his sensors somehow. Maybe someday soon. But not right now."

She nodded slowly. "It's probably for the better anyway. Things aren't great here. I mean, we still have what we have. But there's so much trouble everywhere. There are demonstrations almost every day now. People are angry. Not just at the Alliance. At each other, too. Nobody wants to admit they were for the war, but everyone knows it was some-one else's fault that we lost."

"I want to talk to you again," Aden said. "Now that I am out in the world again. I want to get to know you. We have seventeen years to catch up on. If you want," he added with some haste.

"I would like that, Aden. I'm still not sure what to make of all of this. I'm not quite sure things will ever go back to normal. But we haven't had *normal* in a long time."

Solveig gave him that little smile again, and this time there was no sadness in it.

"I remember how it was when I was little. All my memories of you are good ones. That's why I replied to you and set up this call. If I believed you had turned out to be like Papa, I never would have answered."

"It sounds like you have as much love for him as I do."

"He's our father," she said. "Yours and mine. Of *course* I love him. But he's a hard man to deal with. And I think that one of his kind is quite enough in my life."

She glanced at something off to her right Aden could not see.

"Time's almost up," she said. "If we keep the link up too long, corporate intelligence will crack the encryption and pinpoint the origin and destination. If they find out it was me, they'll let Papa know. And then he will know about you. I scrubbed your inbound message from my queue, but they'll check the time stamps for that terminal pod you're using and link it to the ID pass that was used to rent it."

"I'm on Oceana," Aden said. "Papa has no pull here. Not anymore."

She smiled at that statement, and the melancholy had returned to her expression, as if he had just made a charming and naive statement that was innocently but utterly wrong.

"Papa still has pull *everywhere*, Aden. Don't think for a minute that just because he's out of the company, he doesn't still have his fingers in everything."

"You really do think like an operative," he said and shook his head with a smile of his own. "How do I contact you again?"

"I'll send you a one-time node address. Write it down; don't save it to your comtab directly. When you want to talk again, send a blank message to it."

"Okay." He paused and looked at his sister's face, trying to commit every detail to memory one more time. "Thank you for coming out to see me. I missed you. I want to set right what I messed up. I never meant for you to have to go through all of this. If I had known we were about to have a war, I never would have left."

"It wouldn't have made a big difference, Aden. They would have drafted you anyway. At least you got to choose to not have to fight. I'm glad you're not dead. I like still having a brother."

She tapped an invisible control screen in front of her, and her hologram began to fade.

"Goodbye, Aden. I'll talk to you soon. I love you."

Her hologram disappeared before he could reply, and for a few moments, he sat in the make-believe café, surrounded by computer-generated people, and felt the tears welling up in his eyes. He hadn't heard those last three words in a long time, and he realized just how much he had wanted to have someone say them to him again and mean it.

Aden closed down the simulation, and the café dissipated in front of him until he only saw the inside of the pod and the soft glow of the control screen. He opened the pod door and left the terminal quickly, making it look like he had a purpose and somewhere to be in a hurry. When he stepped out into the bright day, the sun hurt his eyes after the darkness of the pod, and he shielded them with one hand and hurried down the main vein in search of a shop to buy a set of solar foils while the conversation with his sister played itself out again in his head.

If I believed you had turned out to be like Papa, I never would have answered, she had said. There was always the possibility that she had turned out like Papa, that she had set up the meeting as a lure to get his location and the details of the ID he was using right now. If that was the case, his father could do with him as he pleased. Maybe his existence would mess up the line of inheritance and succession at home, and Solveig would just rid herself of him on her own initiative. But his instinct told him that she wasn't duplicitous. Something in that weary smile of hers made it clear to Aden that they both had shared experiences when it came to their upbringing, and that her paranoia regarding her privacy wasn't an act any more than his own cautiousness.

His comtab vibrated, and he looked at the incoming message. As Solveig had said, it contained only a comms node address, and the message was flashing a two-minute scrub timer. Aden hurried into a store and wrote the node number down on one of the order pads, then copied the information. Two minutes later, the original message erased itself from his comtab.

The comtab in his hands was linked to his ID pass. The measures Solveig had taken were hard to detangle, but it wasn't impossible, especially for a good corporate intel division with the resources of a company like Ragnar Industries. If they found out his current ID, there was no way for him to stay out of the reach of his father. Every time he spent money from his ledger, the transaction was watermarked with his ID. He would not be able to eat a meal, stay at a capsule hotel, or book travel without them being able to track every little move he made. The only way to remain anonymous and obscure was to ditch his temporary ID pass and get a new one.

Aden looked at the expiration date laser engraved into the tamper-proof polymer mix. He had twenty-five days of free movement before he had to be back on Gretia. And if the corporate intel division had traced Solveig's comms by then, his name would pop up on all kinds of alerts the moment he scanned himself in at the immigration and customs terminal at the Sandvik spaceport. And even if they hadn't traced the comms, time was not on his side. He didn't know yet when he was ready to return to Gretia, but he knew it wouldn't be in the next twenty-five days, and getting arrested by the Oceana police for overstaying his waiver would see him hauled back home for certain.

On every planet, there were services available for people who preferred to move outside of the official networks. When he was stationed on Oceana, Aden had to be familiar with them because the black markets were an important source of intelligence for any occupying force. His knowledge of the law-averse entrepreneurs in Adrasteia was half a decade out of date, but he knew that those networks were as resilient and entrenched as the legal corporations back home. If the people he knew from years ago weren't in place anymore, there would be others willing to take his ags.

He looked at his ID pass one last time, watching the sun reflecting off the intricate holographic pattern etched into the face of the pass, before he slipped it into his pocket again and closed the fastener with finality. Aden Robertson had existed for seventeen years, and maybe this was a good time for him to be laid to rest for good.

Chapter 17
Solveig

When the Mnemosyne session ended, Solveig scrubbed the access log of the comms pod even though she had used a randomly generated employee ID. Then she climbed out of the pod and left the corporate meeting room she had locked down for fifteen minutes. If anyone went through the logs, they'd find that the room and one of the pods inside had been used by an authorized midlevel manager in the R & D department. If they dug any deeper than that, they'd discover that the midlevel manager in question hadn't existed in the employee database until this morning, but that would require some thorough network forensics, and Solveig had bounced the database access for the entry between half a dozen existing manager IDs. She had gotten top marks in mathematics and network technologies at the university, and she knew she would have been far more useful to Ragnar Industries as a corporate intelligence manager than an executive-floor placeholder avatar for her father.

The R & D area she had picked for her private conversation was on the fifteenth floor, and she stopped by the employee canteen on the twenty-first to make the way back upstairs as circuitous as possible. She got an Acheron-style noodle salad with fermented vegetables and a fizzy mead and sat down for her meal in a quiet corner of the canteen to let the jumbled thoughts in her head sort themselves out.

Aden was still alive.

Solveig had had little doubt about the source of the message she had received, but she had also inherited her father's habitual distrust, and a small part of her had still suspected a cruel prank or a fraudster. But seeing him in the Mnemosyne had wiped away the last bit of that doubt. No AI could simulate or replicate the look in Aden's eyes, the way the corners of his eyes crinkled when he smiled, or the tone of his voice. She hadn't seen him in seventeen years, but everything about the man she had seen today matched her memories of him. And nobody else could have known his term of endearment for her. He had called her "Shorty," but only ever as a private mode of address, usually when they skirted the house rules together under his tutelage. He had shown her how to override the biometric lock on the freezer unit in the kitchen where the staff kept the frozen dessert components, and she had made good use of that knowledge for years after he had left. Aden had been the first person in her life to show her that their father's rules and regulations could be circumvented, even turned on themselves sometimes. And the danger of getting caught and punished had made the ice cream taste that much better.

She ate her lunch while she replayed the short conversation with her brother in her head over and over, focusing on the details of his appearance, the tone of his voice, the way he pursed his lips a little when he listened intently. He looked so much like their mother that it was a little unsettling. But he didn't have the same airy everything-will-be-fine attitude as Mama, who could wave away any inconvenience with a little eye-roll and a huff. Whatever had happened to him during the war and after had beaten him down and made him weary and tired looking. She couldn't even imagine the things he must have seen. They'd had reports from the ongoing campaigns throughout the conflict, and even the heavy government censorship hadn't been able to excise all the circumstantial evidence that the war was a bloody stalemate for most of its duration.

How lost he must feel, she thought. *All these years away from home, and now he has nothing left, and nobody knows he's alive except for me.*

———

When the elevator doors opened on the executive level, Solveig was greeted by the sight of three uniformed police officers standing in the middle of the sky lobby. The surprise gave her an unpleasant little jolt.

They found out about the Mnemosyne session, she thought, and panic welled up in her. Then she took a deep breath and stepped out of the elevator. Whatever their business was on the executive floor, there was no way anyone could have connected all the dots and traced them back to her, not even if they had cracked the encryption the moment she placed the call. And even if they had found her out, she wouldn't have police waiting for her already. She'd be greeted by corporate security instead, to take her in for a chat with Magnus, her father's hand puppet.

Two of the officers were Gretian uniformed police, wearing the green-and-white skin suits of patrol officers. The third was in the dark-blue uniform of the JSP, the Alliance military police that patrolled jointly with the Gretian police force. One of the Gretian officers waved her over to them.

"Good morning, miss," he said. "May I see your ID pass?"

Solveig took it out of her pocket and handed it to him. In suspense thrillers on the networks, people usually said something like *What's the meaning of this?* but she didn't even manage to respond to the greeting, taken completely aback by the unexpected interrogative. She collected her composure while the officer scanned the ID pass with his hand terminal.

"Miss Ragnar," he said. "The executive floor is currently locked down for an official police investigation. Would you please follow me to your office?" His tone and demeanor made it clear that she didn't have an option to refuse the request, so she took her ID card back and nodded.

"Lead the way," she said, but he shook his head and gestured for her to go ahead.

"After you, miss."

He wants to make sure I don't dump anything on the way, she thought, and her concern grew. This couldn't be about her clandestine call, but whatever they were after seemed pretty important if they felt the need to lock down the entire executive floor. She wondered if someone had gotten killed or assaulted up here but then dismissed the idea as unlikely. Marten ran a tight ship when it came to executive security.

As they crossed the floor, Solveig saw that more officers were standing on the executive floor in regular intervals. Other police officers, dressed in civilian clothing and with identification shields around their necks, were walking around with employees by their sides. She walked over to her office, and her assistant Anja walked toward her, a nonplussed look on her face.

"Miss Solveig, I've already . . ."

"Not now," the police officer with Solveig said firmly and held out a hand. "Please do not talk to Miss Ragnar until after our business is concluded."

Anja stopped in her tracks and gave the officer an unfriendly glare, but she turned around and walked off without further protest. Even though the Gretian police did not have the sweeping authority and heavy-handedness they'd been known for in the old order, old habits died hard, and Gretians were still conditioned to defer to people with badges and uniforms.

When she walked into her office, someone was already sitting in her chair. He was one of the plainclothes officers, a good-looking younger man with wavy hair that was long enough to touch the collar of his coat. When he got out of her chair, she saw that he wore his police badge on his waistband, right in front of the holster for his sidearm.

"Miss Ragnar," the uniformed officer announced. Then he left the room and closed the door behind him, leaving Solveig alone with the plainclothes officer.

She gave him a frosty look, irritated by the fact that he had claimed her chair without permission.

"And you are?"

"I am criminal police detective Berg. I apologize for the intrusion, but we are conducting a criminal investigation with our colleagues from the Joint Security Force."

He gestured to the chair he had just vacated.

"Please, have a seat."

"That's my line," Solveig said. "You're in my office. I'm the one who's supposed to offer *you* a seat."

"Of course. My apologies." He smiled curtly. His wavy hair was dark brown, and he had green eyes. She guessed him to be in his late twenties or early thirties, much younger than the police detectives she'd had to deal with in the past. The war had stolen too many young men his age from Gretian society. Solveig found herself thinking that he wasn't bad looking at all, which somehow managed to irritate her more.

"Aren't you all supposed to wear your hair short?" she asked, and his curt smile turned into a broader one.

"They relaxed the regulations last year because they had trouble recruiting new people. So I just started growing it out. I like how it annoys the older guys."

Solveig bit back a smile of her own.

"You look young for a criminal detective."

"You look young for a corporate vice president," he replied. "Most of those old guys on the floor behind you look like they're in the same social club as my grandfather."

"A lot of the young ones went off to war, remember?" Solveig's expression darkened a little again as she thought of Aden. Without the war, he would be sitting in this office right now instead. "What can I do for you, Detective Berg?"

"I was hoping you could assist me with an ongoing investigation."

"Do I have a choice?"

He shrugged. "You always have a choice. You can refuse to cooperate. That's not against the law. But I don't know how my colleagues from the JSP would feel. They'd probably try to find out why."

"Well, I don't have anything to hide. But I'd say that even if I did, wouldn't I?"

She sat down behind her desk and turned on her terminal.

"Can I call my assistant to bring in a chair for you?"

"Sure, as long as you don't talk about anything else," Detective Berg said.

Solveig touched the comms panel.

"Anja, could you bring in another chair, please?"

"Of course, Miss Ragnar," Anja replied. Ten seconds later, the door opened, and Anja came in, pushing a chair with one hand, which she rolled in front of Solveig's desk.

"Thank you, Anja," Solveig said.

"Of course, Miss Ragnar," Anja said again. She gave Detective Berg a cold look and walked out briskly. The door closed behind her silently, and the sounds and murmurs from the executive floor fell silent again. Detective Berg took the chair and rolled it around the desk until it was next to Solveig's.

"I hope you don't mind the proximity, but I have to be able to see what you bring up on those screens while I am in here."

He pulled a comtab out from underneath his coat and brought up a screen projection of his own that he flicked around in the air and placed above the desk in front of him. Solveig watched as he scrolled through some screens and tapped on various fields. Then a picture appeared on his screen. It was clearly taken in a police evidence lab, with scaled rulers on all four sides of the image. The object in the middle of the evidence grid was an armored glove that looked like it was police or military equipment.

"A few days ago, one of the Alliance patrols down in the Palladian sector got ambushed by unknown attackers. They managed to kill a good number of soldiers. This is one of the few pieces of evidence recovered at the scene. Our forensic analysts have concluded that it was manufactured here on Gretia, by a company that's a wholly owned subsidiary of Ragnar Industries."

He spun the image around to show her the glove from all angles. The material was dark and strangely reflective. It seemed to change hues slightly as the light shifted the angles.

"Ragnar hasn't made military gear since the end of the war," Solveig said. "We're not allowed. All the R & D on weapons and armor has stopped. The subsidiary that made this is probably long shut down."

"I'd like to see what your access level can tell you about this object. My colleagues are busy asking some of the other executive officers for the same information right now."

"And then you'll compare notes. So you can be sure that no one is cooking up fake evidence."

Detective Berg shrugged again and brushed a rogue strand of his hair away from his forehead.

"That's how it works, Miss Ragnar."

"Fine." She opened a screen above her terminal and moved it next to the image from Berg's comtab. Then she logged into the corporate network and readied her entry interface for a system-wide forensic search.

"There would be microstamping on the component fibers. All the subsidiaries had their own. It was a three-letter code," Solveig said.

Berg shunted the relevant data over to her screen, and she examined it.

"Your forensic people are right," she said. "But that's not hard. The codes are public knowledge now. This one's marked 'byf.' That's Lagertha Land Systems."

She cross-referenced another data field.

"Lagertha Land Systems was dissolved four and a half years ago. They made combat armor and ballistic clothing, among other things. Their nonmilitary operations were absorbed by a different subsidiary. Did you have your people check the embedded serial number? If it's military armor, it's serialized on the molecular level."

"We did. But we had no access to whatever database has those records. That's part of the reason why we are here."

"I should be able to look that up," Solveig said. "But be patient if it takes me a bit of time. It's my first day, and I'm still figuring out the system."

"Take your time," Detective Berg said. "I'm in no rush. And those JSP troopers will be here as long as it takes. They *really* want to find out who's behind this."

Solveig set the AI to retrieve the details on the embedded serial number. Berg idly drummed his fingertips on the tabletop as they waited for the system to collect the information. His fingers were long and slender, the nails well manicured. He looked like someone who could have been sitting next to her in lectures at the university just last year.

"How many died?"

"Sorry?"

"How many soldiers died in that attack?" she asked.

"Seven. All Pallas Brigade."

"Gods," Solveig replied, shocked. She had heard of the incident on the newscasts, but none of them had mentioned the number of casualties. She had seen plenty of the tough, no-nonsense–looking Pallas Brigade troopers out on JSP patrol with the Gretian police. Whoever managed to kill seven of them at once wasn't just a lone patriot taking potshots at the occupation forces.

"Here we go," she said when the AI returned the query results. Berg leaned closer to her to look at her screen. He smelled faintly of shaving lotion, and whatever brand he used had a pleasant scent.

"That glove belongs to a set that was delivered to the War Ministry in the fourth quarter of 917. The system says it was part of a small-batch contract."

"Can you tell which unit received it?"

Solveig shook her head. "That would be in the War Ministry database, but I don't have access to that. But from the size of the contract, this wasn't general issue. It was just sixty units. Maybe a field trial."

"Who would do new field trials of stealth armor not six months before the end of the war?"

Solveig shrugged. "I don't know the military. But I know finance and networking. If you can figure out which budget paid for it, you can usually tell where it went."

"I see." Detective Berg studied the screen for a little while, scrolling through data fields and poking at various entries. "Corporate finance is about as transparent to me as nuclear-fusion engineering."

"It's all just numbers," Solveig said. "But when it comes to budgets, everything has to come from somewhere. You can't just add zeroes in a database and create money out of nowhere. Give me an ag in my ledger and sufficient network access, and I can trace it back all the way to when the central bank hashed it."

Berg looked at her and smiled.

"You'd make a good police detective, then," he said. "You'd be a superstar in the network forensics division."

"Oh, no." Solveig shook her head and reflexively returned his smile. "That's not my calling at all."

"I'll need a copy of all that data for our own investigators. And if I could call on you if I need any more information, that would be much appreciated."

"If I am authorized to give it to you, certainly," she replied, and he nodded.

She sent the data stream for the query results to his comtab and authorized the data release with her own network ID. The transfer only took a few seconds, and when it was finished, Detective Berg got out of his chair and pocketed his comtab.

"Thank you very much, Miss Ragnar. I appreciate your cooperation with this investigation. Can I ask you to refrain from talking to anyone on the floor until the chief inspector gives the green light?"

"You make it sound again like I have a choice," she said, and he smiled.

When he was gone, she took a deep breath. The air still smelled faintly like his shaving lotion. He was terribly easy to agree with, and she wondered if it had all been a setup, that they had assigned the young and handsome police detective to her on purpose because they knew she was less likely to dig in her heels than if they had made her talk to a grumpy old one.

She looked at the data still up on her screen, the hundreds of transactions between Ragnar Industries and the War Ministry, billions of ags of material delivered to the war machine that had fought the rest of the system to a draw for years.

Doesn't matter in the end, she decided. *They'll get that information anyway, from all the other executives. And it's not like I have a reason to foil a murder investigation.*

Or do I, and I just don't know it yet?

CHAPTER 18

DUNSTAN

The best thing about running silent is not having to talk to anyone, Dunstan thought.

Minotaur was coasting through the space between Rhodia and Acheron quietly, listening intently into the void. Trying to catch pirates was a lot like trying to catch burglars. You could respond to alarms and hope you made it in time to catch them in the act, which was difficult when the alarm went off half a million kilometers away. Or you could sneak around in the darkness with them and keep your eyes and ears open.

Running silent meant that *Minotaur* was coasting on thrusters, without lighting her main drive. Even the artificial gravity was turned off because some of the more lavishly equipped pirate ships had sensors that were sensitive enough to detect the EM noise from spinning grav-mag rotators at a distance. The crew didn't like to run silent for extended periods of time because it was a pain in the ass to do regular tasks in zero g, and everyone hated not being able to access the Mnemosyne, which meant that the off-duty shifts had to resort to watching locally stored entertainment and keeping their outgoing message traffic in a hold queue. But it also meant that Dunstan wasn't obliged to acknowledge incoming comms except for priority fleet traffic, and that was a relief after the chaos that had followed the scuttling of the Gretian internment fleet.

"Halfway done," Lieutenant Bosworth said.

"What's that, Bosworth?"

"Three and a half days in, three and a half to go," the lieutenant replied.

Dunstan looked at the time display on the forward bulkhead of the AIC.

"And we're halfway into this watch," he said. "I swear, time moves more slowly when you're running silent."

The holographic map above the plot table showed a whole lot of nothing. Sixteen hours earlier, *Minotaur* had passed the frigate RNS *Agamemnon*, which was on a reciprocal heading back to Rhodia at an easy one-g burn. Now *Minotaur* was about to dip into the region between the Rhodia-to-Acheron transfer that cut through a slice of Oceanian space because of the way the planets were aligned in their orbits. The problem with protecting interplanetary trade routes between six planets with differing orbital durations was that the routes changed all the time as the planets moved in relation to each other, and no navy could cover all that space or escort each ship individually.

"Astrogation, can I get a fix on the nearest merchant in the neighborhood?"

The astrogation station was staffed by Midshipman Boyer, a new member of the crew who had joined *Minotaur* just before the patrol. She was the youngest person in the AIC by at least ten years, and Dunstan had felt ancient when he saw her service record and noticed that she had joined the fleet as an officer candidate a full two years after the end of the war.

"Aye, sir," she replied and consulted her screen. "The nearest civilian ship is RMV *Orestes*. They're three million kilometers ahead of us on the track and burning at point seven g."

He brought up a screen on his command display and checked the database entry for *Orestes*. She was a big ore hauler, and the flight plan on file told him that she was delivering ten million tons of Palladian titanium ore to an orbital refinery at Acheron. The load she transported was expensive, but ore haulers weren't attractive targets for pirates, who preferred a much higher value-to-mass ratio than unrefined ore offered. It was hard to make off with millions of tons of ore and harder still to sell it without attracting notice.

"All right, we'll cut this one short in about ten minutes. Prepare to end silent running. On the next burn, cross the track to starboard and then put us off *Orestes*'s starboard stern. Let's keep pace with them for a while."

"Aye, sir."

"Helm, do a wake check before we light off the drive," Dunstan ordered.

"Aye, sir. Commencing wake check."

Even when *Minotaur*'s main drive wasn't cluttering the EM spectrum to their rear, the ship had sharper ears and eyes on the front, so it was standard fleet practice to swing the nose around and check the space astern before resuming a drive burn. Dunstan watched the dotted line on the plot spin around as *Minotaur* changed orientation relative to the transit track. They were just finished with the 180-degree thruster spin when a new symbol appeared on the plot.

"New contact on passive, relative bearing ten by negative thirty," Lieutenant Bosworth called out.

"Belay my last and keep the ship in silent running," Dunstan ordered. The new contact was roughly following the transit track toward Acheron, but was offset by several thousand kilometers and was a few degrees off course from the ideal lowest-energy trajectory that most ships used.

"Designating new contact *Sultan One*. Distance eighty-three thousand. They are burning at point nine g. No active radiation, just a drive plume," Lieutenant Mayler reported. "And their ID transponder isn't on. They're running dark and dirty, sir. I'd say we've got ourselves some illicit activity here."

"Track them on passive, but stand by to turn on the light," Dunstan said. "When we paint them with our active sensors, I want to have a firing solution ready in case they do something stupid. And run that drive plume signature through the AI."

"Already on it, sir," Mayler replied. He watched the data stream on the passive array's display he had opened in front of him and frowned. "They're bow on to us, so the AI can't make much of it yet. And there's something off about their power output. It's fluctuating."

"Technical problems?" Dunstan looked at the icon that crept toward them on the plot, still well in front of the line that marked the outer edge of *Minotaur*'s optimal missile engagement range. If the unknown contact was a ship in need of technical assistance or rescue, it wouldn't be half as gratifying as flushing a pirate, but at least they'd have something to show for the reactor fuel they'd burned on this patrol already.

"I don't think so, sir. Looks more like someone messed with the output curve. It keeps fluctuating back and forth randomly by a few percent."

"To make it harder to get a read on their drive signature," Dunstan guessed.

"Either that or they have a rickety boat and a shitty engineer."

"I'd buy that if they weren't also running dirty. I think your assessment about the illicit activity is correct, Lieutenant Mayler. No good reason to run dark either. Especially not if they're having drive trouble."

He leaned forward and studied the plot. The contact marked "S1" was closing the distance slowly but steadily, moving at almost a full g while *Minotaur* was coasting silently. If they were pirates, Dunstan wanted to keep them at a distance before challenging them. With her military-grade drive and gravmag system, *Minotaur* could sustain ten g, and most pirates used small ships with commercial civilian drives and no gravity compensators. If they turned and ran, he knew he'd have no trouble catching them, but if they fired missiles at him, he wanted to be on the outer edge of their reach.

"Could this be one of our friends from the internment lot?" he asked.

Lieutenant Mayler shook his head.

"I don't think so. The stealth boat that shot at us was much closer to us, and we never even got a whiff of them on passive. And whatever this thing is, the drive plume is way too small for a Sleipnir."

"We'll know once we light them up with the active array. Stand by to come out of silent running."

"Aye, sir. Standing by on the active."

———

The unknown ship was still two minutes out of *Minotaur*'s weapons range when the display on the plot changed, and the icon for the contact turned from gray to blue. Next to the symbol, a name and registry number appeared: "OMV-83291 Cirrus."

"They turned on their transponder, sir. Oceanian merchant ID," Mayler said.

"Think they spotted us?"

"At this range? Doubtful. But not impossible. Depends on how good their passive gear is."

"All right." Dunstan shifted in his seat. "Cancel silent running. Go active on that contact. And give me an open comms channel."

"Go ahead, sir."

"Attention, unknown vessel. This is the Rhodian Navy warship *Minotaur*. Do you copy?"

The reply came ten seconds later over a connection that sounded tinny and full of static, like someone was using a handheld low-power comms unit and holding it out of an airlock.

"*Minotaur, this is the Oceanian merchant vessel* Cirrus. *We read you, but we're having trouble with our comms gear. Stand by.*"

Dunstan turned to Lieutenant Bosworth. "Check on that transponder ID. If that's a legit registry, see where that ship is supposed to be right now."

"Aye, sir."

"*Cirrus*, you want to explain why you are outside of a transit lane with your transponder turned off? Because that's not a good look right now."

"*Minotaur, we've been having issues with the central AI. We've had to cold start the system, so we're out of comms and without transponder for three hours while we restored the AI from backup. Everything's coming back online now.*"

Dunstan exchanged a look with Lieutenant Mayler. They'd heard plenty of excuses for shady behavior from suspicious ships in the past, and this was one of the more plausible ones.

"Sir, that merchant ID checks out. And their last docking record was at Hades, four weeks ago," Lieutenant Bosworth said.

"That's a long way off," Dunstan said. "But I suppose they could have made the run to Rhodia and then out here in that time."

"In theory. But there's no active flight plan on file for them. And they didn't dock at Rhodia."

Dunstan looked around in the AIC and addressed the room.

"So we caught someone flying dirty who is now broadcasting valid Oceanian ID, but for a ship that shouldn't really be in this part of the system. What is your best guess?"

Midshipman Boyer was the first to take a stab at an answer.

"Sir, they spotted us on passive, and now they're spoofing a genuine transponder ID."

"And serving us the least unlikely story they could think up," Dunstan added. "Very good, Boyer."

"They're entering weapons range for the ASMs, sir," Lieutenant Mayler said. On the plot, the blue icon for the ship pretending to be OMV *Cirrus* crossed the curved red line marking the outer edge of the ideal engagement range for *Minotaur's* antiship missiles.

Dunstan tapped the TRANSMIT field on the comms section of his command screen.

"*Cirrus*, cut your main drive and maintain heading. Prepare to receive a boarding party for inspection."

"*Understood,* Minotaur. *Cutting propulsion and maintaining course.*"

"They're not even trying to argue with us," Lieutenant Bosworth said when Dunstan closed the channel.

"That could be either really good or really bad," Dunstan said. Nine out of ten merchant skippers resented inspections and the time lost to them, and would try to bitch their way out of them by offering up cargo manifests and live cam feeds, everything to avoid the delay and hassle of having to wait for a warship to match their speed and course and then have a marine boarding party poking around on their ship. If this crew was instantly compliant, either they were among the 10 percent who didn't argue or they had something up their sleeve. Considering the circumstances of the initial contact, Dunstan was almost certain it was the latter.

"You're a pirate who just got flushed by a warship. They've announced they're coming alongside for inspection. What do you do?" Dunstan asked.

"Run, shoot, or comply and surrender," Lieutenant Bosworth said.

"Well, they're not running. So that leaves the other two options."

He looked at the blue icon on the plot, which was now ten kilometers inside *Minotaur's* weapons range and no longer accelerating.

"Burn and set an intercept heading, but make the convergence angle sharp," he ordered. "I want to keep as much space between us and them as we can until we know what we're dealing with here."

———

They spent the next half hour slowly closing the distance on a roughly parallel heading, burning their main drive to match the speed of the other ship. If the captain of the merchant vessel was annoyed with their slow approach, he didn't voice it on comms, which was another indicator that something wasn't quite right. Real merchant skippers didn't usually keep their grievances to themselves, especially when the ship that held them up wasn't even from their own planet's navy. But whoever was in charge on OMV *Cirrus* just held their bearing as ordered, patiently waiting for *Minotaur* to come alongside as the distance between the two ships shrank to seventy, then sixty kilometers.

"We've mapped their hull with the side array," Lieutenant Mayler said. "Snout to tail."

"Let's see it," Dunstan replied. Lieutenant Mayler pulled up the scanner model on his screen and tossed it over to the plot table. Dunstan expanded the image and spun it around slowly.

"Now give me whatever the database has on OMV *Cirrus*."

Mayler repeated the process and added another image to the plot table, where it floated next to the first one. Even without aligning them and putting them directly next to each other, Dunstan could see that the two models were completely different ships. The actual OMV *Cirrus* was a long and slender freighter that had the typical boned-fish appearance of a modular container tug, a command pod connected to a drive section by a two-hundred-meter spine. The ship coasting along sixty kilometers off their starboard right now was much smaller. The stubby cylindrical hull shape seemed vaguely familiar to Dunstan, but he couldn't quite remember where he had last seen a ship that looked like that.

"Combine the model with the drive profile and let the AI take a crack at a proper ID. And set the point defense to standby. Whatever that thing is, it's not an Oceanian container hauler."

He expanded the 3-D scan on the screen until the details started to pixelate. It was an unusual configuration for a civilian ship, and he mentally added and subtracted hull details to make the shape match something filed away in his memory. He knew that ship, or at least the class, but he also knew that it had been a long time since it had come across his awareness.

The AI was just a little more efficient than his synapses. A few seconds after Lieutenant Mayler had fed it the scanner and drive-signature data, it came back with an analysis that made Mayler let out a little whistle of surprise.

"Sir, that's not a commercial vessel. It's a warship. One of ours."

"Say again, Mayler?"

"It's Rhodian, sir. The AI gives a ninety-one percent match for an Axius-class corvette escort." Mayler brought up a third window with a schematic of an Axius and lined it up with the other two shapes to let Dunstan compare them. The overall shape of the ship was the same, even though the crew that ran it now had added a variety of hull attachments that were either functional additions or camouflage.

"Should have seen that earlier," Dunstan said. "But there hasn't been an Axius in the fleet since the beginning of the war."

"Database says one was lost during the war, and the other three were decommissioned and scrapped."

"What was the lost one?"

"RNS *Daphne*. Went missing at the First Battle of Oceana in '14 and presumed destroyed."

"Guess they presumed wrong."

He glanced at the specifications for the armament of the Axius-class ships. They were light even for corvettes, only intended for orbital patrols and escort duties to free up the bigger multipurpose frigates and cruisers. The design had two missile tubes, one fixed rail-gun mount, and two point-defense turrets that still used slug-throwing guns instead of directed-energy mounts. *Minotaur* had twice the mass and was far better armed, but even a long-obsolete Axius still had a credible bite, enough to take out any merchant and even pose a threat to a frigate with a lucky hit in the right spot. And that was just the design spec, without considering whatever the new owners might have added to enhance the ship's combat value in the last nine years.

"The marines are suited up and ready for boarding action, sir," Lieutenant Bosworth said.

"Thank you, XO," Dunstan said. "Helm, decrease the convergence angle by twenty degrees. Let's get this thing secured or blow it out of space. Whichever way they want to play today."

"They're not thinking we are buying their fake ID, are they?" Lieutenant Mayler asked.

The answer to the lieutenant's question came twenty seconds later, when the other ship crossed the thirty-kilometer distance line on the plot. Two bright-red V-shaped icons appeared next to *Cirrus-Daphne* and accelerated toward *Minotaur*.

"Missile launch," Lieutenant Mayler shouted. "Incoming ASMs, threat vector ninety by zero. They've launched at us."

"Activate the PDS," Dunstan ordered.

"PDS is tracking in automatic mode. Good lock on both birds. Contact *Sultan One* is accelerating again. Sir, they're turning away from us and burning at four g."

"Of course they are. We'll deal with them in a minute. Go fully autonomous on the PDS."

For the second time in two weeks, Minotaur's point-defense AI took over the ship to fight against incoming live fire. This time, the computer swung the hull around with the lateral thrusters until the nose of *Minotaur* faced the antiship missiles streaking toward them at thirty g. On the plot, *Cirrus-Daphne* was sprinting away, its transponder shut down again.

"Weapons, get a firing solution on *Sultan One* and stand by on tubes one and two," Dunstan ordered.

"Aye, sir. Warming up one and two."

The enemy missiles crossed the twenty-kilometer line in just a few seconds, then rushed toward the ten-kilometer line. Dunstan knew that the point-defense AI would do a better job than any living human, but he'd never fully get used to seeing incoming ordnance on the plot and not having a button to push or trigger to pull. At the ranges and velocities involved in ship-to-ship warfare in space, it was almost always a duel fought between computers.

Just as the missiles crossed the ten-kilometer mark in front of *Minotaur*, one of the icons disappeared from the plot.

"Soft kill on the first bird," Lieutenant Mayler reported. "Second bird still tracking."

"Come on," Dunstan implored the AI. "Make it two for two."

"Soft kill failed on bird two. Distance eight thousand. Seven. Six. Five."

The lights in the AIC dimmed as the directed-energy mounts unloaded at the incoming warhead, focus firing at it with four emitters. A moment later, the second icon was blotted from the plot as well, a mere four thousand meters in front of *Minotaur*'s bow. Just like in the engagement two weeks ago at the internment lot, the inert debris of a broken-up missile glanced off the armor plating on the nose.

"Hard kill on bird two," Mayler said with satisfaction in his voice. "Standing by to return fire. We have target lock."

"Hold fire on the ASMs," Dunstan ordered. "Lay in a pursuit course and open the throttle. Go to seven g."

The maximum design acceleration of *Minotaur* was well beyond that number, and they could maintain seven all day long without straining either their reactor or their bodies. *Minotaur* was a frigate and the smallest warship class that had a military-grade gravmag compensator. The other ship was too old and too small to have one of those, and Dunstan knew that without compensators, four g was unpleasant to endure for any length of time even in a good acceleration couch. He watched the plot as *Minotaur* leaped forward and followed the track left on the display by the fleeing corvette.

"Send a message to all ships in the AO and tell them we're in pursuit of a pirate vessel that appears to be a stolen Rhodian corvette," Dunstan said. "Transmit all the sensor data and the drive profiles for the ship and the ASMs to the fleet. And advise that ore hauler to watch their six and increase their burn rate."

"Aye, sir."

Dunstan watched the display, where the gap between the two ships started to shrink again as *Minotaur*'s acceleration advantage came into play. The corvette had opened the distance to five hundred kilometers while *Minotaur*'s point defense had maneuvered the ship defensively, but now that number was rapidly decreasing, and *Minotaur* had another two and a half g in reserve.

"We have them by the scruff, one way or another," Dunstan said. "Keep that targeting lock active, and make sure they know it."

"We've got our targeting lasers all over that hull. I'm sure their threat detectors are screaming their ears off right now," Mayler replied.

"Give me a tight-beam connection to that ship."

"You're on, sir."

Dunstan tapped the TRANSMIT field on his control screen.

"Attention, vessel pretending to be the *Cirrus*. We know that your ship is Rhodian Navy property. We are coming to reclaim it. If you fire at us again, we will shoot back. You do not want to test the point defenses of that museum ship against our missiles. Cut your drive now and maintain heading. This is your only warning."

The other ship kept up its four-g burn for another ten seconds. They were solidly inside the ideal engagement range for *Minotaur*'s antiship missiles. The pretend-*Cirrus* had used a spoofed ID code and opened fire on an Alliance naval unit. Under interplanetary law and their rules of engagement, *Minotaur* had the right to shoot them out of space without another warning.

On the tactical display, the numbers next to the other ship's icon changed as they dropped acceleration down to two g, then one. Soon, they had stopped accelerating and were coasting at a steady speed.

"Minotaur, *hold your fire,*" the pretend-*Cirrus* sent a few seconds later. "*We are standing down.*"

"You don't just toss your gun and raise your hands after you've taken your shot," Lieutenant Bosworth growled.

"We'll get no intel from a debris field," Dunstan said. "And I want to bring that ship back to the fleet where it belongs. Who knows what these bastards have been doing out here with our hardware. Helm, resume the approach and go for a least-time intercept."

"Aye, sir."

The helmsman entered the trajectory into the computer, and the ship's AI turned the hull around to counterburn and scrub velocity for the rendezvous. To step on the brakes, the ship had to open the throttle to nine and a half g briefly, which was close enough to the limit of the compensator that the AIC crew started to feel heavy in their gravity chairs. Then the ship flipped itself around end over end again, now only slightly faster than the corvette coasting in front of them.

"Sir, if we come alongside and they turn on their point-defense guns, they can stitch us up pretty badly," Lieutenant Bosworth warned.

"Weapons, set our own point defense to target their gun mounts and keep a good eye on them. If they start tracking us with those things, blast them off their hull."

"Aye, sir," Mayler replied. The corvette had an old point-defense cannon system that threw a few hundred metal slugs per second at incoming warheads. That sort of system had been rendered obsolete by directed-energy emitters like the ones on *Minotaur*, which worked at light speed, never ran out of ammunition as long as the ship's reactor was running, and didn't need a mechanical mount because they had no physical gun barrels to aim.

It took another ten minutes for *Minotaur* to match the other ship's course and speed precisely and line up the airlocks of both ships. Dunstan watched the feed from the optical arrays and magnified the view of the corvette's hull. When she disappeared, RNS *Daphne* would have worn the flat titanium-gray paint that had been standard at the time. Now she was painted in a roughly textured, nonreflective black, and she had no external identification markings. It offended him that this corvette, designed to protect merchant shipping, had been turned into an instrument of ambush and robbery. It was the first time he had seen pirates using a military ship, and taking down a pirate and reclaiming a Rhodian Navy ship in the same action would make this week end much better than it had begun.

"We are lined up for docking ops," Lieutenant Bosworth announced. On the screen in front of him, Dunstan saw the camera feed from the airlock. Ten meters away, the airlock of the corvette seemed to hang motionless in space even though he knew both ships were coasting along at hundreds of meters per second.

"Marines are in the airlock and ready for boarding, sir."

"Extend the collar and give me a comms link to Sergeant Bosca."

On the screen, the image changed as half a dozen magnetic rappelling lines bridged the distance between the hulls and attached themselves to the corvette. Then the flexible docking collar from *Minotaur*'s airlock extended toward the lock on the pirate ship and latched into place.

"Seal confirmed. Go ahead for Sergeant Bosca."

Dunstan addressed the leader of the ship's marine detachment. "Sergeant, this is the CO. Seize and secure that ship. Arrest and restrain everyone on board. Shoot them if they resist or try to destroy any evidence."

"With pleasure, sir," Sergeant Bosca replied.

On the screen, Dunstan saw the reflection of the airlock's warning strobe lighting up the docking collar as the marines cycled the lock. He had no doubt that the other ship's crew was watching the whole thing from their side. The marines floated out into the connector and over to the other ship, drifting in practiced formation and propelled by the thrusters in their suits.

"*Cirrus*, open your airlock. When our marines board, you will keep your hands visible and follow their commands. Anyone who holds or aims a weapon will be shot without warning," Dunstan sent on the ship-to-ship channel.

"*Affirmative*, Minotaur. *The crew is waiting on the maneuvering deck. We are unarmed and will not resist.*"

Lieutenant Bosworth looked offended.

"That's awfully cooperative from someone who just launched two ASMs at us a few minutes ago. He has to know he's looking at twenty years for that charge alone."

"They rolled the dice hard, Bosworth. We sent everyone their coordinates, so they know we won't space them on the spot. They're probably more than happy to take the twenty years at this point."

———

The corvette was a small ship, usually crewed by only a dozen people, and the Rhodian marine detachment was ten strong, but it still took them the better part of an hour to secure the eight prisoners and search the ship from top to bottom.

"Ship is secure," Sergeant Bosca finally reported. "Sir, you may want to come over here and take a look at this command deck."

"I'll suit up and come across with the engineer," Dunstan replied. "Sit tight. We'll be right there."

When Dunstan floated up into the command deck of the reclaimed RNS *Daphne*, an acrid smell hung in the air.

"What have they done to this poor thing?" Petty Officer Reen exclaimed behind him as he followed Dunstan into the command deck. Sergeant Bosca and one of his marines were waiting for them by the helm station, weapons stowed and helmet visors raised.

"We're going to have a fun time getting this ship back to the fleet," Sergeant Bosca said and pointed at the comms station, which was splashed with fire suppressant foam. "They torched half the stations on this deck with thermal charges."

Petty Officer Reen floated over to the comms station and wiped off some of the foam with his glove to look at the damage.

"Slagged it good," he said, with what sounded like grudging professional admiration. "Long-range comms, ID transponder, Mnemosyne node. All fried. I can't even tell who made this console. It's not what was installed at the fleet yard, though."

"Same with weapons control and electronic warfare," Sergeant Bosca said. "Looks like they prepped everything while we were playing catch-up. This is the strangest pirate op I've ever seen, sir. They made a pile of stuff down on the maneuvering deck and slagged that, too. Comtabs, ID cards, that sort of thing. It's like they really don't want us to know who they are and who they've been talking to."

"We'll find out who they are soon enough when we run their DNA profiles," Dunstan said. "How many?"

"Eight, sir. That's a mighty slim crew even for a little corvette."

Behind Dunstan, Petty Officer Reen floated from station to station and inspected the hardware.

"This is all commercial gear. Looks like they ripped out most of the original stuff and replaced it with off-the-shelf components. To be honest, they probably gave it a major upgrade. The original Axius boats never got the new integrated AI stations." He tapped a control slab, and a screen popped up on top of the console, displaying an interface that looked unfamiliar to Dunstan.

"That's civilian navigation software," Reen said. "I know the interface. It's an Oceanian company. The UI is set to Rhodian, though."

He lowered himself in front of the station and touched the floating display to bring up the UI functions, but a red warning message popped up as soon as his finger intersected with the hologram.

"Can't access the processing core. They've scrubbed the navigation database. Maybe just erased the whole core. Right down to the star charts. No way to tell where they've been in this ship."

"They had an action plan for getting boarded," Dunstan said. "Just like we would have done in the war. Burn the codes, kill the comms, erase the core. Leave no intel for the enemy. They even slagged their personal comtabs?"

"Yes, sir," Sergeant Bosca said. "We tossed the whole boat from bow to stern. They didn't have much personal gear with them. What they did bring all went into that burn pile they made."

"Fleet intel will find something. They always do. Some data buffer somewhere in a comms terminal that didn't get cleared. We just have to get this ship back to Rhodia One."

"The helm is functional and the main drive works," Petty Officer Reen said. He shut down the screen in front of him and rotated himself upright again in the zero-g environment. "She's got fuel for the reactor, and we can fit her with short-range comms. No reason why we can't drive her home at an easy one g. *Minotaur* can lead the way and do all the navigation work."

"Get whatever you need and put together a prize crew," Dunstan said. "And then check every system on this ship and make sure she's safe to drive back home. Once you are done, give me a time estimate for any repairs or retrofits."

"Aye, sir."

Dunstan looked around on the command deck and shook his head.

"A prize crew," he repeated. "I don't think anyone's had to put one of those together since the end of the war. Things are getting strange out here. I don't like the way any of this feels."

"The pirate crew are secured and under guard in the brig, sir. We couldn't separate them because the brig isn't big enough," Sergeant Bosca said.

"Let's go see the catch of the day and listen to whatever bullshit story they've cooked up for us. If they talk at all. Crew that slags their transponder and wipes their nav system clean probably knows how to keep their mouths shut."

"Someone always ends up talking sooner or later," Sergeant Bosca said. He flashed a grim little smile. "Even the tough ones get chatty on the way to the airlock."

CHAPTER 19

ADEN

"What you're looking for costs a lot of money."

"I have some," Aden said.

"No, I mean a *lot*."

The bar was a dive. It had been a dive when Aden was last here five years ago. It was still the same seedy mix of drinking, gambling, and assembly-line sex work he had known during the occupation. And Aden thanked the gods that the management hadn't changed either. The man in the booth in front of him was Piet, the owner of the place. Piet was in his sixties or maybe even seventies by now—Aden had never asked—and he was built like a suit of powered infantry armor, if those were available with a potbelly. But even Piet's belly looked hard. Piet was a head shorter than Aden but twice as wide, and Aden had once seen the man carry two drunken Oceanian fleet-yard workers out of his bar by the backs of their necks without their feet touching the ground at all between barstools and door.

"I can pay," Aden said. "But it's a bit urgent."

"How urgent?"

"Three days or less."

Piet whistled through his teeth. "That is urgent. Not sure I can get someone on that job with that short a notice. Not for the quality you need. If I can, there'll be an expedite charge."

"Whatever it takes, Piet. Just let me know soon, so I can go ask somewhere else if I have to."

"Don't give me the 'comparison shopping' pressure. You know better. Hang on while I send someone a message."

Piet got out his comtab and worked the display with hands that looked like they could crush the device to dust if he squeezed it reflexively while sneezing.

"Where have you been, anyway? Haven't seen you since we kicked the fuzzheads off the planet, and now you walk in again like it's the summer of 918."

"I got a job on Rhodia," Aden said. "Last-minute thing."

"Fucking liar," Piet said, and Aden's heart sank for a moment.

"It was about a woman," Piet continued.

Aden suppressed a sigh of relief and shrugged. "It was about a woman."

Piet finished writing his message and tossed the comtab onto the table.

"I knew it. Pretty boy like you. When you were still in here every other night, half the girls in the place would have given you free time. Half the boys, too."

"I've had a rough five years, Piet."

"That why you're asking me to find you a pro? Did you kill someone?"

"No, I didn't kill someone. I just need to be someone else right now. And it can't be shit work."

"I don't deal with people who do shit work. Well, I deal with some people who do shit work. For customers who can only afford shit pay."

"I can afford a little better than shit pay right now."

"We'll see. You know I'll take a commission off the top if you go through me."

"Yeah," Aden said. "I figured as much. I'm willing to pay it because I don't have the time to do all the legwork. This city has changed in the last five years."

"For the better. Business is booming again. I get to take money from tourists from all over, not just from fuzzheads on shore leave."

Piet's comtab buzzed, and he picked it up and looked at the incoming message.

"Got you a guy. He's about as not cheap as you can get, but he's good. And fast."

"Well, you know what they say. Good, cheap, fast. Pick any two."

"You got that right."

———

The man who slid into the booth across from Aden fifteen minutes later didn't look at all like what he had expected people in his field to look like. He was in his thirties, with a full head of long blond hair he kept tied back, and he wore a suit jacket with a tasteful star-shaped embroidery pattern over a white silk shirt.

"This is Henk," Piet said and got up. "I'll leave you to it. But remember—you come to an agreement, you pay me; I pay him. Just add ten percent to whatever he quotes you."

"Five," Aden said.

"You don't shut up, I'll make it fifteen, pretty boy. Good to see you again," Piet said and wandered back to his spot by the bar.

"That's top-shelf stuff you're asking for," Henk said once Aden had explained his needs. "Top-shelf price tag, too."

"What's top shelf?"

"Your package, in less than three days? Twenty-five K."

"Gods," Aden said, shell-shocked. He had expected maybe half that at the most. With Piet's commission factored in, he'd be down to under ten thousand.

"What you're asking for isn't your standard shitty-ass fake ID pass. You want what we call 'real-fake ID.' Means it has to be issued by the actual authority. Means you have to have people inside you can pay, and they don't risk their jobs for shrimp legs. You have to have matching database entries, DNA profiles, the whole thing. You have to make a credit ledger file and fill in a decent history. That's a lot of palms to grease."

"And how watertight is it going to be?"

"It'll be real 'cause it is. Customs, police checks, residence, everything. You'll come up green everywhere. The only thing it won't stand up to is a detailed check. But you have to get into some bad shit before that's an issue. If they bust you for something else, and they have reason to believe you're flashing a real-fake ID pass, they can take it apart. But that would take a while. Good idea is to not give them a reason to look at you twice to begin with."

"Good advice in any case. I don't have much of a choice, so let's do it."

"Transfer in advance. And I'll need your current ID pass so I can clone the data off it and put it on your new one."

Aden pulled out his Gretian POW ID reluctantly and gave it to Henk.

"Don't tell Piet that's a Gretian pass," he said. "He'll kill me, and then nobody will get paid."

Henk raised his hands in a dismissive gesture. "I don't care about that political shit. I just care about data files and money in my account."

"Still. Keep it close, please."

"One more thing. Whatever comtab is linked to that ID, you have to get rid of it. And that includes whatever's left on your ledger. No way to transfer it without leaving a trail."

"That's all I have left," Aden said. "I'll have no money to get off the planet."

"But you'll have a shiny new you to go find yourself a new job with. Unless you want to stay the old you. That's up to you."

"That's not an option."

Henk did his dismissive hand-shrug gesture again.

"I agree with your terms," Aden said. "Just be quick, please."

"You want me to pick a name at random, or do you have one in mind? They have to know what to seed the database with."

Aden thought for a few moments.

"Same first name. Change the last name to Jansen."

"Jansen. That's good. Nice, common name. Aden Jansen. You sure you want to keep the first name?"

"Yeah," Aden said. "I'm kind of used to it by now."

"Go pay Piet, and I'll get started. I'll send a message to your comtab when you can come back and pick everything up. And you know Piet. Bring the police in . . ."

"They'd never find any piece of me if I brought the police into Piet's business," Aden said.

"Obviously," Henk said matter-of-factly, like he had just been told that on Oceana the sky was blue and water was wet.

———

"I can help you with the rest of your ledger," Piet said after Aden had transferred the funds for Henk's services.

"How so?"

"How much you got left?"

Aden checked his balance. "Nine thousand."

"If you transfer that, too, I can bounce it around between a few accounts and then transfer it back to your new ledger whenever Henk is done doing his shit. Any transfer over ten K, it starts throwing up red flags. But nine, nobody's going to notice that."

"What's your commission for that?"

Piet shrugged. "Fifteen percent. For the extra work bouncing the transfers around. But I'll chalk up some credit for you with the girls or the dice. Whichever way your boat floats these days."

Aden didn't have to think long. He'd get skinned on that deal, but nine thousand ags was more than zero.

"I'll do it," he said. "Just let me leave a few hundred on here so I can eat and sleep while I wait for that new ID pass."

"You leave extra on there, it's gone as soon as you drown that comtab," Piet said. "Go and make sure you eat well."

When he got back to his hotel room, he followed Piet's advice and ordered a big, expensive dinner. Then he turned on the network news screen so he would have something other than his soon-to-be-defunct comtab to look at.

The hotel food was excellent as always, but his mind was somewhere else, and he only managed to eat half the vat-grown steak and most of the greenhouse asparagus and potatoes on the side. Then he put the leftovers into the service terminal for recycling and started packing his bag. He'd have to find somewhere else to stay once he got his new ID pass, or it would be really easy to trace a direct line from his old self to his new one. All the paranoid rules of intelligence-gathering operational security were still in the back of his brain, even though he hadn't used any of it except his language skills for five years. When you were pretending to be someone else, the smallest and dumbest little details could trip you up and get you captured or killed. At least he hadn't had to worry about his ID not passing muster because the Oceanian authorities were under Gretian control at the time, and his ID pass had been officially issued by the proper authority.

He went to bed early, but it took him two hours to fall asleep, and his sleep was interrupted and restless until he got up and closed the balcony door for the first time since he had moved into the room. With the outside world shut out, he finally fell asleep and stayed that way until the morning.

———

The next evening, not even twenty-four hours after he had paid his money in Piet's bar, Aden's comtab buzzed with the message he had been waiting for. The forgery workshop must have had a slow week, he guessed, but that was fine with him. He hadn't done any research on flights off the planet or jobs here on Oceana because he didn't want to leave traces for someone to find if they tracked back the data on his current comtab. Instead, he had spent a long and boring day watching network news and eating more food off the automated delivery menu. Now he scooped up the old comtab and threw it over the balcony railing. It sailed toward the water of the canal in a neat arc and disappeared with just a tiny splash that sparkled in the lights from the nearby buildings. Then he grabbed his bag and left the hotel.

When he slid into the booth across from Henk fifteen minutes later, the younger man pushed a blue plastic envelope across the table.

"You are now Aden Jansen, upstanding and unremarkable citizen of Oceana. Middle-of-the-pack credit rating, good health record, mostly law-abiding except for a few minor run-ins with the police in your exuberant youth. It looks weird when there's no grease spots on the record. I nuked your old ID pass. It was three weeks from expiring anyway."

"That was quick. Thank you."

"Piet called in a few minor favors on your behalf to grease the gears a bit."

"Guess he earned his expedite charge." Aden opened the envelope and looked at the ID pass briefly before slipping it into his pocket. People didn't study their IDs in public.

"So I can go out and get on a flight to Acheron or Hades right now, and the ID pass scanner at the spaceport won't light up."

"Correct. There's a memchip with your new life history in that envelope, too. Buy a new comtab, ditch the old one, and learn a bit about your new self before anyone asks you questions you can't answer."

Aden shook the memchip out of the bag and stuck it into his pocket as well.

"Are we good, then?"

"I got paid. I'm good. Enjoy your new life."

Piet wasn't at the bar or anywhere in the front room, and Aden didn't bother to look for him. The man had delivered as agreed and ahead of time, but he had also taken every ag he said he would. He liked the tough old bastard, but he was under no illusions that Piet wouldn't feed him to the crabs if he learned that the man hanging out in his bar every other day during the Gretian occupation had been one of the occupiers himself. Wherever else he would go from here, he knew that he'd never come back to this bar—and probably never set foot on the eastern leaf again even if he decided to stay on Oceana.

He walked out of the bar into the cool evening air, regretting that Henk hadn't returned his Gretian prisoner-of-war ID to him so he could fling it into the nearby canal as well.

There were half a dozen personal electronics stores on the nearest stretch of the main vein, and Aden walked into the cleanest and most inviting-looking one. He asked for the same model comtab he had bought in Rhodia—he was used to the shape now and had just learned most of the functions—and the clerk activated it for him so he could pay for his purchase. When the clerk scanned Aden's new ID, Aden held his breath for a moment, half-convinced that Henk and Piet had fucked him over and that the verification light would blink red. But it flashed a friendly green instead, and a few seconds later, a new data screen appeared on the comtab, showing the balance of the bank ledger linked to his Oceanian ID pass—seven thousand eight hundred and twenty-five ags. Aden paid for the comtab and pocketed it, satisfied to have the now-familiar weight back in the right spot.

Outside, he took a public pod all the way to the end of the leaf at the central island. Then he got out, walked halfway up the stairs, and took a right turn onto the sea promenade, which was moderately busy with tourists tonight. He figured it was appropriate to start a new life with a move into a new neighborhood, so he circled half the island and walked off at the western leaf, as far away as possible from the hotel room he had rented on his first night on Adrasteia.

The western leaf was a neighborhood for locals, less tourist oriented and with fewer shops and hotels, but he found a new place to stay on a side road half a kilometer into the leaf. It wasn't a seafront hotel, but that was fine with him. He checked himself in at the self-serve terminal with his new ID pass and comtab and rented a single-room unit that was half the size and a quarter the daily rate of the place he had stayed before. There was a single bay window that was stepped down from the level of the main living space, and it overlooked the canal in front of the building. The area in front of the window was just big enough for a little comfort chair that could spin 360 degrees. Aden put his bag down on the bed and sat down in the chair, then swiveled it around to face the canal. Then he took the memchip out of his pocket and inserted it into his new comtab to read the biography that Henk had cobbled together for him in the official databases in less than twenty-four hours. It was clear that he'd had access to Aden's actual records, because the fictional Aden Jansen had an education that roughly matched his, with all the right linguistics degrees, this time from two Oceanian universities instead of the military language school.

You'll have a shiny new you to go find yourself a job with, he remembered Henk saying. It was the first time in his life that he'd really had this power, the absolute freedom to decide what he would do with himself next. The military had been a forced choice, the only way to get away from home and to drop off the sensors reliably, so that hadn't counted. And ever since he had first put on a uniform, other people had told him where to go and what to do. With this ID pass, he could go anywhere in the system and do anything he wanted.

Seven thousand ags won't get me far, though, he thought.

On a whim, he flipped to the Mnemosyne page listing the job openings on Adrasteia. He narrowed it down by skill parameters until he had filtered out the listings on his screen to only the calls for language specialists and translators. Most of them were for tourist-oriented businesses. One was for a government job at the spaceport authority that he knew would require an in-depth background check his ID wouldn't withstand. But the last one on the short list caught his eye, and he expanded the listing on his comtab and flicked it over to the room's wall-mounted big screen.

LOOKING TO HIRE: Language expert to join courier freighter crew as communications specialist. Must be native-level fluent in Rhodian and Gretian. Fluency in all other system languages a plus. Must be willing to travel system-wide. Private shipboard quarters provided. Trial period required. Payment is 1/8 crew portion of contract net profits. Contact node 28651222.89 for an interview if interested.

Aden paced in front of the big screen for a little while, reading the ad a few more times, as if additional readings would reveal some more information. But that was all—a paid way off the planet that seemed to be tailor-made for his particular skill set. He could stay here and burn through the seven thousand ags he had remaining, but that would not carry him for very long before he'd have to find some money somewhere. Requesting an interview and talking to the people behind that job offer couldn't hurt things. He'd had enough leisure time to last him for a few years.

He opened a new text window on his comtab and addressed it to the node listed on the employment call. Then he wrote a quick message and sent it before he could think too much about it. Whatever his future held now, it couldn't turn out worse than his past had. And if it did, at least he was the one holding the controls this time.

CHAPTER 20

IDINA

One day, someone is going to bring a grudge and a gun to one of these, Idina thought as she surveyed the crowd on the plaza.

The JSP was out with two full companies today. Idina and her platoon had been on the night watch since she had joined them, and if she hadn't already held a grudge against the Gretian loyalists for having the balls to wave those flags around by the hundreds right in front of her, the lack of sleep and forced overtime would have kindled one. Principal Square was a rectangle with sides that were 250 meters long, over sixty thousand square meters of ground, and this demonstration was the first one she had seen that managed to fill most of it. People weren't packed shoulder to shoulder, but the crowd was still many thousands strong. If things went sideways, even the two companies of JSP lining the periphery of the square would have a hard time cleaning up the mess. They had the fast-response company on standby at AOFB Sandvik for backup, but even with combat gyrofoil deployment, it would take them at least five minutes to get here once someone sounded the alert. When people were trying to beat you up or kill you, five minutes was a very long time.

Idina's platoon had the north side of the square, forty Palladian troopers in riot armor, reinforced by their Gretian police patrol partners. Eighty JSP troops were forming a multicolored line of dark blue and green, one trooper every three meters. They had deployed in alternating formation, one police officer in Gretian green next to each Palladian. From JSP experience with crowd control, it was easier to keep crowds in check when they weren't facing just one authority in their immediate field of view. There were people who would get aggressive with a foreign occupation soldier, and there were some who would stand up to their own planet's police force, but very few had enough anger and bravery to take on both authorities at once. The arrangement strengthened the legitimacy and authority of both the Gretian police and the Alliance military components of the JSP. It was also symbolic—Gretians standing side by side with Palladians, Rhodians, and Oceanians.

"What are they shouting again?" Idina sent to Captain Dahl, who was standing to her right, hands clasped in front of her belt buckle.

"No serfdom," Captain Dahl replied. "They do have a terrible lack of variety, don't they?"

Idina smiled grimly.

"I wonder if they had the same concerns for the Oceanians. Do you recall any demonstrations back then?"

"There were some peace protests, actually," Captain Dahl replied. "For the first few weeks. Until the High Council passed the Sedition Act."

"The Sedition Act," Idina said.

"Punishing expressions of disloyalty in speech, writing, or action," Captain Dahl said. "If it's found to cause others to view the national institutions with contempt."

Guilty as charged, Idina thought. A month ago, she would have said it out loud, but during her nightly patrols with the woman, Idina had learned that she couldn't get a rise out of Dahl by bad-mouthing anything about her planet. Every time Idina had tried to land a snarky or biting remark, Dahl had either shrugged it off or agreed with it.

"JSP Purple Four and Blue One, be advised you have counterprotesters converging on the street and advancing on the northwest corner of the plaza. Head count is a hundred plus."

Idina looked to her right, where the northwest corner of the plaza opened onto a street. She couldn't see any of the counterprotesters yet from where she was standing, but the command gyrofoil patrolling in the sky high above the square had everything in view with multiple camera arrays, and she switched to an overhead view on her data monocle to see the group marching down the road, less than a hundred meters from the edge of the plaza.

"Purple Four Actual, copy that," she replied. "I see them. They'll come out right between us and Blue One." She switched to the company channel. "Hey, Blue One, we have a few adds coming in from that diagonal feed road. Suggest we shorten the line and put ourselves in between before things get heated."

"Purple Four, I concur," the Oceanian lieutenant in charge of Blue One platoon replied. *"Close it up, everyone, and clip the corner."*

"You heard it, Purple," Idina sent to her platoon. "Straight line twenty meters in. We'll decide which way to face once we see who gets all riled up first."

The two platoons started to shorten the deployment line across the northwestern corner of the plaza. The crowd of protesters here at the fringe was loose enough that the JSP troopers and police officers didn't have to push anyone back. As they reconfigured the line and advanced into the square a little, the protesters just ebbed back slowly. But the police activity drew attention to that corner, and when the first loyalist demonstrators spotted the group of reformers approaching the square, Idina could practically see the wave of shouted updates rolling across the crowd. Where before the attention of the nearby loyalist activists had been on the protest chant leaders and speakers in the middle of the square, the redeployment of Purple and Blue platoons caused a sudden redirection of eyeballs. Soon, a sizable crowd had mimicked remaking the line, and more kept reinforcing them from behind. Cutting two opposing factions of protesters off from each other was standard procedure, but Idina felt exposed, wedged in between two groups that both didn't want her there. She had felt safer with the crowd in front of her and a solid building at her back.

Once the loyalists spotted the reformers entering the square, the mood became hostile almost instantly. Both groups started shouting at each other. The reformers were waving their own flags, which showed the silver star of Gretia on a vertical green band, with large white stripes on either side. Before long, Idina's platoon was wedged in between two groups of angry people who exchanged heated insults across the barrier of armored police and soldiers between them. Captain Dahl used the public-address system of her suit's helmet to speak to the crowd in Gretian, and the people standing closest to the line backed off just a little. For a few moments, it looked like things would cool down on this corner of the square, but then the first objects started flying out of the ranks of the loyalists and over the heads of the JSP line. Behind them, the reformer protesters replied with indignant shouts.

A beverage bladder came flying toward Idina. She didn't know whether it had been intended for her or just poorly aimed, but it glanced off her shoulder armor and burst on the pavement between her and Captain Dahl. The liquid that splashed against her side looked like piss.

"Oh, for the sake of all the gods," she growled. "That's it."

She toggled into the platoon and company channels simultaneously.

"Purple, deploy your shields," Idina ordered.

She reached for the extendable shield on her belt and activated it in front of her. It was a padded and insulated handle that deployed a cruciform frame when she pushed the button. Each limb was the thickness of a finger and half a meter long. Two seconds later, the shield's panels expanded between the limbs, forming a transparent square. The top and bottom limbs extended even more until the shield covered Idina from shoulder to shoulder and from the brow of her helmet down to her knees. She turned on the repulsor and smiled grimly at the sight of the bright-blue ionized field covering the outer surface of her shield. The repulsor layer shocked or stunned anyone who touched it, and the flexible panels behind the electrified outer layer of graphene were made from a transparent ballistic carbon blend that turned rigid as sheet steel when it had current running through it.

"Shields up!"

All along the joint JSP-police line, troopers extended their own shields and brought them up to form a wall.

"Purple, lock shields and advance by ten meters," Idina ordered. "Start in courtesy mode. Add power as needed, if needed."

Courtesy mode was the lowest power of the repulsor field. It would hurt anyone who touched it, but it wouldn't knock them out. For most demonstrations, the sight of the shimmering blue fields on the fronts of the riot shields was usually enough to make crowds disperse voluntarily. Cranked up all the way, the repulsor field would stun anyone who touched it and ionize the air five meters in front of the shield. Idina glanced over her shoulder to see the reformer protesters start to move with them, emboldened by the police lining up to face their opponents.

"Blue, stand by to swing your line around and cover our backs," she sent to the lieutenant of the Oceanian platoon holding the line to their right. "Those assholes seem to think we're fighting for them now."

Something about seeing a bunch of Gretians retreat from her with fear in their eyes was cathartic to Idina. From her patrols with Dahl, she had come away with the conviction that she would make a terrible police officer, and that the JSP was probably the worst possible assignment for her temperament. Dahl was excellent at defusing conflict and only using the least amount of violence necessary to end a fight once she was forced into one. For Idina, deploying martial tools released a sort of safety switch in her brain. Dahl seemed to hate conflict, but once the course was set for a fight, Idina almost relished the prospect.

A few of the protesters in front of the group let their mutual anger override their wisdom and stood their ground. They seemed aware of the capabilities of the riot shields because they put up the hoods of their jackets and lowered their sleeves. Then they linked arms and made a push against the gap between Idina and the Gretian cop to her left. Idina changed her direction a little and took two fast steps out of turn to intercept them. She caught one of them full-on with her shield, but he brought up his arms and threw himself against the repulsor field before she could twist the handle and increase the field strength. His jacket seemed to be made of insulating material because he did not cry out in pain when the sleeves touched the field. They crashed together, and the Gretian protester tried to shove her backward. He was a tall guy with an athletic build, and Idina was a head and a half shorter, but she had grown up and trained all her life in a gravity that would have this man panting with exhaustion if he had to do a brisk hundred-meter walk in it. She dug her heels in, and he looked surprised when he saw that his push had failed to move her. Then she flexed her arms and pushed back with all her upper-body strength. He took the impact of the shield on his raised arms, which she smashed back into his face. This time, he yelped in pain even as he stumbled backward. The crowd behind him quickly made way in a very haphazard fashion, and he backpedaled five meters before falling hard on his ass. It was satisfying to see his look of loathing replaced by one of shock and hurt. She had always felt that the Gretians hated Palladians the most of all the Alliance nations because they looked the least alike—tall and light skinned versus short, stocky, and dark skinned.

Not so superior now, are you, shithead? she thought as she brought up her shield again and took a half step back to tighten the formation and close the gap she had opened between herself and Captain Dahl. The Gretian police officer to her left had increased his field strength in time to knock one of the other brave demonstrators out even through his insulating jacket material. The third one had unlinked arms with the first two and changed his mind about his odds, retreating into the crowd instead. They were all yelling at the JSP and police troopers just as much as they were shouting at their opponents, and despite the danger, Idina was enjoying their expressions of anger and frustration.

Something shook the ground below her boot soles. A second later, the dull thunder of an explosion rolled across the plaza, and people in front of her started shouting and screaming. All the flags and signs in the crowd seemed to come down at once.

"Bomb," someone announced on the company channel.

"Oh, shit," Idina said without transmitting.

All political disagreements seemed forgotten in an instant. Behind the police line, the reformers broke and ran out of the plaza, away from the now hundreds of people surging at the police in blind terror. Behind the loyalists, a smoke column started to rise into the sky above the square.

"Purple, Blue," she barked into the company channel. "Wedge formation, shields turned to low. Push if you can, but stand your ground."

She waded into the approaching crowd and dug in her heels. Behind her, she could sense the other members of her platoon following her order and shifting formation to get out of the way of the human flood coming toward them. People bounced off repulsor fields, oblivious, in their fear, to the pain, then pushed along in the stream of bodies flooding past the groups of police and JSP huddling together in tight wedges with shields facing outward.

The gaps in their formation acted like a pressure valve. People who saw the blue glow of the police shields in front of them instinctively steered away from them and into the spaces between the JSP sections. If the square had been packed shoulder to shoulder, Idina knew that her force would have been swept away like driftwood in a mountain stream, repulsor shields or not. But there was just enough space for the panicking crowd to thin out a little in their uncoordinated surge away from the center of the square.

"*Bomb, bomb, bomb,*" the hovering airborne command section called out. "*Explosion in the center of the square by the main podium. Twenty-plus casualties at least. Medical units alerted and reported inbound. All units, secure the center of the plaza and establish a perimeter for the emergency responders.*"

"You heard the man," Idina shouted to her platoon. "Advance to the center and re-form."

———

From the look of it, the bomb hadn't been large, but in the more densely packed crowd around the podium, it had been enough to cause carnage. Idina counted at least a dozen unmoving bodies on the ground. Some had severed limbs. Others were bleeding from gaping wounds in their heads. In a wider ring around the dead that had caught the full force of the blast, the wounded were squirming on the ground, trying to crawl away or holding wounds closed with their hands.

Overhead, a police gyrofoil thundered into the square with a medical unit right behind it. Both gyrofoils pulled up to bleed off forward speed, then hovered over the middle of the square. The combined downwash from their rotors dispersed the rising smoke. On the pavement near the podium, Idina saw the characteristic star-shaped scorch pattern of a ground-level high-explosive detonation. The ground was littered with dropped signs and flags, which were now getting blown around by the engine wash from the gyrofoils overhead.

"Face out, deploy, standard dispersion," Idina ordered. The platoon formed a skirmish line and started moving toward the edge of the plaza again. The protesters didn't need much encouragement to clear the square. Within two minutes, the combined JSP force had cleared a hundred-meter circle in the center of the square, and the medical gyrofoil set down behind their security line. Idina glanced at Captain Dahl in the line to her right again. The older woman looked shaken for the first time since she had met her. Idina had seen what high explosives could do to a human body many times, but she guessed that this was new territory even for an urban police officer. Gretia had chosen to surrender before the Alliance had to invade the planet and beat it into submission, so the Gretians who hadn't served in the military had no direct experience with war and its implements. A lot of them seemed to believe their planet hadn't really lost the war because nobody ever saw an invasion fleet coming down from orbit, and Idina supposed it wasn't hard to believe that when war had never visited your doorstep.

In front of their line, the initial rush of people fleeing the plaza had abated a little. There were still hundreds of people in the square, but not all of them were looking to get away. Some small groups had reassembled and moved against the general flow of the crowd toward the middle of the square again. When they were in shouting range, they yelled at the JSP line and started throwing objects once more. Idina raised her shield over her head and deflected a stick that looked like it had been ripped from a flag or protest sign.

"What the hells are they yelling now?" she asked Captain Dahl.

"They're idiots," Dahl replied tersely. "They're saying we did this. I mean—you." She glanced at Idina. "The JSP. The Alliance."

"We're going to need more boots on the ground," Idina sent to the company commander. "The crowd is getting hostile again, and we can't make this circle any wider."

"Be advised that the fast-response unit is on the way from Sandvik Base," command replied. *"ETA two minutes."*

"We have backup coming," Idina told her platoon. "Two minutes out. Hold the line."

When the combat gyrofoil from Sandvik arrived, it was an imposing sight. The huge machine swooped in and turned in place, then hovered twenty meters above the center of the square. The rappelling lines dropped, and a whole company of Alliance troops descended onto the plaza. The sight of that spectacle made the protesters pause and watch the gyrofoil, like they were watching an air-show demonstration. As soon as the troops were on the ground, they disconnected from their lines and rushed over to reinforce the JSP line, and the combat gyrofoil ascended again, its engines creating a small storm on the plaza that blew around flurries of debris. By now, there were half a dozen medical gyrofoils on the ground inside the circle her JSP company had formed, and more were hovering overhead, waiting for their turn to land. Idina saw flashing blue lights on the periphery of the square, medical pods on wheels slowly making their way through the exiting crowds. It seemed like every emergency responder in the city was in, around, or above this square now.

When the huge combat gyrofoil had cleared the airspace above the plaza again, another medical gyrofoil moved in and began its vertical ascent. The crowd in front of the JSP line seemed disheartened by the sudden influx of more soldiers shoring up their line from behind, and the objects stopped flying at the police shields. Idina marched forward with her fellow troops and the Gretian officers to widen the circle again so more gyrofoils could land and take on the injured. The center of the square was busy with medics rushing between the dead and wounded for triage. Idina glanced over her shoulder and saw the medical gyrofoil extend its landing skids and set down on the pavement a hundred meters behind the police line in a free spot between two other emergency foils. The ship rotated until its back was toward the center of the square and the nose faced the police line. Then it settled down on its skids. Idina could see right into the cockpit, but there were no pilots behind the controls.

That's against regs, Idina thought, just a fraction of a second before the alarm bells went off in her head. *Why would anyone remote-land a medical—*

She never heard the explosion. The hearing assist in her helmet cut off, and by the time she realized what had happened, she was on the ground, twenty meters closer to the perimeter of the square than when she had lifted her foot to take her next step. The shockwave from the blast felt like a physical thing, as if some giant had plucked that huge combat gyrofoil out of the sky and swung it at the back of the JSP line like a bat. She tumbled like a rag in a storm, helplessly, unable to stop her forward motion, until she collided with something semisolid, and the impact knocked the breath from her. Three different voices were shouting into her helmet's headset all at the same time, and she couldn't make sense of any of them as she tried to force air back into her lungs.

She got to her knees after what seemed like minutes of effort. All around her, bodies were strewn on the ground. Most of them were Gretian civilians, but she saw a few green police uniforms and dark-blue JSP suits as well. The front of the closest building was pockmarked with shrapnel, and every window in the first five floors had been blown out. Her hearing returned slowly to the sound of hundreds of emergency sirens, people screaming, and the roar of many gyrofoil engines overhead. She turned around to look at the center of the square, dreading what she knew would be there—or rather, what wouldn't.

The middle of the plaza was carpeted with burning wreckage parts. The explosion had torn apart all three of the medical foils that had been loading patients or offloading medics. Strewn between the flaming bits of aircraft were bodies dressed in white medic jumpsuits. The last time Idina had seen carnage like this, she had been in battle, in the middle of the worst part of the war with Gretia, when they were fighting to take back one of the cities the fuzzheads had captured, and both sides were willing to trade hundreds of dead for each city block they gained. This was a calculated massacre, designed to kill as many people as possible. Follow-up bombs to kill emergency responders were a classic guerilla and terrorist tactic, and this bomb had killed dozens of whiteshirts and hundreds of civilians.

"Purple, anyone injured?" she asked into her headset when she could make sense of the radio noises again. Instantly, her squad started sending in nonverbal status reports that popped up on her data monocle. Most of them came up flashing between yellow and red, the color codes for wounded or injured.

"All right, anyone *not* injured?" she said. Only one status icon came up green.

"Gods be damned," she muttered. Her suit's automatic medic unit was busy injecting her with something that made it a little easier to take breaths again, and she could feel the nanofibers shift around and try to steer the blood flow in her limbs.

She got to her feet, which made her momentarily dizzy. Then the fuzziness in her head cleared, and she took stock of her immediate surroundings. The riot armor she wore was designed to shield her from blunt impacts and low-level piercing attacks, and while she was sure she'd be dead without it, she felt pain in half a dozen places on her back and legs where shrapnel had managed to make it through both the gel-backed armor plates and the ballistic nanofiber suit she was wearing underneath. The explosives specialists and heavy assault troopers of the brigade had extra-heavy armor that used electromagnetic reactive plates capable of shrugging off the blast from an antipersonnel mine at point-blank range, but this riot control gear was not it. The civilians who had been in front of the police line, however, had taken the worst of the blast by far because they had no armor at all.

No, she thought. *This is worse than even the battles on Pallas. At least they had all tried to avoid killing civilians, even the fuzzheads.* This was wholesale slaughter of unarmed and unprotected people, torn and mangled bodies everywhere she looked.

There was movement to her right, and she drew her sidearm out of instinct, but lowered it when she saw the familiar dark blue of JSP riot armor.

"Colors Chaudhary." Corporal Chandrakhar staggered up to her, his helmet missing from his head, a long gash on his face that went from the bridge of his nose to the corner of his jaw. She could see the muscles underneath poking through the cut when he spoke. Blood ran freely down his neck and into the collar of his armor.

"Hold still, Chandrakhar." She steadied herself on him and pulled a pack of wound gel out of her belt pouch. Then she squished it onto the gash, which had missed his left eye by less than a centimeter. He let out a slow breath and closed his eyes for a moment.

"Bad happenings, Colors."

"Bad happenings," she agreed. Underneath her armor, she could feel the automedic applying the same adaptive gel to her wounds. The gel produced a weird sensation, hot and cold at the same time, but it was better than the pain it replaced.

"Your fuzzhead captain, she's over there," the corporal said and pointed. She followed his gesture with her eyes and saw a tall figure clad in Gretian green lying motionless between three dead civilians.

"Fuck all the gods," she said. "Sit down and wait for the medics, Corporal."

"I'll help you, Colors."

"Sit down," she repeated in her command voice, and this time he obeyed with a little groan.

She staggered over to Captain Dahl, whose riot armor had been peppered with shrapnel as well. A jagged piece of alloy the size of Idina's palm was buried in the armor plate covering Dahl's lower back, right above the belt line. She couldn't tell how far in the shrapnel had gone, but Dahl wasn't moving. Idina got out another gel pack and wedged it underneath the armor plate on Dahl's back until her fingers caught on the ragged edge of the shrapnel. She squished the gel around the metal a bit so it could creep down the alloy and into Dahl's skin suit to seal the wound. There was no way to tell if Dahl was still alive because her Gretian police suit didn't link with the telemetry in Idina's armor, but this was the one thing she could do right now that might help at least a little if Dahl wasn't dead. Then Idina sat down hard next to Dahl and the dead Gretians. There were no more medical foils waiting their turn to land. The sky had been wiped clear, and the only sirens she heard came from the wheeled emergency pods rolling into the square.

"Fuck all the gods," she repeated. Then she toggled her comms into the company channel.

"This is Purple Actual. All my troopers are wounded except for one. One of my Gretian officers is down. Get a medical evac to my position. We have no perimeter security left. Purple is combat ineffective."

She looked around at the sea of dead bodies around her. The vast majority of them were Gretians, the people who had invaded her planet and killed her fellow troops by the thousands, and these Gretians had been out here demanding a return to the same system that had started the war. But as much as she had enjoyed knocking some of them on their asses, nobody deserved to die like this. Bombs were a coward's weapon, anonymous and without the burden of proximity, the polar opposite of a kukri. There was no honor in killing like this, no bravery. At least the Gretians who had invaded Pallas had come halfway across the system and taken the fight to armed people who were stronger and better adapted to the environment than they were.

A medical pod pulled up ten meters in front of them. For a moment, she wondered if this one would blow up in a cloud of shrapnel, too. At this range, she would die instantly, armor or not. She didn't even bother pulling out her sidearm again.

The doors of the pod opened, and two whiteshirts jumped out, civilian Gretian medical personnel. They grabbed their kit bags and came rushing over.

Beside Idina, Captain Dahl's leg moved just a little bit, and Idina reached out and patted the armor on Dahl's forearm lightly.

You'd make a decent brigade trooper, you tough old goat, she thought. *Don't you die yet, gods be damned.*

CHAPTER 21
SOLVEIG

At first, Solveig had thought that the lunch delivery on the executive floor was an indulgence, but after a few days with Ragnar Industries, she found that eating in her office was less of an interruption than making the trek down to the company canteen. When she started immersing herself in a subject, she had a tendency to forget mealtimes, and today, she only remembered that she had ordered food from the executive delivery menu earlier in the morning when her assistant walked in with a covered tray at precisely noon.

"Thank you, Anja," she said when the woman placed the tray on the table in the middle of the office. "I'll take it over here."

"Of course, Miss Ragnar." Anja dutifully picked up the tray and delivered it to Solveig's desk, where she put it down and removed the cover. Solveig hadn't really spent a lot of time looking over the menu and had just repeated her order from yesterday—salad topped with mustard egg wedges and bread rounds on the side.

"They are still at it out there." Anja glanced over to the window, which afforded a panoramic view of Principal Square below and the masses of protesters that were gathered.

"Every day this week," Solveig said. "And the crowds keep getting bigger."

"People have their grievances," Anja said.

It sounded tentative, as if she wasn't sure of the sentiment or whether it was appropriate to voice it in front of her boss. Solveig knew that most of the people on the executive floor were still trying to read her. *They want to know if I'm anything like my father,* she thought. It felt strange to see people twice her age tiptoe around her deferentially, as if she would carry word back to her father if someone offended her. Falk Ragnar had been cut out of the company for half a decade, but her presence seemed to cast her father's shadow in front of her.

"Just let me know when you are finished, and I'll come and collect everything," Anja said. "Do you need anything else, Miss Ragnar?"

"I'm fine for now. Thank you." She smiled at the older woman, who returned the pleasantry in a curt and professional way and walked out of the office, closing the door behind her without a sound.

Solveig got out of her chair and stretched with a little groan. Then she walked over to the window and looked down at the amount of people in the square. It seemed that as the crowds had grown every day this week, so had the number and size of the Gretian flags they were waving among the protest signs. The planet had been under Alliance military rule for five years now, and Gretia wanted to govern itself again, but it seemed like nobody could agree on how things should continue. The loudest voices were the ones in the square now, the loyalists who wanted to go back to the way things had been.

Solveig sympathized with them, and as the daughter of a plot holder, she would have much to gain if they all went back to the old ways. The plot holders had enjoyed a hereditary place in the legislature, 128 High Council seats passed down from parents to children, political power that did not have to bow to the capricious will of the common vote. But that old social structure had thrown the whole system into war, and it didn't seem right to her to pick up exactly where they had left off. Something needed to change, but until enough people could agree on that something, Gretia would be run by the Alliance, atoning both for its sins and the inability to get its own affairs in order.

On her desk, she had three screens open, each one subdivided into several tasks. Solveig returned to her chair and picked at her salad while she refocused her attention on the numbers and flowcharts that made up the substance of Ragnar Industries. She had been using her high-level access for three days now, and she still had only barely scratched the complexities of the organization her father built. But one thing was clear to her already—Ragnar was doing more than its share when it came to atoning for Gretia's sins. As an intern, she had only been allowed to see a small slice of the business, but now that everything was in front of her, the magnitude of the disaster had become clear to her. Ragnar Industries was a shell of the company it had been before the surrender. With the military contracts gone and its export business only slowly recovering, the company did less than half of the order volume from before the end of the war. And 15 percent of every ag earned by the corporation had to go into the war reparations fund.

Every company that had been involved in arming and equipping the Gretian military during the war had to pay into the fund. None of their owners or executive boards could stay on, even if they were family owned, and nobody in the owner families who had been at least eighteen years old on the day of the surrender could take them over either. Half the family-owned corporations on Gretia had been decapitated, with no hope of the original owners regaining control. Some, like Ragnar, had family heirs who hadn't been of age yet on that day. Solveig had missed it by luck of a late delivery. Her mother had been overdue with her for a week and didn't want to be induced, so Solveig was born three days after what would become the cutoff date eighteen years in the future. That was before they had known the significance of that day—the terms of the treaty had only been established a few months later, when it was too late for anyone to try to extend pregnancies past the deadline. But back then, everyone had been cowed, beaten down by the defeat, glad to have peace after four years of war that had felt like twenty, and nobody would have dared to show up on Principal Square waving Gretian flags in protest. They had to take what was served because they had lost, so they did. And Solveig, who had been too young to have a voice and a vote in the old order, had become her father's one hope of keeping the sign on the side of the building from turning into an anachronistic fiction. That weight had been on her shoulders since her first day at university, but sitting here in this building, at this desk, it felt like it was about to crush her.

———

Solveig was halfway through her salad when something shook the Alon panes of her office windows hard enough to make them rattle in their mountings. A second later, she heard a deep, rumbling thunderclap outside. She dropped her fork into her salad bowl and rushed over to the window.

Below, the mass of demonstrators was streaming away from a spot in the center of the square like a swift-moving tide. There was a haze of smoke spreading out over the square, and she could see people lying on the ground. At least a dozen motionless bodies were sprawled out on the concrete, and even from fifty floors up, Solveig could see pools of blood spreading between them. Others were on the ground as well, but moving, scrambling away from the source of the sudden devastation or getting dragged away. Everyone in the square seemed to be in motion now, thousands of people in sudden panic and moving away from the danger. With the sound-dampening office windows, the scene seemed eerily silent.

Behind her, the office door opened, and Anja rushed in, closely followed by Marten. Both of them came over to the window and surveyed the scene.

Anja let out a shocked gasp. "What happened?" she asked.

"I didn't see it, but I heard it," Solveig replied. "It shook the windows. Looks like someone set off a bomb. Gods."

Down on the square, the police line that had ringed the plaza and kept order during the demonstration was now moving into the center, toward the carnage, fighting against a current of panicked people. Then Solveig saw the blue glow of deployed plasma riot shields, and the crowds began to part, away from the advancing police.

"We need to get you out of here, Miss Solveig," Marten said next to her. He pulled out his comtab and started punching input fields rapidly. "I'm having one of the secure gyrofoils start up and stand by on the roof."

"Marten, we are fifty floors up," Solveig said. "And I don't think that was meant for any of us."

"It's a terrorist attack two hundred meters from your desk. I am obliged to get you to safety until we know what's going on." He held out an arm and made a motion to usher her away from the window. She took a step away from him to evade the gesture. Outside, a police gyrofoil soared past the building and descended into the square with its emergency lights flashing, followed by two medical foils a few moments later.

"I think I'm plenty safe at the moment. Nobody's trying to storm the building." She turned to Anja, who was still staring at the scene on the plaza with unconcealed horror on her face.

"There are dead and injured people out there. Don't we have a medical facility in this building?"

Anja tore her eyes away from the chaos outside and looked at her.

"Of course we do. The company medical station, on the tenth floor."

"They're for employees with headaches or scraped elbows," Marten said. "They're not set up for mass casualty events."

"There are people hurt right in front of our building, Marten. We can at least see if we can do something."

"This is Principal Square. That plaza is going to have every medical pod in the city on it in a few minutes. They'll take care of the casualties much faster than we could. We'd just add to the chaos if we sent our medics out there."

Down on the plaza, the initial surge of the crowd away from the explosion had slowed down. Some people were even moving back toward the center. There were at least a hundred police officers down in the square now, forming a solid skirmish line with their riot shields and nudging the crowd back. Within a few minutes, they had cleared out enough space around the dead and wounded to allow the hovering medical gyrofoils to land safely. Solveig was amazed to see that some in the crowd were throwing objects at the police line and shouting things she couldn't hear through the glass all the way up here. As many police as there were down on the plaza, Principal Square was huge, and the line of riot shields looked pitifully thin in front of the crowd that was still present.

Just as Marten had predicted, a few minutes later the sky above the plaza was full of emergency gyrofoils looking for a landing spot, and the foils were setting down in the square as quickly as the police line could clear more space. Wheeled medical pods were converging on the square from seemingly every direction as well, crawling through the crowd with flashing emergency lights. Then a large military gyrofoil appeared overhead and dropped rappelling lines, and dozens of figures in blue Joint Security Patrol uniforms and green Gretian police suits descended onto the plaza and immediately rushed to reinforce the existing police line around the scene.

As soon as all the police and soldiers had put their boots on the ground, the military gyrofoil cleared the airspace, climbing straight up while still retracting the rappelling lines, and the air disturbed by the rapid ascent of the huge six-engined foil made the windows of Solveig's office vibrate a little even from this distance. On the plaza, the down-draft blew around dropped protest signs and Gretian flags in a flurry of silver and green. Solveig tried to count the number of people on the ground but gave up when she had reached twenty and hadn't even counted half the bodies. By now, medics in white skin suits were swarming all over the center of the plaza and tending to the many injured. It looked like the aftermath of a battle. No, Solveig corrected herself. With the skirmish line of police and JSP troops still clearing the crowd out of Principal Square while the medics saw to the dead and injured, it looked like an ongoing battle.

Another medical gyrofoil descended into the square. In the room behind Solveig, Marten was talking on his comtab. He had turned on the big holoscreen that projected against the wall of the office, and a news feed was running silently, footage from news drones showing the events happening below from different angles even as Solveig was watching them unfold with her own eyes. She saw the emergency gyrofoil landing between the police line and the cluster of casualties and medics. MAJOR SECURITY INCIDENT AT PROTEST IN PRINCIPAL SQUARE—MANY CASUALTIES, the scrolling headline tape under the footage read.

Behind Solveig, another thunderclap pounded the windows, and the floor seemed to shift underneath her feet. She lost her balance and fell backward against one of the window panels. The news footage on the screen shook violently, then blinked out. She hadn't seen Marten begin to move, but he was suddenly above her, pulling her away from the window and shielding her with his body. Solveig glanced back, dazed, and saw gouges and cracks in the Alon panel behind her. Outside, a deep, angry boom rolled across the plaza and reflected back from the sides of the surrounding buildings until it sounded like a slow-moving thunderstorm rumbling across the city.

Marten pulled her to her feet. He had dropped his comtab when he started to move, and he guided her toward the door with one arm and scooped up his device with the other hand.

"We need to go *now*, Miss Solveig," he barked in a tone that left no doubt he would not entertain any debate. Solveig was too dazed and frightened to argue, so she let him pull her along and rush her out of the office and toward the nearby elevator bank. One of the executive assistants came rushing up to them and started talking to Marten, but her bodyguard just shoved him out of the way with enough force to make him stumble backward with a yelp and fall on his ass.

When they reached the elevator bank, Marten swerved right and opened one of the emergency-staircase access doors with his comtab. He slipped the comtab into his pocket and reached under his suit jacket as he peered around the door, then brought out a pistol and scanned the stairwell beyond the door before ushering her through.

The gyrofoil landing pad was directly above the executive level. With Marten rushing her along and keeping one arm wrapped around her, Solveig felt like her feet only touched the stairs two or three times before they had climbed the flight to the top landing. Marten opened the rooftop access door and checked the outside, then pulled her along with him.

The world beyond the soundproof insulation of Ragnar Tower was awash in discordant noise. On the street level fifty floors below them, countless sirens were blaring their ascending two-tone emergency alerts. A column of dirty-looking smoke was billowing into the sky in front of the building. Two police gyrofoils shot past Ragnar Tower, so low that the downwash from their engines blew Solveig's hair out of her face.

There were four landing pads on the rooftop, arranged like the petals of a water lily. Two of them had gyrofoils parked on them. One had its engines running and its position lights blinking, and Marten rushed her onto the landing pad and toward the waiting machine. He helped her up the short boarding ladder and into the passenger compartment. It was one of the company's own secure gyrofoils, used for executive transportation, the type of perk her father had wanted her to use from her first day. She had considered the idea wasteful, but right now she was thankful that she wouldn't have to venture out into the streets below, which sounded like the end of this world had just begun.

Solveig buckled herself in with shaking hands that felt like she suddenly had ten thumbs. Marten strapped himself in across the cabin from her. The door closed with a soft whining noise. The interior of the gyrofoil was soundproof, and as soon as the door sealed and locked into place, it shut out the aural chaos of the outside world again.

"Get us up and out of here," Marten said into the intercom on the armrest of his seat. "Back to the residence."

"Sir, they just declared the area over the inner city closed to all air traffic," one of the pilots replied.

"Do I look like I give a shit?" Marten said, raising his voice just a little. It was as much irritation as he had ever shown in her presence. "They're not going to shoot us down for taking off without permission. We'll pay the fine. Now take Miss Ragnar out of here before you find yourself flying traffic drones for a living."

"Yes, sir," the pilot said. A moment later, the slight vibrations from the rotors increased, and the gyrofoil rose into the air. They pivoted away from the square and smoothly accelerated away from the rooftop landing pad. Solveig caught a glimpse of the sign on the side of the building near the roofline, her family name in titanium-oxide white letters ten meters tall. Then they were past Ragnar Tower and the Principal Square area, soaring up and away from the center of the city as fast as the gyrofoil could climb.

"I respect your position, Miss Solveig. And I recognize your authority. But I have been in charge of your safety since before you could walk. And the next time I tell you that we need to leave a place, you need to listen right away," Marten said. "That second explosion left shrapnel marks on the window where you were standing."

Solveig nodded, too shaken to argue. Dozens, maybe hundreds of people had been killed within sight of her office, and she had been standing at the window and watching everything happen as if it were a news broadcast playing on a holoscreen.

The gyrofoil banked into a sweeping turn to the left as it ascended into the midday sky. It was sunny and only lightly overcast, which made the column of smoke rising from between the tall buildings around Principal Square all the more obvious. The entire city center was a sea of flashing blue emergency lights.

Her comtab buzzed with the notification of an incoming message. She didn't have to take it out of her pocket to know who was trying to reach her. But they'd be home in ten minutes anyway, and she was still too upset to trust herself to hold a coherent conversation with her father about what just happened. She hadn't even processed the whole event yet, but her father wasn't the kind of man who was used to waiting for answers.

"Can you message him and tell him I'm safe and on the way home, please?" she asked Marten.

"Of course, Miss Solveig."

Marten took out his own comtab and did as she had asked. She nodded at him in thanks, closed her eyes, and let her head rest against the side of her seat back. They were ten kilometers away from Ragnar Tower, and the cabin of the gyrofoil actively dampened all sounds, but in her mind she could still hear the emergency sirens screaming behind them, the sound following her all the way home.

CHAPTER 22

DUNSTAN

"We are about twelve hours out from Rhodia One," Dunstan said. "There will be a very eager detachment of naval intelligence officers waiting for our arrival."

The man in front of him didn't look intimidated or impressed. He just looked slightly bored. All the pirates they had captured were wearing off-the-rack flight overalls of the kind you could find anyplace that catered to commercial shipping, and this prisoner's overalls had the most stripes on the shoulder boards—the four parallel gold bars of a commanding captain. Dunstan had never seen a pirate outfit that bothered with rank insignia, but he could tell from the bearing of all the prisoners that this was no ordinary collection of freelance thieves.

"Do you want to tell me how you came into possession of a Rhodian Navy corvette that was reported missing and presumed lost at a major naval engagement early in the war?"

"No," the pirate captain said. "I really do not."

His Rhodian was too generic to be native, but Dunstan couldn't place the accent at all. It didn't have any of the foreign inflections he was used to hearing, the uvular R sounds of a Gretian accent or the tapped Acheroni version. He spoke Rhodian like a translating AI, which made him even more unsettling than a merchant murderer already ought to be. And according to Dunstan's engineering chief and the weapons officer, there was little doubt that the three remaining missiles in the magazines of the repurposed RNS *Daphne* matched the drive signature of the ones that had destroyed the Acheroni merchant ship *Cloud Dancer* a few days ago.

"What I am trying to tell you is that they might take it into consideration if I tell them you were cooperative. You may get out after ten years instead of twenty-five."

The pirate captain shook his head slowly.

"I gain nothing from talking to you. Let your naval intelligence people get a crack at the job. They get so little work as it is."

"Oh ho. That's a good one. Could have come from any of our fleet COs." Dunstan couldn't suppress a little grin. The pirate captain rewarded his reaction with a tiny smirk.

Dunstan pulled out his comtab and activated it. Then he opened a screen on the table between him and the captain and brought up the schematic of the ex-*Daphne*'s missiles the chief engineer had sent him earlier.

"This is something else," he said. "Those are Gretian M7c missiles. We found them in the magazine of your ship. But they don't have Gretian seeker heads. In fact, someone took the missiles, added polymer drive bands so they'd fit Rhodian 550-millimeter missile tubes, stripped all the Gretian electronics, and substituted commercial ones with custom target AI and encryption."

"That's very interesting," the captain replied. "You should let your friends at naval intelligence know about that. Because that would indicate some degree of technological sophistication."

"Yes, it would. But let me guess. You wouldn't know anything about that." Dunstan closed the screen with the schematic again.

The captain shook his head in the same slow, deliberate fashion as before. He was a trim and fit man, with a full beard and hair that curled down over the edge of his uniform collar. Dunstan guessed him to be his own age, mid-to-late forties, and something about his bearing and behavior shouted "military."

"I do not," the captain said. "We were just heading for Oceana in a ship that has been legally salvaged in interplanetary space. I know we came across a Rhodian frigate that ordered us to cut our drive and stand by for boarding, and I know that we complied immediately."

"You think your tribunal judge is going to swallow that?" Dunstan asked. "I hope you don't have any big plans for the next twenty-five years."

"I think your justice system is going to do what it does," the captain said. "It's going to give us the maximum benefit of the doubt. And it's going to make the prosecutor's evidence subject to the maximum burden of proof. Because you are a planet that values rights and due process."

"We are. But we've been known to make exceptions. Space is a big place, and this ship has two fast-cycling airlocks. We're still half a day away from civilization, you know."

The pirate captain chuckled softly.

"You're threatening to space my crew. After you already told everybody in the AO you were intercepting us. Try again, Lieutenant Commander. Because that kind of thing will get you ten to twenty-five years in military prison. If you wanted to make us disappear, you shouldn't have sent a broadcast in the open."

Dunstan smiled without humor. He had the feeling that he could be sitting here all day trying to scare this man into talking and just have a wasted day and an anger headache to show for it. He could either make good on his threat and start spacing that crew, or leave the headaches to the professionals of the military intelligence team that was already waiting for them at Rhodia One, and he had a distaste for summary executions. Even ambush killers deserved their day in court.

"Well," he said. "You don't want to tell me who you are or why you've retrofitted one of our warships to kill merchants. I'm not going to play out the whole embarrassing bluff theater where we walk you all to the airlock and pretend we're going to space you one by one. So we're both just having a really unproductive afternoon."

Dunstan stowed his comtab and stood up. The pirate ship captain was shackled to a restraint loop under the table, which prevented him from trying to bash in Dunstan's head or taking any position other than sitting down.

"Have it your way," Dunstan said. "And here's what's going to happen now. Once we get to Rhodia One, they'll get approval for a DNA scan on you. Then we'll know who you are. And you'll have a lot of people trying to get information out of you. They are good at what they do. And then, depending on what you and your men give them, you are looking at anywhere between fifteen and thirty years in a Rhodian prison arcology. And not a nice, low-security one."

The captain could only raise his chained hands ten centimeters above the table, but he still managed a passable dismissive gesture with them.

"That's what you think is going to happen," he said.

"I know that's what is going to happen."

The captain laughed softly.

"You really don't know anything yet," he said. "You have *no idea* what's coming for you."

———

On his way back to the AIC, Lieutenant Bosworth caught up with Dunstan in the main top-to-bottom ladderway.

"Sir, we got an approval on our emergency DNA sample request from the fleet legal division. Lieutenant Foster ran their samples through the database."

"And who are our new smarmy, well-organized friends in the generic uniforms?"

They stepped off the ladder on the AIC level, and Lieutenant Bosworth ran a hand through his hair and let out a sharp puff of breath.

"Here's the thing, sir. We don't know. They're not popping up in any of the data banks. Not Rhodian, not Gretian. No hit on Hades or Oceana either. They don't look like they're Palladians or Acheroni, but we ran everything through their systems anyway just in case. No hits at all. They're in no civil or military database anywhere in the system."

Dunstan frowned. The Rhodian military was the main component of the Alliance, and they had access to every security database. If you didn't have your DNA profile in the Mnemosyne anywhere, you didn't exist, but the eight men and women locked up in his brig right now certainly weren't figments of their imagination. Even intelligence operatives didn't draw a blank when someone captured them and forced a DNA scan. They usually had waterproof real-fake IDs tied to their genetic profiles.

"Lieutenant Foster wants to let fleet intel run the scans again just in case our equipment is defective."

"They'll run the scans again anyway. But I think we have caught ourselves some really odd fish. The intel people are going to piss themselves with joy at the challenge."

"They'll spend a month just plucking apart *Daphne*. The chief engineer says there's barely anything original left on her."

"Any intel from the comtabs and the other stuff they slagged?"

"No, sir. Maybe the intel forensics people can get something."

"We'll see," Dunstan said. "But we've done our part. I can't even remember the last time anyone brought in eight live pirates and their ship. Never mind that it's one of our own. Too bad we can't claim salvage on it."

Lieutenant Bosworth chuckled.

"That would be something. Even at scrap value, we'd all get pay and a half this year."

"But it's fleet property. Always has been, even when these people were doing gods know what with it."

"If they verify that the birds in the magazine match the ones that destroyed that Acheroni merchant, they're each looking at seven counts of murder," Bosworth said as they both stepped across the bulkhead threshold and into the AIC.

"Plus the piracy charges. And a long list of other sins. I hope there's a formal charge for fucking up a perfectly good escort corvette."

"From what the chief says, they did that ship a favor. Those were expensive retrofits. Better than what we can do with our own old escort gunboats. The only mistake they made was to use missiles with commercial-grade brains against a warship."

"Yeah, that wasn't too smart," Dunstan said. "Which is odd. Because that crew has its act together otherwise."

Bosworth returned to his own duties, and Dunstan walked up to the plot table to check the display. This far into Rhodian space, their surroundings were busy with dozens of ship icons—merchants and passenger liners heading toward Rhodia One or away from it—a steady stream of commerce that went on around the clock. Any of them could be flying with a spoofed transponder ID, but you couldn't really dock anywhere with fake credentials because the dockmaster AI would verify your ship's hull and drive profile against the official entries in the registry and alert authorities if it found a mismatch. You couldn't just park a stolen warship at Rhodia One or Eudora Station above Oceana and refill your tanks, and reloading a magazine with military-grade ASMs would definitely get the dockmaster's attention. There were armed privateers and security contractors out there with rail guns and missile tubes, but that sort of firepower was tightly controlled. Wherever RNS *Daphne* had been for the last nine years, Dunstan was sure she hadn't been docked anyplace that was linked into the Mnemosyne. But pirates didn't have clandestine stations floating around in the void. Stations were so expensive to run that no amount of stolen pallets of electronics or courier containers of precious metals could make the operation worthwhile.

"We're in the queue for Rhodia One, sir," Midshipman Boyer said from her post at the astrogation console. "Going for turnaround and two-and-a-half-g deceleration burn in seventeen minutes."

"Very well," Dunstan replied. "Steady as she goes."

They were coming home with an intact ship and a prize in tow. They'd taken a pirate craft out of business and suffered no casualties. By every measure, it had been a successful patrol. But as Dunstan watched the dozens of ship icons on the plot, he couldn't shake the unsettling feeling he'd had since they had captured the former RNS *Daphne*, which had only intensified after his interrogation of the pirate ship's captain. Every other pirate he had questioned before had been meek, resigned, or frightened, and Dunstan had been able to use any of those states to fashion a lever to get what he wanted out of them. This man had been unafraid and dismissive, and the sincere certainty of his words and their almost pitying delivery had given Dunstan a discordant feeling of foreboding that he hadn't been able to shake.

You have no idea what's coming for you.

CHAPTER 23

ADEN

"You look like you've been around the block a bit," the woman said to Aden.

The bar at the spaceport catered to travelers, so it lacked the dangerous and dingy element of Piet's shadowy establishment down on the eastern leaf. However, the two people sitting across the table from Aden wouldn't have looked entirely out of place in one of Piet's booths. The woman who had started the conversation was Oceanian, and she looked like she spent a lot of time in zero g. She was tall, but slender like an Acheroni, as much as Aden could tell her body shape underneath the flight suit she was wearing. The man in the booth next to her was obviously Palladian. His skin had the darkest shade of brown Aden had ever seen on a Palladian, and the man studied Aden over the folded hands he had propped up on the table in front of him like he was appraising him for value.

"I've traveled some," Aden replied.

The woman consulted her comtab briefly and put it on the table.

"Aden Jansen, trained linguist. My name is Ronja Decker. I am the captain of a courier ship named *Zephyr*." She nodded at the Palladian next to her. "This is my executive officer, Henry Siboniso."

"Pleased to meet you." Aden nodded an Oceanian greeting.

"We have three more members on our crew, but they're not available right now, so we are the hiring committee," Captain Decker said. "So tell us a bit about your language skills."

"Native Oceanian and Gretian," he said. "My mother is from here, my father was from Gretia. Picked up Rhodian in school and got very good at it, right up to native level. I can get by in Hadean, but not enough to sound like a local. Basic Acheroni, but very basic. Like, 'order a drink and rent a hotel room' basic. No Palladian, unfortunately."

"We have that covered," Siboniso said. He had a deep, soft voice that made the statement sound almost mournful.

"That's a good variety," Captain Decker said. "Our crew is Oceanian except for Henry here. We had a Rhodian comms specialist, but he left for greener pastures recently, so we need someone to take his slot. We don't do any illegal stuff as far as Oceana is concerned, but we often take contracts to get stuff into jurisdictions that are a little more uptight. And when we do, we sometimes need to pass ourselves off as locals, or understand their slang when they don't want to be overheard. As you probably know, the translator AI isn't good enough for that."

"What kind of stuff do you transport?" Aden asked. Decker looked at Siboniso and smiled a little.

"Well, *Zephyr* is very expensive to run. She's a fast ship with very little cargo space. So we mostly take high-value courier and delivery jobs. More often than not, it involves crossing through parts of space that aren't entirely safe for other cargo ships. Would you feel comfortable with that?"

Aden chewed on his lower lip. "That depends entirely on the ship. I've been on the receiving end of pirate missiles, and I've had my share of time in an escape pod. As a general rule of thumb, I'd like to avoid logging any more."

Siboniso laughed. It sounded smooth as silk.

"There's always the chance," he said. "But *Zephyr* isn't a normal courier ship. We've been in business for seven years, and we've never had to take to the pods."

"And whenever we do take riskier contracts, the pay is worth it," the captain added. "But if you want a no-risk job, you're probably better off applying somewhere else."

"I don't mind risk," Aden replied. "Especially not when it comes with hazard pay."

"Do you have military experience?" Siboniso asked.

"I was in signals intelligence for ten years."

"What was your rank?"

"Major. I was a company commander at the end."

Siboniso nodded, and for a moment, Aden thought he spotted the shadow of a frown on the Palladian's face.

"So you know how to handle a gun?"

"I had small-arms training. But that wasn't my job. I haven't fired one in years. Still remember the how-to, though."

"The two men who pointed you my way when you showed up for the interview were native speakers of Gretian and Rhodian," Captain Decker said. "They say you check out. If Henry here has no objections, I want to offer you the job."

She leaned across the table a little.

"Here's the deal, however. This is on a probationary basis. We will take you on the next job. When it's done, the crew gets to vote on whether you'll get to stay. There's five of us, so there won't be a tie, and every vote has the same weight. The kind of jobs we do, we have to have team cohesion. It's no good if you're competent but don't play well with the rest of the crew."

"I understand. If they decide they don't like me, I am no worse off than now. I'd like to take you up on the offer."

Captain Decker turned to Siboniso.

"What do you think, Henry?"

The Palladian looked at Aden with a gaze that felt like it was scanning him all the way down to his skeletal structure.

"He's hiding something. But most of us are, in this line of work. And he's not lying about the military service or his language skills. I'd say we give him a try. If he doesn't work out, we can drop him off at Oceana again after the next run."

Captain Decker smiled and leaned back in her seat.

"All right, let's give you a try, Aden Jansen."

She held out a fist, and Aden bumped the side of it in Oceanian fashion.

"Why don't you head back to the docking port, Henry? I want to have a few more words with our new hire before we take off for the station."

"Sure thing, Captain," Siboniso replied. He unfolded himself out of his seat, gave Aden a friendly nod, and walked off. Aden saw that he had a blade hanging off the belt around his flight suit's waist. He didn't recognize the shape of the weapon, but he knew what the biometric security sheath for a Pallas Brigade blade looked like, and he had to control himself not to flinch a little as the big Palladian walked by.

"He was in the brigade," Aden said when Siboniso was out of earshot.

Captain Decker nodded. She looked like she was around Aden's age, maybe a little older, with blue eyes and blonde hair, which she wore in a short braid that barely hung past the edge of her flight suit's collar. One of the front teeth in her lower jaw was slightly turned inward, but she hadn't bothered to get it straightened, and the minor imperfection somehow made her smile more appealing.

"He was," Captain Decker replied. "Corporal Siboniso, First Regiment. He fought on Pallas for a year and a half during the Gretian invasion. The man has stories that would make your toenails curl. But he needs to be very drunk to tell them."

She drummed her fingertips on the tabletop and then slapped it lightly with the palm of her hand.

"All right, Aden Jansen. Henry says you are hiding something, but he doesn't think it's enough to turn you down for the job. Here's your chance to come clean and tell me what you're keeping from us. I told you everyone on the ship gets an equal vote, but ultimately I'm the captain, and I'm responsible for my crew. I need to know what I am dropping into their midst."

Aden hesitated. If he put his cards on the table, she'd have good cause to reject him. Oceanians had no love for Gretians, especially not occupiers. But Siboniso had even less love for his kind, and if the former brigade member found out that he was working side by side with a former Blackguard, Aden had no doubt the man would use his blade on him with abandon and chop him into pieces. And if Captain Decker rejected him, he'd be no worse off than before.

"My ID is forged," he said. "I didn't lie about my mother and father, but I'm not Oceanian. I'm Gretian."

Decker let out a low whistle through her teeth. Then she chuckled.

"How good is that ID pass?"

"As good as you can get for money. It's real-fake. It'll stand up to any official checks. Just not to detailed forensic attention."

She looked at him with a slightly amused expression for a few moments, and he steeled himself for the rejection he was sure would follow.

"Here's the deal. I'll pretend I have no idea. If you want to tell Henry or the rest of the crew, that's up to you, although I strongly suggest you come clean at some point. Most of us have some shady shit in our backgrounds. If anything, the fact that you had the knowledge and the initiative to get that ID pass makes you more suited for this line of work, not less."

Aden let out the breath he'd been holding.

"But if we ever get jacked up by the authorities, and your cover is blown, I'll drop you like you're radioactive and claim ignorance if it's what's best for the rest of the crew. Do I have a solid signal?"

"Yes, you do," he replied. "And that's exactly what I'd expect you to do. No hard feelings."

"No hard feelings," Decker agreed. "Ready to meet the rest of the crew, then?"

He took a deep breath and let it out slowly.

"I am," he said. "I just need to go back to the hotel and grab my stuff."

Captain Decker brought up a note on her comtab and flicked it over to his device.

"That's the shuttle we're taking back up to Eudora Station. It leaves in two hours. If you miss it, you'll have to buy your own ride up. If you're not on the station by 1500 hours, we are leaving without you. Schedule's tight."

"I'll be on time," Aden said, and she nodded.

He got up from his seat and walked out of the bar. Outside in the concourse, the light from the rising sun streamed in through the tall windows of the spaceport and painted the latticework of the building in vivid shades of orange and red, a new day and a fresh beginning.

Chapter 24

Solveig

Solveig was relieved that her father wasn't waiting on the landing pad near the house when the company gyrofoil landed. The walk from the pad to the house led through the gardens, which would give her a few more minutes to settle her mind. Behind her, the gyrofoil took off again to take Marten back to Ragnar Tower. She had feared that he'd want to walk her to the house personally to make sure no assassins or terrorists climbed out of the fishpond or jumped out from behind one of the apple trees, but his comtab had been chirping constantly with incoming message requests by the time they had landed. It had been easy to convince him that his time was better spent at the locked-down corporate headquarters right now. He was not just her personal body-guard but also one of the company's senior security officers, and the building had thirty thousand employees to calm down and reassure in the wake of the bombing.

Her father was pacing in the living room in front of the muted holoscreen, holding a glass in one hand and his comtab in the other. He was in the middle of an animated conversation with someone, but when Solveig stepped through the patio doors he had left wide open, he instantly terminated the comm and chucked his comtab onto a nearby counter. He hurried over to her and embraced her in a firm hug. She could hear the ice cubes clinking against his glass as he did.

"Are you okay?" he asked.

"I'm fine, Papa. I was in my office when it happened. All the way upstairs."

"Did you see it?"

"I was at my desk. I heard the first explosion and went over to the window to look. Someone must have placed a bomb. We watched the medical foils come in, and the police started clearing the square. And then . . . I don't know what happened exactly. I was standing with my back to the window to watch the newscast. And something else went off. Much bigger. It shook the whole building. And Marten grabbed me and got me to the landing pad."

Falk Ragnar let go of his daughter and paced back into the middle of the room. He pointed his glass at the holoscreen that was showing news footage and scrolling updates silently. Solveig's stomach twisted a little when she saw the aerial shot of Principal Square, smoke still rising from its center. Several wrecked and burning gyrofoils were strewn across the plaza. The magnification of the drone's camera was just enough to see that there were many bodies littered between the gyrofoil wrecks.

"They say that one of the medical foils had a bomb in it," her father said. "They're not saying that the first one that went off was just to get all the emergency responders to the scene. But that's what happened."

"How do you know, Papa?"

"Because it's a common terrorist tactic, Solveig. You want to hurt someone, you take out their police and their medical personnel. Those loyalists, they'll have no shortage of bodies for the next protest. But the police and the medics? Those take years to train."

Solveig watched, aghast, as the scrolling news update on the screen listed the preliminary casualty count.

AT LEAST THREE HUNDRED PROTESTERS KILLED OR INJURED; NINE POLICE AND JSP CONFIRMED DEAD. MEDICAL PERSONNEL CASUALTIES UNCONFIRMED, BUT SAID TO BE IN THE DOZENS.

"I saw the breaking news update," Falk said. "Do you have any idea what kind of agony you go through when you know your daughter is in a place where two bombs just went off, and you're not even allowed to send her a comm because she's at work?"

He threw the glass he was holding through the open patio door, where it sailed toward the edge of the pool. It didn't quite make it into the water and instead shattered on the marble of the raised pool rim, spraying glass shards and ice cubes. Her father walked over to the bar in the corner of the living room, got another glass out of the rack, and slammed it down on the bar counter. Then he dropped in a few ice cubes and poured a healthy amount of amber liquor from an expensive-looking decanter.

"They geo-fenced all my comms. I can't talk to anyone at Ragnar Tower. I have to wait until they leave the building. And I had best not talk company business unless I want to go to corrective lockup for six months. On the first offense. All because of the Alon. Because we sold fucking windows to the military."

"I saw the balance sheets this week. Well, some of them," Solveig said. "There's so much to go through."

He took a long sip from his glass and nodded at the bar.

"You want something to drink? You're a working professional now. And you're of age. Might as well enjoy the perks." Falk smirked. "Not that I don't know what goes on at university."

"Some mead maybe, if we have any," she replied.

"Of course we do."

He went to the wine cooler built into the counter and pulled out a bottle, then opened it with a swift twist of his hand. He took a goblet from the rack that held the drink ware and filled it for her.

"Thank you," she said. The mead was far better than the stuff they'd smuggled into the dormitories at university. Falk Ragnar did not waste his time with cheap spirits.

"What else did you see at work? Not that you're allowed to tell me details."

"We're not doing well," Solveig replied. "Less than half the pre-armistice gross. And two-thirds of the plants are running at less than sixty percent capacity. Can't get raw materials from Pallas, can't get tech from Rhodia. And I'm pretty sure the plants are throttling back on purpose to slow down production."

"You figured all that out in your first three days? Damn." Her father shot her a smile. "You know, it's the family business, but I can't blame them. Even as the former president." A shadow of anguish darkened his expression for a moment. "Fifteen percent of gross goes to that gods-be-damned reparations fund. Not even net, mind you. Gross."

He shook his head and took another sip from his glass. "That's what all the protests are about. The poor bastards who got blown up in the square today. Just taking to the streets for fair treatment. War's been over for five years. And now someone's killing them for speaking up against the occupation."

"Who would do that sort of thing?" Solveig asked. "I mean, there's nobody who stands to gain from that."

"Who knows? The reformers, maybe? I don't think they have the guts. Or the means. That was cold and calculated. You don't just pull something off like that out of the blue with a bunch of weak-wristed collaborators. Somebody knew how to punch right where it would hurt the most."

He looked at the holoscreen and scowled. The news network was still showing the scene of the bombing from multiple angles and altitudes. She knew that he had turned off the sound because the vapid and inane commentary from the talking heads usually irritated him to the point of rage in short order.

"This is going to create strife. On a whole new scale. The loyalists are already blaming the reformers. The reformers are saying it was a false-flag operation. And a bunch of people on both sides are suspecting it was the Alliance. Trying to keep both the reformers and loyalists at each other's throats. So we don't unite against the occupation. So they can keep milking us for fifteen percent of everything we produce."

"Only until the reparations are paid," Solveig said.

Falk barked a humorless laugh.

"Have you seen the amount they claim we owe? Three hundred billion ags. Even if we get lucky and our economy pulls itself out of the toilet, it'll take us fifty years to pay that off. And that's if they don't just decide to move the goalposts. They said we could satisfy the terms with intellectual property instead of cash. You know how much they offered us as debt relief for the Alon patent? A billion and a half."

"That's our most valuable patent. Without that, the Rhodians can make Alon, and we'll go bankrupt in a year."

"Exactly." He raised his glass at his daughter. "You paid attention in business college. Very good. So we told them no. And they threatened to confiscate the patent. Just take it from us."

"And why didn't they?"

"Because a bunch of us got together and told them what would happen if they started stripping Gretia down to the bones. Told them they could kiss their reparations goodbye if we got to the point where we couldn't even feed ourselves. They ended up seeing reason." Falk slugged the rest of his drink and dumped the ice cubes in the bar sink.

"Damn," he said. "I'm not used to talking to you like this. Like a grown-up, I mean. Someone who understands gross and net and implications of patent law. You were seventeen when the war ended."

"I knew about those even back then," Solveig replied.

"Of course you did." Her father smiled at her. "It runs in the blood, I guess."

They covered that in math and economics in class-level eight, she wanted to reply, but the family legacy was her father's sore spot, his one overriding concern, and if he wanted to believe that she was a natural prodigy at interplanetary business, she knew she wouldn't be able to counter that notion even if she tried. He walked back to the bar and repeated the refill routine without taking his eyes off the holoscreen. Now the newsies were showing eyewitness interviews with people on the street in Sandvik, and the general camera direction had been changed to surface-level shots of the plaza, now cordoned off by heavily armored JSP troops in bulky powered exosuits.

"That war has cost us so much," Falk said. He left open whether he meant the planet, the company, the family, or all of those at once.

"Why did you vote for it?" Solveig asked.

He tore his eyes away from the screen and looked at her in surprise. "What?"

"You voted for the war," she said. "In the High Council. Right before they invaded Oceana. I saw it in the files during history-and-civics class one day. One hundred and one votes for the war, twenty-seven against. You didn't vote to stop it. Why not?"

He pursed his lips, and the surprise on his face morphed into irritation. For a long moment, he looked at her without saying anything. Then he sighed, turned away from her, and walked over to one of the lounging chairs. He sat down and let the chair morph to adjust itself to his body before taking a sip from his fresh drink.

"Because I made a bad call, Solveig."

He gestured toward the holoscreen, and it turned itself off and vanished.

"A bad call," she repeated.

"I know that sounds perfectly awful," he said. "Four years of war, a quarter million of ours dead. And now we have Rhodian masters. And we'll be paying them for a generation. I left you a fine mess, I know."

"So why did you vote for war?"

"You mean they didn't teach that in that history-and-civics class of yours?" He smiled dryly. While she had been away at school, he had taken to wearing a neatly trimmed mustache, and she still wasn't quite used to seeing his face like that. His facial hair was also white, and it brought out the blue in his eyes even more, making the color look brighter and colder somehow.

"All wars are about resources," he said. "And all the strife in this system is always about the same resource. The one you can only mine on one planet."

"Palladium," she said, and he nodded.

"The stuff that makes our worlds go round. Everyone needs it. You can't make gravmag generators without it. Unless you're Hades and have enough solar energy to not give a shit about efficiency. You can't have low-loss power conduits without it. No vactrains, no high-yield fusion plants, no fast AI networks. Whoever controls the palladium supply controls the technological development of all the planets, not just their own. Until someone finds something else that's a superconductor at room temperature. And believe me, we've spent billions looking for alternatives. But the Rhodies control the supply, and they get to set the price. And they only ever turned that screw one way for Gretia."

"If it was about palladium, then why did we invade Oceana? That just got all the other planets aligned against us."

"We never had much of a use for the place," Falk said. "We don't need the protein or the water anymore. But we needed to put pressure on Acheron. They do need that protein and water. And they were starting to take a page out of the Rhodian playbook and raising prices on us for their graphene."

He sipped from his drink and looked past Solveig. His blue eyes had become a little less focused, and she wondered how many drinks he'd had already while waiting for her to return home.

"The military wanted to open a theater that would tie up the Rhodies so they'd bleed themselves out before we made the move for

Pallas," he continued. "We couldn't take on both the Rhodians and the Palladians at full strength. Beat one, then beat the other in turn, so you don't have to deal with them as a unified force. It was a gamble, and it backfired. Like the whole fucking war."

He looked up at her again and gave her a lopsided smile.

"I don't have an excuse for my vote, if that's what you're looking for. I did what I thought was best for the planet. And we left you all a terrible mess. I'm sorry for that. I wish I could do it over."

Solveig walked to the patio doors and stood in the breeze coming from the lake in front of the house. There was no other building in sight. The Ragnar estate was in the middle of twenty-five square kilometers of carefully managed forests, meadows, and lakes. Before she was born, her father had rebuilt the family home and made every building single level, to preserve the views and make the estate blend in with its surroundings more harmoniously. Even in defeat, they had more private space than almost any other family in the system, trees and soil and water that belonged to them and nobody else, a privilege earned by their ancestors for taking on the burden of feeding everyone on their plot, back when food was scarce and a lot of agriculture was done on costly trial and error.

"I wish the war hadn't happened," she said. "With everything we lost. Everything they lost. I know it's hard for you, Papa. But even if we didn't go to war, I don't think I'd be doing anything different right now. I'd be sitting in that office anyway. Just with you next door."

Her father slurped one of the ice cubes out of his glass and crunched it slowly between his teeth.

"Maybe. Or maybe you'd be off on a tour of the system. Or doing a practicum with one of our partner firms on Acheron. Partying with your friends on an Oceana cruise. And if you were at Ragnar Tower already, you'd be a few levels lower than you are now."

He put his drink down on the table in front of him and stood up to join her at the patio door.

"But the war happened. For better or worse, we old farts chose to make it happen. And I don't have time for training wheels, Solveig. You'll be vice president for a few years, and then you will be company president and chief executive officer. Because I am seventy, and I am running out of time to make sure that our company doesn't get plucked apart like a dinner chicken. That it stays the family enterprise."

Falk stepped past his daughter onto the patio and took a deep breath of fresh air, then exhaled it slowly.

"And who knows," he said. "Things are changing out there. The Alliance may decide that it's too much of a burden to oversee us forever. You may have your office next to mine after all in a few years."

"There's a treaty," she said.

He turned and grinned. His teeth had always been the whitest and straightest of any person she knew. If he colored his hair, he could pass for fifty instead of seventy.

"Treaties are words on a page, Solveig. They're only worth anything if you have the ability to enforce them."

Falk's comtab chirped, and he walked back to the table and picked up his drink again while he read the incoming message. Then her father made the strangest sound she had ever heard him utter. It sounded like a strangled shout that was almost a moan. His drink shattered on the floor, the harsh sound of the bursting glass breaking in the quiet. Solveig whirled around.

"*Papa!* Are you okay? What is it? What happened?"

Her father stood in the middle of the living room, a small pool of liquor forming by his feet among the shards of broken glass. A moment later, the service door next to the kitchen opened, and one of the house-keepers came rushing out with a rag and a debris remover in hand. Falk waved him off with a curt hand gesture.

"Not now. Give us the room, please."

The housekeeper disappeared as fast as he had popped in. Her father stood, hunched over, his left hand closed around the comtab, his knuckles white.

"Do you need a medic? What's wrong?" she asked. "What happened?"

He looked up at her, and for the first time in her life, Solveig saw her father with tears in his eyes. She rushed toward him in concern, disregarding the pool of liquor she was stepping into, but then she saw that her father was smiling through his tears.

He held up his comtab. She waited for him to gather himself.

Mama, she thought. *It has to be about Mama. She's decided to come back to us. They've made up, and she's coming back.* There was nothing else she could think of that would have her father react so emotionally in front of her.

"It's Aden," he said. Then he smiled, and this time it was a genuine expression of joy, not his fake, toothy grin.

"Corporate intel traced an encrypted comms session from our network to a public pod on Oceana. The comtab that was used to rent it was found discarded in a canal. The last name is different, but the DNA profile was a match for Aden. *Your brother is still alive, Solveig.*"

For a moment, his sudden outburst of vulnerability moved her, and she considered telling him everything: that she had been in touch with Aden, that she had been the person who placed that comms session. But something in the back of her head threw the safety switch just in time, and she sat down on one of the nearby living room chairs and started sobbing. The tears she had meant to conjure up as a deflection came easy and felt surprisingly genuine.

Everything is going to change now, she thought as she buried her face in her hands. *And I'm not at all sure it will be for the better.*

CHAPTER 25

IDINA

Just the smell in the hallways of the Rhodian military hospital brought back unwanted memories to Idina. She had spent two days here after the ambush that wiped out her section, and now her olfactory recall was forever tied to the impotent anger she had felt after she had woken up in this place. She gripped the handle of her kukri tightly as she walked down the hall.

The hospital was the busiest place in Sandvik right now. The civilian hospitals in the city had been overwhelmed with the stream of wounded victims from the double bombing on Principal Square, so the Rhodian Army had taken the overflow of both civilians and JSP wounded alike. Now Alliance military surgeons were patching up people who would have spit in their faces or tried to brain them with flagpoles just a few hours earlier. But that was before those bombs had gone off, before everyone on that square had been reduced to a shrapnel target, loyalists and reformers, Gretian cops and Alliance soldiers. The JSP had lost three troopers, thankfully none from her platoon, and 139 Alliance soldiers had been wounded. The Gretian police had lost six and suffered ninety-six wounded. The civilians had gotten the brunt of it, unprotected by riot armor, helmets, or ballistic nanofiber skin suits. The civvie death count stood at 312, many of them whiteshirt first responders. Over nine hundred had been wounded, and many of those were now filling up the treatment and patient rooms all over the city.

She found the room she had been looking for at the end of a long, sterile, bright white hallway. Captain Dahl was on a medical zero-gravity couch, covered from neck to toe in a nanofiber blanket that held her in a snug embrace. The monochrome environment made Dahl's hair look even whiter and her eyes even bluer than usual. Idina made sure her translator earbud was seated correctly and turned on.

"It is good to see you, Sergeant Chaudhary."

"I'm glad you aren't dead," Idina replied. "You're the first Gretian I don't completely hate."

The other woman smiled weakly. "I'm afraid I will not be going on patrol with you for a little while."

"You'll be back on your feet before you know it. They can do miracles in here. Ask me how I know."

"Those bombs killed many of our people. Yours and mine. Someone wants us to fight each other, I think. We should not do them the favor."

"That's already happening, I'm afraid. Your loyalists are blaming the Alliance. Those who aren't blaming the reformers, that is. Everyone thinks everyone else is out to get them."

The two women looked at each other in silence. So much was standing on the edge of a kukri right now, and what happened in the next few days and months would determine where it fell.

"This is the second time I've gotten wounded on patrol during this tour," Idina said. "That means I have the right to go home on medical release before my tour ends."

Captain Dahl sighed a little.

"You have earned it, Sergeant. But I will miss you. I will have to get used to a new partner again once I return to duty."

"Oh, I turned them down," Idina replied. "I'm staying for another five months."

Dahl raised an eyebrow and smiled wryly. Idina had never seen a woman who could lift a brow so effectively.

"Why would you do that? You do not like it here, on Gretia."

"No, I don't. But I don't want to have to come back here and make war again a year from now. And I think that's what the people who laid those bombs want us to do."

Idina crossed her arms in front of her rib cage and drummed the fingers of her right hand on the handle of her kukri.

"So you need to get fixed up and back on your feet. So we can look for the people who did this. Find them, arrest them, or chop them into little pieces if we have to."

Captain Dahl's smile widened ever so slightly.

"I used to think those big knives of yours are a bit barbaric," she said. "But after yesterday, I think a little chopping might be in order here and there."

———

She had only intended to make her visit a brief one, but when Idina left the hospital, the sun had started to set, and she realized she'd been talking to the convalescing Dahl for two hours. The shrapnel chunk that had pierced the police captain's armor had missed her spine by only a centimeter or two, but that had been the difference between a crippling injury and a merely painful and annoying one. According to the medics, Dahl would be back on the street in a few days, and if Idina had judged the police captain correctly, she'd try to have her recovery time cut in half.

The steady stream of emergency pods and gyrofoils to the hospital had slacked off, but the perimeter was still busy, and security was as tight as Idina had ever seen it around a military facility—dozens of troops in heavy armor guarding all access points while gyrofoil gunships patrolled the sky. In the distance, the column of smoke from the explosions had dissipated above the buildings of downtown Sandvik, and Idina saw that the evening sky above the city was busy with dozens of position lights from police and military aircraft. Idina hadn't seen that many gyrofoils in the air at the same time since the last days of the war. The city was temporarily closed for business until the military knew it had the situation fully under control again.

She checked her comtab for the current duty schedule and found that it hadn't changed from the regular assignment she'd had this week: ten to six, the graveyard shift. Her section had worked an extra watch during the demonstration to augment the daytime watch, and that usually meant a twenty-four-hour break the next day, but with all available forces on deck in the city, she had already written off that perk tonight. It would have felt frivolous to sleep in and spend the day doing nothing when almost every other soldier in this sector was in armor and out on the streets. There was little else for her to do until ten, so she decided to go back to base early and perform some maintenance and diagnostics on her gear and weapons.

When the time came and she walked into the liaison room where her platoon was assembling for the watch, Idina double-checked the roster on her comtab to see that none of her troopers had reported in as sick or otherwise unable to go on patrol. Every member of the platoon was present, and Idina was sure that most of them hadn't taken a break since yesterday either. The Gretian police officers had turned out in full strength as well despite the losses they had suffered. She had been with the platoon for long enough now that she remembered the faces of the regulars on the other side and recognized the obvious replacements.

There was little levity in the room tonight. The troops were gearing up without the usual banter, and conversations were quieter and more subdued. Idina walked the ranks to check the individual sections, nodding encouragement along the way. Both her Palladians and the Gretians who knew her returned the nods solemnly. The Gretians, tall and fair skinned, would never look like Palladians, but it was amazing to her just how well those police officers meshed with her combat troopers already, working in paired teams and pulling on the same rope. A few years ago, they would have tried to kill each other with any weapon and method at their disposal. And not long ago, Idina would have felt apprehension at the thought of serving alongside armed Gretians again. But as she walked the floor and checked on each team individually, she realized that whoever had been gunning for them with those bombs had not differentiated between the Palladians and the Gretians in her JSP company. When they all hit the streets again tonight, they'd all accept the same risks, wear the same targets on their armor. And yet, all the Gretians had shown up again, not to be outdone by their Palladian counterparts. If anything, they were showing even more fortitude than her own troops, because their armor was lighter, and they carried outdated civilian-grade weapons.

I'm respecting their guts, Idina thought and shook her head. *The world has truly turned upside down.*

Captain Dahl's temporary replacement as Idina's patrol partner was a police lieutenant named Thomsen. She was blonde and very pretty for a Gretian as far as Idina could judge, and she was at least twenty-five years younger than Dahl. Idina was surprised when Thomsen introduced herself in halting Palladian.

"Your pronunciation isn't bad," she told her. "Where did you learn that?"

The Gretian lieutenant gave Idina a sheepish smile and switched back to her native language.

"They offer it at the police school as an elective now," she said. "I had a choice of Hadean or Palladian, and there are no Hadeans in the JSP. But my knowledge is still basic, so please excuse any mangling of your language."

"I will give you full credit for the effort. If Palladian is as hard for you people to learn as Gretian is for me, you picked the steeper path to climb by far."

The other woman rewarded the compliment with a shy smile. She looked very young to be wearing a lieutenant's stars on her shoulder boards.

"Are you new to the police?"

Lieutenant Thomsen shook her head. "I have been on patrol duty for two years. This is my first time as supervisor, though."

"You *are* new," Idina concluded.

"I will just be filling in for Captain Dahl until she is back on the force. I will try not to mess up in the meantime."

Idina felt strangely maternal as she looked at Thomsen's armor and the gear on her belt. She suppressed an impulse to hand check the fasteners to make sure the young woman had latched them all the way. Thomsen didn't look quite young enough to be her daughter, but that margin was only a few years thin. She wondered if Dahl felt the same way whenever she looked at Idina—someone to take under her wing and keep from getting herself hurt or killed.

"I'm sure you'll do fine," she said. "Whatever else your government messed up over the years, at least they know how to train their police well."

Idina put on her helmet and brought up the data display to make sure everything was connected. Then she nodded at the door to the flight pad, where the police gyrofoils were waiting for the joint JSP patrols.

"Ready to go keep the peace, Lieutenant?"

Thomsen voiced her affirmation in Palladian, and Idina nodded.

"At the very least, I'll be able to teach you some more vocabulary while we're going on patrols together. *Fifth Platoon, move out,*" she added in a louder voice. "Let's go, JSP. And watch your backs out there, all of you."

She strode toward the flight pad door, and this time, she waited for her Gretian counterpart to catch up with her and lead the way to the gyrofoil.

CHAPTER 26

ADEN

The hotel wasn't very far down the western leaf's central vein, so Aden didn't bother to take a pod. Instead, he walked the distance, an easy ten-minute stroll in the morning air. He didn't know how long he'd be out in the darkness of space again after he got to Eudora and met his new crew, and he wanted to soak up all the fresh air and sunshine he could until he left.

There wasn't much to collect at the hotel, but with only seven thousand left on his ledger, he wasn't about to discard five hundred ags' worth of good clothes. He assembled everything and put it into a travel pack he had bought with the clothing. Then he left the room and used his comtab to check out and make the final transfer for the room rate.

When he was almost back at the bridge that connected the western leaf to the central island, some faint alarm signal that had been dormant for a long time turned itself on in the back of his mind. After years of intelligence fieldwork, he'd developed subconscious sensors that told him when something didn't look quite right, and he had learned to stop and listen to them whenever they got tripped.

On the far end of the bridge, right where it connected to the central island, there were three men standing in a loose line across the street, facing west and out onto the leaf. The flow of foot traffic was streaming around them, going both ways, but those three didn't seem to have a destination. They were just kind of milling in place, with their comtabs out and in front of their faces. Something about the way they were interacting with the devices intensified the faint warning buzz that had made Aden stop in his tracks when he had felt it first, and his training reasserted itself. People who used comtabs for comms or data access interacted with the device. They talked to whoever was on the screen, or they tapped data fields and scrolled through them with their fingers, maybe typed out a response. But these three just held out the devices in front of them as they were milling around at the end of the bridge, and an unpleasant jolt went through Aden when he realized what they were doing.

They're scanning the crowd, he thought. They were either running a near-field scanner to check embedded ID pass signatures, or they were running facial-ID AI on their comtabs to look for someone in the passing stream of people. And there were three of them because one person alone couldn't cover the width of the bridge with just a near-field scanner.

Aden got out his own comtab and pretended to look something up on it so he could use the built-in optical sensor to magnify his view of the men at the end of the bridge. They were very stealthy about their business, but now that he had a few seconds to observe them, it was crystal clear to Aden that these men were combing the crowd and doing dragnet surveillance. He'd done it himself more than once. Even their location supported the hypothesis. Each of Adrasteia's eight leaves was five kilometers long, but they all came to a point where they connected to the central island. If he wanted to set up a dragnet with the least amount of available bodies, he would park them right where these men were standing, at the bridge that was the chokepoint between each leaf and the hub.

Adrasteia had almost a million residents, and tens of thousands of visitors were in the city on any given day. If these were Oceanian police officers, the chance they'd be looking for him was so minimal as to be mathematically insignificant. And he had a new ID pass that could stand up to the scrutiny of a near-field scan in passing. But his old, habitual paranoia was reasserting itself, and he was almost certain they were looking for him, whoever they were.

He heard Solveig's voice in his head.

Papa still has pull everywhere, Aden.

There was no reason for the Oceanian police to be looking for him. If his real-fake ID was compromised, all they'd have to do was to wait until he used it, or he walked past a security scanner, and they could pinpoint him and come pick him up. They wouldn't have to resort to near-field skimming or facial recognition on a handheld. These men were not here in any official capacity, which meant that if they were looking for him, they were sent by his father. And even if there was only a small chance they *were* on the lookout for Aden, he wasn't willing to ride the odds, not with his self-determination at stake.

Aden decided to find another way onto the central island. He turned around and walked back west, but as soon as he had taken a few steps, he knew that he'd made a mistake. He looked back over his shoulder—another beginner's error—and saw that his sudden movement against the flow of the foot traffic on his side of the bridge had attracted the attention of one of the men on the far side. He'd acted just like a fugitive and given them exactly what they were looking for. All three men were now walking out across the bridge, still forming a loose blocking line. They moved smoothly, without fuss or drama, but he knew that they were tracking him. One of them held up his comtab casually, and Aden turned his head so the facial-recognition AI couldn't get a good lock on him. Any Oceanian cop or intel officer could have just tapped into any of the thousands of public safety cameras all over the city to get a hit on his face. The fact that they needed to rely on their comtabs further confirmed that they weren't local cops.

Aden dropped the pretense and dashed into the first side vein he passed on his right. Just before the nearby buildings made him lose sight of the bridge, he chanced a look to see that two of the three men had broken into a run as well, while the third was standing in the middle of the bridge and holding aloft his comtab. Aden ran down the side vein, weaving his way between pedestrians and people on two-wheeled gyroblades, trying to put distance between himself and the street corner behind him. Another side vein appeared to his left, and he hooked that way to change course. Adrasteia's living modules were all rhomboid shaped, which made for a disorienting street layout if you weren't used to it, but Aden had spent four years here, and he still knew his way around those floating rhomboids and their many interconnecting alleyways. Just as he made it into the side vein, he glanced left to see the two men turning the corner from the main vein fifty meters away, and he cursed and redoubled his sprinting efforts. If they had been unsure about their quarry before, he was certain that he had removed all possible ambiguity with that sudden and obvious flight. For the first time since his release, he felt something like gratitude toward the Rhodies, who had given their POWs access to extensive exercise facilities that included a half-kilometer indoor running track.

He dashed through a succession of narrow alleys and passageways, changing his direction frequently in what he hoped were unpredictable turns. Twice, he shot out of side alleys and almost hurled himself into one of the many canals that were crisscrossing the leaf. When he was completely out of breath, and not even the adrenaline of being chased could force more air into his lungs, he stopped at a store in a side vein and mingled with the customers while he caught his breath again. He half expected his pursuers to come to a skidding halt right in front of the store like in some action feature on the networks, but when five minutes had passed and nobody had followed him inside, he guessed that he had lost them.

Aden bought a snack in the store so he wouldn't look out of place, and checked the time on his comtab when he used the device to pay. Twenty minutes had passed since he'd started running, and the geolocator on the comtab showed him two and a half kilometers into the western leaf, well past the location of the hotel he'd stayed in earlier. The shuttle with the *Zephyr* crew, his new employer and colleagues, would lift off in an hour and a half. If the remaining member of the pursuer trio was still on the bridge, Aden knew he'd never make it onto the central island without being spotted, and he didn't have the time to cross over to another leaf from one of the outer rings to see if they had someone waiting on that bridge as well. With his heart pounding in his chest, he stepped outside and looked around, then made his way back toward the bridge when none of his pursuers were in evidence.

The way back was less of a mad dash, but he still changed directions frequently and zigzagged his way through the side veins and alleys. By the time he was back in the bridge area, his timer had only a little over thirty minutes left on it. He went to a corner where he could get a good view of the bridge. Then he cursed when he saw that the third man was still there. He had moved to the near end on the leaf, and he was talking into his comtab while scanning his immediate surroundings, clearly trying to keep all the passing pedestrians in view.

If he's talking to the others, he can't use his facial-recognition AI or his near-field scanner, Aden thought. Under normal circumstances, he would have backed off and tried to find another way across, maybe even risked swimming the distance and climbing up to the seafront promenade on the central island from the seawall side, but time was not on his side for elaborate evasion tactics.

On the nearby main vein, a particularly big and loud group of young Rhodian university kids walked past Aden's vantage spot and the bridge. The other two pursuers could return at any moment and cast the net tightly across the end of the bridge again, and then he'd either be caught or miss his ride off the planet. Aden steeled himself and walked out casually, but with purpose, until he was bringing up the rear of the noisy university student group. They made their way toward the bridge, where the third man was still talking into his comtab. Aden felt exposed even as he tried his best to move with the group and use their bodies as a line-of-sight block. Whenever someone else had tried to pull this sort of thing on him, it had always been obvious, and he felt like he was broadcasting his presence even as he willed himself not to lose his nerve. In a pinch, he'd be able to hold his own against just one man.

The group started to pass by his pursuer. Aden tensed his shoulder muscles and took a deep breath. When he was three or four meters away from the man, the two kids in front of Aden moved over to the side to get a view of the water below the bridge, and he failed to match their movement in time. The third man's eyes widened, and he lowered his comtab and started to open his mouth. Aden launched himself forward and slammed into the man with his full body weight. Caught by surprise, his pursuer reeled backward and tumbled to the ground, and his comtab flew out of his hand and skittered across the photovoltaic surface of the street.

Aden didn't follow up on the body blow. Instead, he started running across the bridge, dodging and weaving around more pedestrians, not daring to look over his shoulder for fear of losing his footing and giving his pursuer a chance to catch up. The path beyond the bridge on the central island side turned into a staircase, and he took the steps three and four at a time. Behind him, the man he had dropped yelled something at him, but with the adrenaline surging and the blood roaring in his ears, Aden couldn't even tell if he was hearing Gretian or Oceanian. It didn't matter because he had no interest in what they had to tell him. He focused on rushing up the staircase toward the entrance of the spaceport above as fast as he could.

When he was all the way to the top, he chanced a look back. The one he had dropped on his ass was following him, but he had only made it halfway up the hundred-meter stretch of stairs. Down by the bridge, the other two had reappeared, and they were running to catch up, but Aden knew he'd be able to make it into the spaceport before they could reach the top of the stairs. His lungs and leg muscles were burning, but he broke into a sprint again and raced toward the spaceport atrium doors, fueled almost entirely by fear and adrenaline.

Once he was in the atrium, he slowed to a quick walk to avoid drawing attention from the security personnel. Then he made his way to the nearest security lock and got out his ID pass to scan himself into the concourse. He looked over his shoulder again as he did and saw the man he had knocked down rush through the doors and start looking around for him. Their eyes met right as Aden was holding his ID pass down on the scanner field, and he held his breath. If those men were police officers, the system would block his access and restrain him in the security lock, and his flight would be over.

The scanner field lit up in green, and the lock's doors opened on the far end. Aden gave the other man a curt wave and stepped through. His pursuer had stopped in the middle of the atrium, and the man just responded with a shake of the head that looked sad and disappointed. Aden moved on before the other two could catch up with their friend and resume the chase. Whoever they were, it seemed they weren't too keen on following him through the security lock right now, which told him all he needed to know.

Adrasteia's spaceport was huge, and the shuttle terminal was at the far end of it. When Aden walked into the waiting area by the boarding collar, the timer on his comtab only had eleven minutes left. He was more fatigued than he had been since basic training in the military, and his legs were shaking with exertion. Captain Decker and her executive officer were sitting on a bench at the far side of the waiting area, and

Aden walked over to join them. Even sitting down, Siboniso looked towering. He was easily the tallest Palladian Aden had ever seen.

"Run into trouble on the way?" Decker asked. "You look like you just ran a race clear across the city."

"Nothing to worry about," Aden said. "I got held up a bit, and then I had to rush to make it in time."

"Well, being able to stick to a schedule is an important prerequisite for the job, so you're still doing all right."

Aden couldn't suppress a quick glance down the concourse toward the security locks, and when he turned his head back again, he saw that Siboniso had noticed. But the Palladian did not say anything. Instead, he folded his arms in front of his chest and let out an entirely unconvincing yawn.

At the boarding collar, the light ring changed from yellow to green, and a pleasant female voice sounded the boarding announcement for their shuttle. Aden let out a long breath, trying hard to keep it from sounding shaky.

"Ready for some profitable adventures, Aden Jansen?" Decker asked as she stood up and flicked her gear bag over her shoulder.

I'm not entirely sure, he would have replied if he had aimed for complete honesty. But there was no way back into Adrasteia for him as long as those men were looking for him, and the shuttle ahead of them was his only way out, the only path to take if he wanted to remain in charge of himself.

"Absolutely," he said instead. She smiled in response, and he could tell by the knowing quality of that smile that his deception skills had declined somewhat in the last few years. Still, she didn't seem to mind the pretense, and that was interesting by itself.

They stepped through the boarding collar and into the shuttle, and Aden found a seat and strapped himself in. Decker and Siboniso took the seats on either side of him. By the time they rolled down the launchway a few minutes later and lifted off into the clear morning sky, the big Palladian was asleep, and his light snoring was definitely not faked. Aden was gripped by the sudden desire to come clean to the captain while her intimidating executive officer was asleep. They'd find out his background sooner or later, and at least he'd be able to put his sins out front from the beginning.

"I have a few dirty spots on my ledger," he said to Decker. "But I've never killed anyone, and I've never stolen anything."

She looked at him with an amused expression.

"It's an hour-long transit to Eudora," she said. "Fill me in on whatever you want me to know. But here's the thing—it doesn't matter as much as you think it might. What's going to matter to me and the crew is what you do from this point on. As far as I'm concerned, Aden Jansen is as new as his fake ID pass."

Aden nodded and suppressed a sigh of relief.

"But know this," she continued. "Your sins will only count against you from this point on, but some sins count double. Do wrong by me or my crew—*especially* my crew—and I will dump you out of my ship in orbit like organic waste."

He nodded again, this time with more deliberation.

"Fair enough," he said.

The shuttle climbed until the sky outside the tiny portholes on the hull turned from blue to black, and the stars began to glitter in the void, passing the viewport one by one.

ACKNOWLEDGMENTS

True story: when I was writing the original acknowledgments a little while ago, the text editor I was using crashed and deleted everything except for the first three words, just as I was literally on the last sentence of what felt like half a chapter of thank-yous.

I'll take that as a hint to be less verbose, which also means I can be less worried about forgetting to thank people, which happens every time. (Writing dedications and acknowledgments is a task every author dreads because of the danger of leaving someone out by accident.)

So this will be the briefer, more streamlined version. Thank you to my wife, Robin, who's still the most capable person I know, and whose work makes it possible for me to shut out the everyday grown-up world and focus my scatterbrain on putting words down.

Thank you to Evan, my agent, and the crew at Ethan Ellenberg for doing everything you do on my behalf. I like this thing where I sign papers and then money shows up, so let's keep that going as long as we can get away with it.

Special thanks to the 47North crew, especially Adrienne Procaccini and Jason Kirk, who kindly did not throw me into the Deadline Dungeon when I came to visit Seattle for ECCC.

Thank you to my writer friends and colleagues for your friendship, advice, support, and many conversations online or over drinks at conventions, especially George R. R. Martin and the Wild Cards gang, and my Viable Paradise posse, who have become some of my closest friends and confidants over the years. You're all a necessary component of my ability to stay productive and sane.

As always, thank you to my readers, especially those of you who read Frontlines and decided to give this new thing of mine a try. I hope you like this world I cooked up.

And lastly, thank you to John Scalzi—for his friendship and support over the years in general, and for getting a new kitten in particular. Because it gave me a name to steal at the exact time during the writing of my draft when I needed to name a cat. SMUDGE, YOU'RE A SPACE CAT NOW.

ABOUT THE AUTHOR

Marko Kloos is the author of the Frontlines series of military science fiction and is a member of George R. R. Martin's Wild Cards consortium. Born in Germany and raised in and around the city of Münster, Marko was previously a soldier, bookseller, freight dockworker, and corporate IT administrator before deciding that he wasn't cut out for anything except making stuff up for fun and profit. Marko writes primarily science fiction and fantasy—his first genre love ever since his youth, when he spent his allowance mostly on German SF pulp serials. He likes bookstores, kind people, October in New England, fountain pens, and wristwatches. Marko resides at "Castle Frostbite" in New Hampshire with his wife, two children, and roving pack of voracious dachshunds. For more information, visit www.markokloos.com.